Other books in the Os Zahir series:

The Book of Silence (2008)

Crossing Borders (2013)

Casino Princess

Christine Andain

ISBN: 978-0-9931673-0-0

Published and Printed in the UK by Newman Thomson Limited.

Foreword

My late wife Christine completed this, the third book featuring the Northern Cypriot detective, Os Zahir, three months before she died. She had wished to see it published before her death, but, sadly, this was not to be. However, in bringing her wish to fruition posthumously I hope it will be a tribute to her talent and creativity and to a life that was lived to the full.

The appearance of Casino Princess would not have been possible without the generosity of John and Marilyn Thomson who have funded its publication and I am indebted to their friendship and support. I would also like to thank Bob Pointing who spent many hours proof reading Christine's final draft, thereby ensuring that it could be published much earlier than would otherwise have been possible. Needless to say, what errors remain must be attributed to me! In addition I would like to thank Sir Howard and Lady Sheila Newby for organising and supporting the launch of both Casino Princess and Christine's second novel Crossing Borders.

I hope that Christine's family and her many friends will enjoy the third outing of her iconic detective, Os Zahir and her descriptions of a part of the Mediterranean she had come to love.

Ian Andain

December 2014.

Chapter One

Os Zahir, Chief Inspector of Kyrenia Police, Northern Cyprus, poured boiling water over his coffee granules and then carried his mug into the sitting room. He had already lit the gas bottle while he had been waiting for the kettle, but as yet the portable fire had made no impression on his cold fingers. He tightened the cord of his velour dressing gown, a present from Rose last winter, and wondered again how to spend his morning. The mobile broke into his lethargy. A voice exploded in his ear.

"Sir! It's Peksolu here." The desk sergeant spoke quickly as if expecting to be interrupted. "Someone's just reported a body outside Ozonkoy – on the road. Inspector Sahim is supposed to be on duty, but he's just rung in to say that he's at the hospital with his wife – it looks like the baby's coming early." The sergeant appeared to falter at Os's lack of response. "I know it's your day off, Sir. I could contact someone else if you're busy."

Os stared down at the large faded Turkish rug that protected his bare feet from the wooden floor, then closed his eyes. How he regretted the excess of alcohol that had been consumed the night before.

"Sir?"

Os tutted for effect. "Alright, give me a few minutes to get myself together."

The relief in the sergeant's voice was palpable. "Thank you, Sir. I'll get Sergeant Fikri to meet you. He lives in

Ozonkoy, so he can be there in a few minutes."

Os was about to say that he would prefer Sergeant Rafiker, but remembered that Sener was in Yenicekoy, preparing for his assistant inspector's exams. Instead, he asked, "Who reported the body, Sergeant?"

"I've no idea, Sir. I answered the call myself, but he didn't want to say much. When I asked for his name he rang off."

Os tutted again then realised that the prospect of work was lifting his mood. "Right Sergeant, find out the number of the phone he used will you? I'll get out to Ozonkoy straight away."

Because it was a Sunday and early, there was very little traffic about. He took the bottom road, passing the colonial-built, limestone post office and courthouse, turning on to the roundabout, at the side of which stood the marble statue of a young couple holding a concrete wreath; it had something to do with freedom, but he had never got around to asking anyone. As a nation they were always celebrating the "Turkish army Intervention of 1974". In a matter of days the Greek Cypriots had been pushed back over the mountains and a line had been drawn across the island, dividing the Turkish Cypriots from the Greeks. Despite the attempts of numerous interventionists over the years, the line had never been removed; the Greek Cypriots still lived in two-thirds of the country and the Turkish Cypriots occupied the northern area that everyone agreed was the most beautiful. Os had not even been born then, but his generation, alongside that of his parents, seemed permanently damaged by the event.

Ruminating over the country's fractious history, he turned off on to a minor road and, after passing frost-blanketed fields of cultivated olive trees, arrived in the village of Ozonkoy. He manoeuvred his car along the empty narrow streets; the shutters and doors of the whitewashed, cottages were still closed. A mangy dog chewed determinedly through the contents of a bag of rubbish, strewing empty tins and paper across the cobbles. Recalling the sergeant's instructions, Os took the small turning by the mosque that led out of the village. A few yards further on, was the middle-aged, rotund figure of Sergeant Fikri crouched by the side of the road. Os pulled over and turned off the engine. He climbed out, zipped up his fur-lined, brown leather jacket over his jeans and jumper, and then walked over to his sergeant.

Fikri stood up, grimacing with the effort, the buttons of his brown mac strained over his drab brown suit. He flipped open a wallet and nodded to where a motorbike lay in the field. "His name is Jamil Emral, Sir. He's been dead for hours by the look of it. I think he must be the brother of Mehmet Emral who runs a place in the village."

Os crouched down beside the body. The dead man was wearing a leather jacket and his torn jeans were congealed with blood. But it was the head that had received the most damage; the face was unrecognisable under a layer of dried blood. Pieces of gravel studded the raw cheeks and the left ear had been reduced to a bloody mess of flesh. His short hair was, like the face, matted in bodily fluids. Os stood up. A streak of pain flashed behind his eyes. How he wished that he had taken an aspirin before he had left home.

Fikri handed Os the wallet. "His ID's in there, Sir."

Os removed the plastic identity card, noting that there was only one five lira note inside. A handsome man, in his late twenties, grinned out from the photo. By the side were printed his details, including his name, Jemal Emral.

"You live in Ozonkoy, don't you, Sergeant? Did you know him?"

Fikri shook his head. "He didn't live in the village, but I know he helped his brother in the restaurant at the weekends. They're twins. To be honest, I've never really spoken to either of them, or been to the restaurant - just seen them in the street. We don't eat out- my wife thinks it's a waste of good money."

Os grinned. He had never met Fikri's wife himself but, if she was anything like her dour husband, he could only imagine what their home life might be like. The sound of a car engine made him turn around. A shiny new Fiat drew in alongside his own ten-year-old Mercedes sports; Os recognised the doctor behind the wheel.

"What have you got for me then, Chief Inspector?" the elderly man called, as he eased himself out on to the tarmac.

Os grinned again. It was still strange hearing his new title of three weeks' duration.

"I've only just arrived myself, Doctor. He's a mess I'm afraid. He must have come off his bike at speed. He wasn't wearing a helmet so the top layer of his skin's gone."

The doctor pulled his bag from the car boot then joined them.

"Check the bike out, Sergeant, will you?" Os said.

Os looked down at the doctor's fingers as he closed the corpse's eyes.

"I'd say he'd been dead since the early hours of this morning at least. Who found him?"

"The station had an anonymous phone call at nine this morning." Os grunted. "It always annoys me that."

"You know what they're like. It's an accident, but still they don't want to get involved. It was probably a farmer passing by and thought that he would waste too much time having to answer questions."

Another car arrived. A plain-clothed policeman from the station climbed out. He began to take photos.

Os turned back to the doctor. "He must have been going at quite a speed for him to come off like that."

The doctor clucked yellowing teeth. "That's the trouble with those things, no protection. Stupid man! If he'd worn a helmet, he might've survived."

"The front tyre's burst, Sir."

Os crunched across the frozen earth to join his sergeant. Side by side they stared down at the mangle of metal. "I suppose that explains why he came off. He must have hit something in the road." Os closed his eyes briefly; he hated this part of the job. "I'll have to go and see his brother, I suppose. Break the news."

"Do you want me to come with you, Sir?"

Os nodded. It was easier when there were two of them. "I'll meet you there; I'll just have a final word with the doctor. By the way, what's the name of this restaurant?"

"The Half Moon. It's just down the road from the bus shelter, by the statue of Ataturk."

It started to drizzle as Os walked back across the field. The usually quiet country lane was now congested with four cars and an ambulance.

He stuck out his hand and grasped the firm handshake of that of the doctor. "I'm going to the brother's house. I'll call in at the station afterwards to write up my report, so if you need me …."

The doctor shrugged. "We're taking the body away now, but it all looks pretty straightforward to me: a stupid accident."

Os nodded at the two paramedics and the police photographer, and then climbed into the worn, soft leather of his car seat. With the heating turned on full, he drove back into the village.

He had never been to Ozonkoy before. He'd heard there were a couple of good restaurants, but, during the six months he had lived with Rose, they had tended to eat either in Kyrenia or around the village of Karaman where they had lived; before that he had lived in Nicosia.

He passed the mosque, a whitewashed structure in character with the rest of the old buildings. Apart from an occasional stray cat, the narrow lanes were still empty, the occupants presumably preferring the warmth of their beds to the damp, cold Sunday morning. An English bookshop advertised coffee and newspapers, as well as new and second hand books, in its window. A large number of foreigners lived alongside the local population here, in reasonable harmony as far as he knew. Turning right, down another narrow lane, he passed a restaurant advertising a flat-screen TV in the bar, and then there, in front of him, was a sign, painted with the words, 'The Half Moon.'

Os pulled in by the large double wooden doors and turned off the engine. There was an air of deterioration about the place. If this was not a recent business, then they were definitely not making a success of it; if they had just bought it, then they had work ahead of them to make it appear as prosperous as the restaurant a few doors down.

He sighed, knowing he was putting off the inevitable, sitting here examining the restaurant frontage. He opened the car door.

" They live down here, Sir." Fikri was waiting further down the road. Os joined him.

"It's the one with the blue door, Sir."

As they came nearer Os saw that, here also, there was need of paint and renovation. He pushed the bell and stood back, expecting to wait. Two minutes later the door was opened, and a man in his late twenties stood in the doorway. Os stared. It was as if the corpse on the road had miraculously healed and was now standing in clean clothes on the threshold of his brother's house. He was approximately 5'9" slim with dark hair, and a face that would be considered good-looking. But unlike the photo of his brother, this man was scowling.

"Yes?"

In response to the aggressive tone, Os flashed his badge.

"What?"

"Are you Mehmet Emral, the brother of Jamil?"

He licked his lips. "Yes. What's the problem?"

"I wonder if we could come inside." Os said.

Mehmet hesitated and then stood back, allowing the two men into the small hallway. A faded Turkish rug lay on top of stone flags; a selection of shoes lined one wall and a wooden sideboard, covered in papers, took up a large part of the other. It was colder inside than out in the street, reminding Os of the miseries of his own rented accommodation. They followed Mehmet through into the sitting room, where the sudden combination of intense heat and fug of cigarette smoke made Os stop in his tracks. A middle-aged woman was curled up in an old armchair edged close to a roaring fire. She barely looked at them. She was dressed in jeans and a thick jumper, her blonde hair dragged unbecomingly into a short ponytail, revealing a pale, tear-streaked face devoid of makeup. She dragged at a half-burnt cigarette, then ground it into a full ashtray.

Mehmet crossed over to stand behind her, placing a hand on her shoulder."This is my wife."

She flinched. Os wondered if he had interrupted an argument. She was at least fifteen years older than him and her plain, lined face was a shocking contrast next to his handsome one. He was surprised that they were up and dressed; in fact it appeared, by the strength of the fire, they had been up for some time.

Os took in a deep breath. "I'm sorry to inform you that a man was found on the road going out of the village. It appears that he came off his bike sometime in the early hours of this morning." He paused then added, "From his papers, we're almost certain that it was your brother".

The howl of pain that emanated from Mrs Emral was a sound that Os had become used to, though it made it no easier to hear. Her husband, his face white, bent over her and whispered something. She took the handkerchief from him and balled it to her mouth. When he straightened up, Os recognised panic in his eyes.

"And you say that this is definitely my brother?"

Os took the identity card from his pocket and handed it to him. "We need you to identify the body, Sir."

Mrs. Emral's howling turned into sobs, making her gasp for breath every few seconds. Os was about to suggest a doctor when Mehmet pulled her to her feet. Shaking his head in response to offers of help, he supported her from the room.

Fikri raised his eyebrows. Os removed his coat, unable to bear the intense heat any longer. Apart from two armchairs and a sofa, the room contained a small desk, the entire surface of which was taken over by an old computer. Underneath the strong smell of woodsmoke, he could also smell damp. That was the problem with some of these old houses: they kept cool in summer, but in winter they were often miserably cold. Newcomers to Northern Cyprus were often surprised by the temperature of the winter months here; this woman was European and she must be used to the luxury of central heating and double glazing.

Suddenly he found himself comparing her to Rose, his ex-partner. Of course the house, left to her by her dead aunt, had central heating and the building was in a much better state than this one. Rose was also financially independent as a writer of English textbooks. This bohemian room suggested a distinct lack of ready money.

It was not exactly dirty, though there was so much clutter it was difficult to tell. Hundreds of tatty English paperbacks were stacked in piles against a wall. Multi-coloured crocheted blankets were draped over the old settee and armchairs, one of which was occupied by two sleeping cats. Here, as in the hallway, the flagstoned floor was covered in old rugs. Plastic sheeting was taped to the two windows as a form of double glazing. Perhaps he should try the same method on his own apartment windows, he speculated.

Os caught sight of himself in the mirror above the fireplace. Standing in the cold morning air had brought the colour back into his face, a contrast against his black polo-neck jumper and certainly an improvement on his reflection that morning. For a horrified second he wondered if he was turning grey, but then relaxed as he realised that drops of moisture still clung to his short black curly hair.

Mehmet came back in. "I've put her to bed. I'm sorry about that but her mother died last month and this has brought it all back." His eyes slipped to the wall behind Os. "Do you want me to come with you now?"

"If that's alright by you, sir?" Os answered. "Do you think your wife needs a doctor?"

"No. She'll be fine after she's had a sleep - she's just very emotional at the moment." He waved his hand as if to intimate that there was nothing more to be said on the subject.

"Are there any other close relatives that we should be talking to?" Os asked.

Mehmet blinked. "If it's Jamil, I'll tell my father; it would be better coming from me."

"Well, if you're ready? My sergeant will take you to the hospital and then on to wherever you need to go afterwards." Os refrained from adding the obvious, that Mehmet would want to start organizing the funeral.

The drizzle had stopped, and the weak winter sun was

forcing itself through the clouds by the time they stepped out into the street. The shutters of nearby houses were still closed, though a few smoking chimneys suggested that life inside was stirring. Os climbed into his car and waited for Fikri and his passenger to pull out in front before following them out of the village.

His mind revisited the scene he had just witnessed. How fascinating were the parallels of this couple's relationship to the one he once had with Rose. But unlike Mehmet and his wife, Rose was three years younger than he was. He had wanted to marry her, but Rose had refused, even though she had been carrying his child. Now the unborn child was dead and the relationship over.

These two were married, but it looked as if the woman was too old to have children. Their history intrigued him although it was unlikely that he would meet them again. He pulled into a parking space, having reached the street where he lived. Unlocking the front door to the converted warehouse, he went up the stairs to his apartment to shower and change.

As he pushed open the glass doors of the Kyrenia Police Station, the duty sergeant called out, "Morning Sir, this is for you".

Os read the note without surprise. It seemed that the mobile used by the witness had belonged to the dead man himself, Jamil Emral. If the witness had been a farmer, then he might not have had his own phone. Or, alternatively, the phone had been used so that the caller could not be traced.

Minutes later he opened the door to his office and glanced around. The first thing that always hit him was the difference in their desks. He had no idea how Inspector Zelfa Ure managed to keep hers so tidy. Her only permanent items were a small vase of fresh flowers and a mug of pens and pencils; his desk was covered with folders and papers that always needed his attention. He had never been aware before that he was a messy worker until nine months ago when he had been forced to share his office with the newcomer on secondment from Istanbul. But there were definite advantages in this new arrangement.

He picked up the monitor and pressed a button: the air con machine, which doubled as a heater, sprang into life. Hot air poured into the chilly room. Meanwhile his colleagues in the rest of the building sweated in the heat of the summer and used mobile gas heaters in winter with the associated fumes. This bit of luxury was all down to the charms of his roommate. She had the ability to get what she wanted from the surly, toad-like superintendent in a way that Os had never seen before. Rolling his shoulders luxuriously under the blast of hot air, he picked up the phone and ordered a Turkish coffee, then sat down to write his report.

Zelfa arrived at the same time as the porter. Os took his small cup of sweet Turkish coffee from the tray and grinned up at her.

"Do you want one?" he asked, surprised that today she was casually dressed in tight jeans and a jumper.

She dismissed the porter with a wave of a manicured hand. "What are you doing here? I thought it was your day off."

Os told her his news. "The couple were interesting; he must have been fifteen years younger."

"Was she Cypriot?" Zelfa asked.

"British, I think."

Zelfa nodded.

"What?"

She pulled her beautiful features into a grimace. "I assume that he was attracted to her money." She shrugged. "I could be wrong of course."

Os recalled the house and restaurant, both in need of serious cash-input. "I thought I'd get the report out of the way and then drive over to my parents for dinner."

Zelfa lifted some papers out of a drawer and placed them in a neat pile on her desk. "Well, give them my regards. How is your father?"

"He went back to work at the university last week, part-time. He's going to see how he does. If he can manage it then he'll do a couple more years before he retires."

Zelfa frowned. She looked younger and more vulnerable in her casual clothes and today she seemed to be wearing less makeup. Her skirt glowed and her dark hair, styled in a long bob, gleamed. She appeared more relaxed than she had been recently.

"And your mother is pleased about that? She's not worried that he'll have another heart attack?"

"They decided that he would be happier doing it this way and the doctor didn't have a problem with it." Os grinned. "He'll have to develop some hobbies!"

"Well, if you want company next time, just give me a yell."

Os took a sip of coffee so that he would not have to give an answer. He knew his mother had really taken to Zelfa, the couple of times that they had met. Once was when the two of them had been in Nicosia on police business and the other when Zelfa had visited after his father was recovering from a heart attack. But to take her with him on a social call was very different; his mother would immediately think that there was something romantic going on between them. He would not hear the last of it.

At that moment her mobile rang; seconds later she got to her feet. "There've been two burglaries up in Lapta during the night - two shops next door to each other. I'm going up there now." She paused at the doorway and her voice sounded wistful. "If you're free any evening this week, I'd value talking something over with you. We could go for a coffee or a meal after work, if you like, or I could cook."

"Of course." Os mentally ran over his week's social activities and realised that he had nothing planned; the transfer to single life was taking some getting used to. He saw a lot of his married school friend, Aka who lived in the apartment above him, but, apart from a few drinks with friends in Nicosia, there was just work. His eyes met her large brown ones. "When were you thinking of?"

She shrugged. "Tomorrow night; I'll cook if you want?"

"Why don't we meet for a drink instead?" He detected disappointment flash across her face.

"Fine! I'll see you tomorrow then," she said. "You'll be gone by the time I get back here, I should imagine." The door swung shut behind her and Os was left with the citrus tones of her perfume hovering in the warm air.

He was re-reading his completed report when his cell phone buzzed. "Yes Fikri?"

"He's identified his brother, Sir. It wasn't nice; the body was still in a hell of a mess. I thought it would have been washed by the time we got there, but they're short staffed at the moment and Emral didn't want to go back again. He recognised a small tattoo on his arm. I'm just waiting for him to sign some forms, then I'll take him home."

"Thanks for that. I'll be here for another hour, but I'll see you in the morning."

Having no other demands on his time, Os decided to stay and work through the papers. Slowly, the pile began to form into some kind of order. At last, he sat back and stretched, aware of his rumbling stomach; he had not eaten anything all day. If he drove over to Nicosia now, he would be able to have a chat with his father before they ate.

He was unhooking his leather jacket from the back of the door when his land- line rang. Should he ignore it? The duty sergeant knew he was still in the building, but he could easily leave by the back door. The phone continued to ring, so, with a sense of foreboding, he lifted the receiver.

"Chief Inspector Zahir?" Os recognised the doctor's voice and immediately relaxed; he would make his mother's lunch after all. "Yes Doctor, what can I do for you?"

"Some bad news, I'm afraid. They've just washed the body and unfortunately there was something I missed this morning. The dead man's hair was very thick and there was blood everywhere from the gashes in his face. But I'm afraid," he hesitated and for a couple of seconds heavy breathing was the only sound, "Jamil Emral's death was not an accident. He was shot." When there was only silence from Os, the doctor added, "They also found a bullet embedded in the back tyre of the motorbike."

Chapter Two

Os took sips from his water bottle as he strode through the corridors of the basement of Nicosia Hospital. Staying overnight at his parents and having a few drinks with his old school friend, Mehmet, had seemed like a good idea until his mother had broken his drunken sleep at eight o'clock that morning. The clack of his leather soles on the concrete floor reverberated off the grey plastered walls. As always, he questioned why the authorities did not think it worthwhile to spend money on this part of the building. How upsetting it must be to collect someone you love from such a place in order that they can be buried. He turned left and passed the open door of the morgue office, nodding at the supervisor who was sitting at his desk.

Os knocked on the next door, and, not waiting for an answer, walked in. Dr. Gok was bent over a body, a scalpel in her hand. The sudden stench of blood was overwhelming. Glancing up, her eyes immediately crinkled at the corners.

"Ah, Chief Inspector Zahir! I was hoping that it would be you. Close the door behind you, will you." She straightened her 6' 3" frame including heels. She towered over him, her white coat buttoned up over a thick jumper. She pulled down her mask, revealing the high cheek bones and perfect skin of a very attractive American woman. He grinned back.

"So what have you got for me?" he asked.

She parted the man's thick, black hair with her gloved

hand. "You can see where the bullet went in. But there's little scorching of the scalp, so the shot must have come from some distance. It killed him immediately of course."

Os picked up a stainless steel dish. He flipped the bullet over and frowned. "I think this could be Russian, standard use by their army."

His mind raced. There were a small number of American soldiers based in Southern Cyprus alongside the large British force. But as far as he knew, there were no Russian soldiers based there. And he knew for definite that the only soldiers in Northern Cyprus were Turkish and Turkish Cypriot. Maybe he was wrong about the bullet.

Dr. Gok cocked her head to the side and the thick blonde plait of hair slid on to her right shoulder. "If he had been wearing a helmet, he might have stood a chance."

He looked at her, but said nothing.

She pointed to the bent right leg of the corpse. "The tibia broke as he came off the motorbike. Any idea of the speed?"

Os shook his head. "I'll find out."

"And of course all this grazing on his face and hands happened when he skidded along the road. He had several units of alcohol in his blood – under the limit though."

Despite the weals along his cheeks and nose, the similarity to his brother, Mehmet was startling. "Anything else?"

"I'm just finishing off now, but that's most of it."

"And the time this happened?"

"The early hours of Sunday. Any time between midnight and four in the morning. As I said, he was killed immediately - you can tell his relatives that. It might give them some comfort."

"So the body had been lying in the road for hours before it was discovered," Os mused aloud. "I wonder whether the assassin had been waiting for him, or if he'd followed him from the restaurant?"

Dr. Gok moved over to the sink and began to scrub her hands. "That's your department, Chief Inspector."

Os grinned at her emphasis on the 'Chief.'He looked around at the pathologist's working environment. Had she ever got used to the lack of equipment and basic facilities? She had trained in New York before she had met her Turkish Cypriot, businessman husband, and now she was working in surroundings that she must find comparably medieval. She had never complained to him though, so maybe she was content.

"I'll look forward to your report then. Can I take the bullet with me?"

She turned and picked up a towel. "I'll send them both over tomorrow, if you don't mind."

This time Os left by the back door, the one where the hearses waited for the coffins. But it was not until he reached his car that he took out his phone.

"Fikri! I want you to meet me outside that restaurant in Ozonkoy. What's it called?"

The sergeant sounded puzzled. "The Half Moon, Sir. Shall I come now?"

Os glanced at his watch. "Make it quarter past ten. I'm driving back from Nicosia so if I'm not there when you arrive, just wait outside."

"No problem, Sir. I'm just catching up on paperwork here."

Os noted his relaxed tone. His other sergeant, Sener would have questioned him, wanting to know any new details. Os had left a message for Fikri yesterday, informing the elderly sergeant that the biker had been murdered, but Fikri had made no reference to it. He shook his head in exasperation and started the engine.

Fikri was leaning against his car smoking a cigarette. "They're both inside, Sir." And then, "I saw them through the window".

The light was on in the restaurant and Mehmet could be seen behind the bar. Os pushed open the heavy wooden door; Mehmet immediately looked up from washing glasses, a shadow passed over his unshaven face. Despite sensing that they were not welcome, Os felt sympathy for the man.

His superintendent had taken on the task of breaking the news to the couple yesterday: that Jamil's death had not been the accident they had first thought - so the body could not yet be released for burial. In normal circumstances, under Muslim law, they would have buried the body within twenty-four hours of the death.

Os spoke gently. "I'm sorry to disturb you at such a time, but we need your help to catch your brother's murderer."

Mrs. Emral appeared in an open doorway, wiping her hands with a cloth. "Have you any idea how Jamil died, officer?" she whispered.

She looked better today. The dark rings under her eyes were still there, but her hair was washed and there was more colour in her face; in fact she was prettier than he had first thought. He noticed a small area by the main dining room, partitioned off by a Cypriot, curved stone archway; two large sofas were positioned opposite each other, a coffee table in between.

"Shall we sit down?" he suggested.

She glanced at her husband and he nodded. The two policemen followed her across the stone-flagged floor, Os noting the stale smells of wood smoke, cigarettes and alcohol. Only five tables were covered in debris from the night before. The others had not been used.

Mrs. Emral sat down, indicating with a flurry of her hand that Os should sit opposite her. Her husband chose to stand behind her, his hand resting on the threadbare velveteen-covered sofa a few inches from her shoulder. Os attempted to sit upright amongst the sagging springs, uncomfortably aware that the material felt damp. This time he needed the warmth of his jacket.

Os wondered at the sullen-faced Mehmet; it was not the usual reaction of a grieving relative. "I need to know as much as you can tell me about your brother. Was he younger or older than you?"

"We were twins."

"Identical?" Os asked, remembering the obliterated face. Mehmet nodded.

"Were you both born here, in Ozonkoy?"

Mehmet shook his head. "We're from Karalangalou. Jamil was still living with my father in the house we grew up in."

16

Os noted that already he was using the past tense; again, many relatives took a while to adjust."And his job?" Os looked around him, thinking this down at heel restaurant could not financially support three adults.

"He worked in a shop that mended computers."

"I take it he wasn't married. A girlfriend?"

Mehmet became interested in the view out of the window. Os lowered his gaze to Mrs Emral.

Her face suddenly took on the appearance of a trapped animal. "There was a woman, a Russian who worked at a casino. We never met her but he talked about her."

Os glanced back at her husband for confirmation. Although his gaze was still on the window, the skin on his face had tightened.

Os turned back to the wife. "Do you know her name and which casino she worked in?" He prompted her silence gently. "Mrs. Emral?"

"It's Molly. You can call me Molly."

Her accent was very different to the Liverpudlian one he had become used to when he had visited Rose's home city several months ago.

He was curious. "What part of England are you from, Molly?"

She looked startled by the change of subject. "Newcastle," she answered, then volunteered, "I came out here two years ago".

"And how long have you been married?"

She pressed her hanky to her mouth and closed her eyes. Her husband gripped her shoulder and glowered. Although strange, Os made allowances for his behaviour; he could not imagine how he would behave if he heard that his own brother was dead.

"The casino is called, Ruby Royal, out past Karsiyaka, on the main road," Molly answered.

For the first time, Fikri spoke. "I know it, Sir. It's been open for a couple of years."

Os glanced at the sergeant who was sitting astride his hard chair, his notebook resting on the wide girth of his leg. He had always suspected that, despite the fact that gambling was illegal for Northern Cypriots, Fikri dabbled.

"And her name?"

Mehmet cut over her. "Natalia. He never mentioned her last name. As Molly said, we never met her. I never thought that it was anything serious."

"Nevertheless, the more people we can talk to about your brother, the better, Sir," Os placated. "Did you see a photo of her, or did he ever describe her?"

Mehmet shrugged, seemingly uninterested. "I believe she was about twenty- five, tall with long blonde hair. We never saw a photo, did we Molly?"

Instead of answering him, she asked sharply, "Do you think she has anything to do with this?"

Os spread his hands. "I've no idea. At the moment we're just trying to get as much background information about your brother-in-law as we can. Who his friends are, what he liked to do when he wasn't working, and so-forth."

Again Mehmet cut across her. "His death had nothing to do with this Natalia. How could she, he hardly knew her."

"So your brother was a gambler?" Os asked.

"Turkish Cypriots aren't allowed to gamble," Mehmet stated, as if the policeman did not already know the law.

Os held on to his irritation. "We're talking about murder here, Sir. Do you really think I care whether your brother was gambling? It's just an obvious place to start our investigation." Os shrugged, "It's likely that he would have met Natalia at the casino, wouldn't you say?"

"I've no idea, Chief Inspector. My brother spent a lot of time here, but we talked about other things. We've had a few problems with this place," he nodded at his wife. "We couldn't afford to employ anyone else, so Jamil would often help out on a Saturday night if we needed him."

"So he obviously didn't see this Natalia on a Saturday night" Os interrupted. "Normally men see their girlfriends at the weekend."

"If she really existed, she'd be working, I suppose," Mehmet answered. "Weekends are the busiest time in a casino."

"He helped us with our computer records," Molly said, as

if she was part of another conversation. "He put everything on spreadsheets."

"Tell me about Saturday night," Os said.

Mehmet squeezed Molly's shoulder. She stared at the floor, presumably remembering the last time she saw her brother-in-law alive. She spoke so quietly that Os had to lean forward.

"There's not much to say. It was the same as most Saturday nights. Jamil arrived here at about six o'clock. We weren't busy, just a few regulars. He had a meal but he didn't say anything in particular; we've our own worries at the moment so I didn't talk much to him myself."

Os raised an eyebrow inviting further information.

Molly suddenly became garrulous. "We've only had this place just over a year and we're in competition with the restaurant up the road. It's difficult to pay the bills in the winter. You've got to keep the place heated, whether there are two people in or a full restaurant. Otherwise they don't come back. And you've got to judge how much food to have in so it's not wasted."

"So your brother was preoccupied?" Os repeated.

Mehmet nodded. "Then my father rang to say he was unwell and he left to check on him."

"What time was that, Sir?" Fikri asked.

Mehmet considered the question. "About midnight. He was going to spend the night here; he often did so he could have a few drinks."

"But he didn't drink on Saturday then, Sir?" Fikri asked.

Again Mehmet paused.

"Your brother is dead," Os reminded him gently. "Whether he was over the limit is immaterial now. In fact we already know from the pathologist that there was alcohol in his blood when he came off his bike."

Mehmet shrugged. "He was going to stay with us until my father rang. Jamil was worried about him, he's getting old. We'd finished here then; Molly and I were both tired, so, after he had gone, we left everything and went home."

"And did you hear from him at all later?" Os asked.

Again the pause. Mehmet seemed to have some difficulty

breathing. "The next news we had about him was when you knocked on our door, Sunday morning."

"And your father didn't ring again to tell you that your brother hadn't arrived?"

"He must have fallen asleep in the chair. I found him there the next morning when I went around to tell him that Jamil was dead."

A sob brought everyone's attention back to Molly. She stood up, pressing her handkerchief to her face. "I'm going back to the house," she whispered.

Mehmet immediately put his arm around her and led her towards the door. "I'll be a few minutes," he called over his shoulder.

Os and Fikri looked at each other. "I think we've got as much information as we're going to at the moment," Os said. "But we'll need his father's address; we'll have to interview him as soon as we've got time. I'll leave you to get that and I'll meet you in Bozer's when you've finished here."

Os went back into the main part of the restaurant. The wooden bar stretched along part of a wall, and by its side, was a large open barbecue area with a galvanised canopy that dispersed the smoke outside. Logs were stacked neatly on either side of the stone fireplace and the residue of Saturday's fire remained in the grate. The small kitchen was in an alcove to the right. Everywhere looked clean but dowdy. It was not a surprise to hear that they had money worries. There were so many restaurants in Northern Cyprus and everyone was feeling the economic downturn. The sound of the front door opening made him turn round.

"I'm sorry," "Mehmet said. "She's very upset."

"It's totally understandable," Os answered. "We'll get out of your way now. But are you quite sure that you have no idea why your brother was killed?"

Anger distorted Mehmet's face. "Of course not. He was only a computer technician, for God's sake. He didn't do any harm to anyone. It must have been a mistake."

Os nodded sympathetically. "Well, thanks for your time. If you could give your father's address to my sergeant- we'll have to talk to him. And if you do think of anything that would help us find the person who killed your brother, please ring me." Os paused. "This question will sound very odd, but you don't know of any connection he might have had with the Russian army do you?"

Mehmet stared at Os as if he was mad. "No. He's done his military service, like me. But we didn't have anything to do with the Russians. Why?"

Os shook his head. "Just a thought." He handed over his card, nodded at Fikri and left.

Os was stirring his coffee when Fikri walked into the café. He had positioned himself in his usual place, with his back to the wall, so that he had a clear view of the room. The café was mainly frequented by policemen, being only walking distance from the station. However, on Wednesdays it was full of shoppers from the weekly market that took place just across the road. Today, most of the steel tables were empty. Fikri sat down heavily and placed his cigarettes and lighter on the table.

"Well, what do you think?" Os asked.

The sergeant took a sip of the coffee that was placed in front of him, smacked his lips, and then placed the small cup back in its saucer. "I think he's lying, Sir. I'm not sure what about, but he knows more than he's saying. It's in his eyes."

"And her? What do you think of his wife, Molly?"

"I think she's scared of him."

Os raised his hand, indicating to the waiter that he wanted two refills, and thought over what his sergeant had said; sometimes Fikri surprised him with the occasional astute observation. "Why do you think that?"

Fikri shook his head. "I don't know really. When he put his hand on her shoulder, I saw her flinch, as if she was expecting him to hurt her."

"And yet, she's from England and she's older than him by fifteen years, wouldn't you say?" Os mused. She's not some slip of a Cypriot girl without any life experience. You'd better find out who owns the restaurant. Is it in her name only, or both of theirs?"

Fikri tapped out a cigarette and struck a match.

Resisting the temptation to help himself to one, Os added, "It's also strange that Mehmet had never met his brother's girlfriend. They're twins. I'd have thought that they would know most things about each other. And they were obviously close, otherwise Jamil wouldn't be helping them out at the weekends. This Natalia can't be working every night. Why didn't Jamil ever take her over to the restaurant for a meal?"

"Maybe he thought that they wouldn't like her, or maybe, like Mehmet said, it was nothing."

Os sipped his coffee.

"Maybe Jamil made her up," Fikri suggested.

The same thought had occurred to Os. A twin brother, still living with his father, might feel the need to fabricate a little glamour.

"Well I'll soon find out. After we've finished our coffee, I'll drive down to the casino while you go to the office where he worked and find out what you can about the dead man. What did he do exactly and what was his work record like? Anything else you can find out too."

Fikri nodded as he watched two elderly men engrossed in their game of backgammon.

"You'll be able to join them soon," Os grinned. "When are you retiring?"

"Not for a while, Sir. I went to see the superintendent yesterday to let him know my change of plan." Fikri expelled a lungful of air in disgust. "With these new mortgages that Cypriots can get, my wife has decided that we're giving my daughter the deposit for a house. She wants to get married, so the down-payment is going to be a wedding present for her." His broad, lined face grimaced. "My father didn't make such sacrifices for me, but these young ones are different. I can't afford to go now."

Os grinned and gathered up his keys. "So we can expect to see your smiling face around the station for some time then! Well, I'll get off. I'll see you back at the station later."

Fikri lit a cigarette. "What was that question about the

Russian army, Sir?"

Os explained about the bullet and then left Fikri still sitting at the table, his bloodshot eyes screwed up in thought.

The drive along the coast road, through the villages of Karalangalou and Alsanjak was devoid of much traffic. Despite it being January, the blue sea glinted misleadingly in the winter sun. Hugging the road to his left were the occasional houses and orchards of orange, lemon and almond trees, the fields stretching back to the base of the soaring, craggy mountain range running parallel to the coast road. The whitewashed houses of several hill villages clung high up on the grey rock.

He felt the usual sharp pang as he passed the road leading up to Karaman but he was not going to think about Rose now. Lines of advertising hoardings, that for years had defaced this stretch of road, had been removed at last by the present government, this being, in Os's view, one of the few good things they had done since coming to power.

In the distance, towering over low-level buildings, was the minaret of the Karsiyaka mosque. Ten years ago Karsiyaka had been a village with a couple of shops and a cluster of houses, but now, newly-built houses sprawled all the way down the mountainside to the sea. Os put his foot down, grinning at the sudden surge of power. The Mercedes might be old, but there was still plenty of life in the engine. To the right, a tall, newish building came into view. It was midday and the sun was out, but neon lights flashed busily around the front doors. Os slowed down, then turned into the half-full, gravel car park.

The Ruby Royal was all black glass and white pillars. As he locked his car door, he caught his reflection in the towering, mirror-like walls. He quickly buttoned up his custom-made suit; was it his imagination or was he putting on weight? He stared critically at his clean-shaven face. Was that a double chin coming? This new habit of drinking regularly was not doing him any good. He averted his eyes, making a mental note to get down to the gym.

Long white marble steps led up to glass doors, which slid open obligingly to allow him to enter. As he stepped into a foyer, he took in the two, over-large men, dressed in dinner suits, who stood centurion-like either side of a long, shiny-black counter. A young woman, in a close-fitting, black dress, smiled at him.

"Good afternoon, Sir. You've come to play."

Os was not sure whether it was a question or a statement, but he noticed that, although she spoke Turkish well, it was not her first language. He took out his warrant card, and as he expected, the woman's smile disappeared. "I'd like to see the manager please."

She picked up the phone and spoke in what, Os suspected, was Russian. He glanced at each of the two men, but, after momentarily making contact, their eyes slid away. The foyer gave the impression of opulence. A black carpet, with some kind of gold emblem, led into an area that, from where Os was standing, appeared to be full of slot machines. Even at this time of day, men and women sat on padded chairs, staring at the moving numbers, as if it was some fascinating TV programme.

Two women sat just inside the entrance. Os suspected that they were Greek Cypriots, both large with their blonde, dyed hair twisted into elaborate buns. They fed metal tokens into their machines as if they were hungry children.

A man in his forties, dressed in a well-cut, navy blue suit, with a crisp white shirt and a silk tie, stepped through the doors of a lift just behind the main desk. He came from around the counter smiling, his hand outstretched.

"I'm the manager: Petrov Salinsky. What can I do to help?"

Os showed his badge as he wondered whether the manager's tailor was local. "I'd like to ask you a few questions about one of your employees. If we could go somewhere so that we can talk ?"

Salinsky's smile faltered. "Of course. Who you want to talk about?"

In answer, Os held out his hand, indicating that the

manager should lead them to somewhere more private. Salinsky stepped back into the lift. The space was just big enough for the two of them. Os was glad when the tinted glass doors slid open again and they stepped into a large private office.

The walls were the same black glass as the foyer below, but from this side, you could see out onto the parking area and the mountains beyond. Os paused for a few seconds, overcome by the view. He smiled at Salinsky.

"I'm surprised that you get any work done."

The manager revealed perfect white teeth that Os suspected were down to the expertise of a cosmetic dentist rather than good genes. "Can I get you anything to drink, Chief Inspector? And please sit down."

Os shook his head. "I've just had a coffee, thank you." He chose one of the black leather sofas, noting that here in the private office, the black and white theme of the Casino continued. The carpet was white, as were the long, shot-silk curtains.

"I'd like to have a word with one of your employees, a croupier called Natalia."

Salinsky draped himself across the sofa opposite. "Could I ask why?"

"We believe that she is friendly with someone we're investigating."

"Really?" Salinsky's eyes narrowed. "Someone who works in the Casino here?"

Os shook his head. He placed Jamil's photo on the table. "This man - he was a regular here?"

Salinsky frowned at the picture. "We get so many people in our Casino, it's difficult to say. But I can say for definite that he was not a friend of Natalia, if it's the same Natalia that works here. Perhaps you're mistaken with your information." He smiled again with his fine set of teeth, but his eyes watched Os speculatively.

"Perhaps," Os answered. "If I could see her now, then we can get any misunderstandings out of the way."

Salinsky stood up and crossed over to his large, black-tinted glass desk; a phone and a computer were the only items on the polished surface. He picked up the receiver and pushed in several buttons. Os then listened to another burst of Russian. Salinsky frowned, then put down the phone.

"It appears that she didn't turn up for the Casino bus this morning. Someone went to check her room, but there was no answer. I'm surprised that I wasn't informed."

Os was surprised too. This man did not look as if he ran a sloppy ship. If he was telling the truth, which Os doubted, then for some reason her absence had been kept from him.

He stood up. "Is this normal behaviour for her?"

"No. She's never missed a shift as far as I know. Her excuse had better be good."

"Well, let's go and look. She must have friends who are on this shift?"

"One minute." Salinsky returned to the phone and this time Os went to stand by the glass wall. A small basic restaurant was situated on the opposite side of the road. What a country of contrasts it was becoming. Here he was, in a building that must have cost an exorbitant amount to build and opposite was what could only be described as a wooden shack. Metal tables and chairs were grouped underneath the cover of a bamboo awning, and, as with so many of the country's restaurants, only a couple of tables were occupied. Despite the popularity of the Casino, he knew which environment he felt most comfortable in.

Os heard Salinsky disconnect one line and then connect into another. This time he spoke in fluent Turkish. Finally, the phone was replaced in its cradle and Salinsky turned round.

"It appears that no one knows where she is? I've asked for the caretaker of the building to open up her room. He'll ring me back shortly."

"Good," Os answered. He watched Salinsky playing with a pen, twisting it round and round in his right hand. "How long has Natalia worked here?"

Sainsky shrugged. "I would have to look into her records to be exact, but I think a year, perhaps a little longer."

"And she is reliable, a good worker?"

"Of course. Anyone who works here is on a trial for three months. We get rid of them if they're not up to speed. The Casino has only been open for eighteen months. It's important that we employ good people." His phone rang. He listened for a few moments and then replaced the receiver. "That was the caretaker," he explained. "Natalia is not in her room. No one has seen her today."

Os nodded, thinking of the various reasons why that might be so."I would like to talk to a friend of hers or the people who have rooms either side of her." When Salinsky opened his mouth, presumably to put forward an objection, Os added, "Shall we go downstairs?"

"I could bring anyone up here to talk to you in private," Salinsky suggested.

Again Os shook his head. "It'll be useful for me to see the place where Natalia works."

For the first time, Salinsky's smooth veneer slipped. "I don't want any of the punters feeling uncomfortable. It will be obvious to everyone that you are the police."

Os smiled, his eyes cold. He knew that, by now, every Turkish Cypriot who might have been playing the tables, would have left by the back door. As it was illegal for any Turkish Cypriot to gamble in his or her own country, every casino had a warning system, which was operated as soon as a police officer entered the building. Os also knew that some of his own colleagues were paid by the casinos to warn them in advance. There could be no other reason why so few locals were arrested, as gambling, amongst his people, was widespread.

"This won't take long. Shall we go?" Os repeated.

They travelled back down in the lift in silence. Ignoring curious glances from his staff in the foyer, Salinsky swept into the area which held at least one hundred slot machines, which, even during the day, were a quarter-occupied. Again, ignoring curious glances, he walked across the thick carpet to a door at the far side. Seconds later they entered the gaming area for the more serious gamblers.

The décor was burgundy and gold: a thick burgundy carpet, gold and burgundy curtains and gold gilt tables and chairs. It had cost a great deal of money to furnish, Russian money or Turkish mafia, Os assumed. Six tables were manned and all of them were busy.

Although none of the croupiers, distinguishable by their black evening wear, gave the two of them any particular attention, Os was certain that the atmosphere had become more charged. Salinsky strolled over to a woman, sitting on a high chair, overlooking two roulette tables. In answer to his question, she indicated a croupier, behind a half moon shaped table, dealing out cards to three customers.

Os watched the complicated manoeuvres as dealers changed seats, and finally, a young man, in his twenties, went to stand behind the indicated woman and whispered in her ear. Fear slid across her beautiful face as she glanced over at Salinsky. She continued to deal the cards, but, once all the coloured chips were pushed across to one of the players, she stood up and her replacement slipped into her seat.

Os sat down on a velvet sofa and waited for her to join him. He could tell immediately that she was anxious, but that did not surprise him. She was a foreign worker. A policeman asking questions, even if it was about her friend, would be unsettling. He introduced himself. "My name is Inspector Zahir. And your name?"

"Alexandra Budanov."

"And you're Russian like Natalia?"

She nodded, her blonde hair, twisted into a luxuriant knot, glinted in the ceiling lights.

"I'm wanting to talk to Natalia. I believe that she didn't turn up for the bus today and I'm told that she isn't in her room. Have you any idea where she might be?"

She shook her head, her eyes fixed on her fidgeting hands.

Os's patience slipped. "This is important. If you don't feel that you can speak openly here, then I can take you down to the station."

She shot him an anxious glance then at the man who had taken her place. "I'm working. I get in trouble if I leave table for long."

Os glanced at her ring finger. "I'm afraid you don't

understand me, Miss Eudanov, I'm investigating a murder and if you're thinking that you can hold anything back, I warn you, you could be in serious trouble."

Now he had her full attention. She stared at him, two red spots glowing on her slavic, high cheekbones. She whispered. " Natalia she been murdered?"

"No," he reassured her. "I'm sure she's fine, but her friend is dead."

"Which friend?" Her tongue snaked out and ran along her painted bottom lip.

Os took the photo cut of his top pocket and pushed it across the velvet seat. "This man - do you know him?" She stared down at the print but did not pick it up. He kept his tone, icily calm. "Please don't waste my time. I want the truth."

She winced. "I seen this man, yes. He comes here many times. But he not Natalia's friend, it impossible. It is not allowed to be friends with people who come here to gamble." Her heavily made-up eyes darted across to Salinsky, who, although watching, was too far away to hear what was being said.

"So, where do you think she might be, your friend, Natalia? I'm told that this is unlike her to miss her shift."

Tears filled her blue eyes. "I don't know. I saw her yesterday for few minutes. It her day off. She in kitchen making cup of coffee. I was late. I said hello, nothing more."

"And how did she seem then?" Os asked.

She shrugged, her beautiful but now miserable face. "I don't know. Okay I think. I was late."

"You had no idea what plans she had for her day off?" he persisted.

She shook her head but not before Os saw her hesitation. "We sleep and sitting around in the sun. The hours are very long here, we get tired." Again, she glanced across at her replacement as if worried that he might be permanent.

"And you're still telling me that this man was not her friend?" Os tapped the photo.

"When Natalia turns up she tell you herself. Friends with customers bad for business."

Os placed the photo in his pocket and stood up. "Well thank you for your time, Miss Budanov. I'm sure we'll speak again."

She sprang to her feet and strode back to her table. Within a few minutes she was back in her seat, shuffling the pack of cards.

Os crossed the room to the waiting Salinsky. "Now I would like to see where Natalia lives."

He frowned. "But why? I've already explained to you that Natalia Sakalova isn't connected to the person you're investigating. When she turns up for work, I'll let you know, if that's what you want."

The two men stared at each other. There was something intimidating about Salinsky; Alexandra Budanov was obviously scared of him. The manager had already intimated that if any of his workforce failed to keep up to his high standards, then they would be dismissed. As the Casino held their work permits, it would mean that they would have to leave the country.

Os shrugged. "Come with me if you like, or ring ahead and tell your caretaker to expect me. I'm relaxed either way."

Salinsky snorted out his annoyance. "I'll send someone with you so that you don't get lost. As you can appreciate, I can't leave the Casino."

"That's very kind of you," Os smiled, understanding Salinsky's frustration. He took one last look around the room. All the workers appeared on task, seemingly oblivious to the activities of their boss and the man who had just been talking to one of their colleagues. But Os had no doubt that, by now, they all knew that he was police and that he was making enquiries about Natalia.

Salinsky had a private word with one of the black-suited men in the foyer, and a few minutes later, Os was following a shiny and new, black Mercedes, out of the car park. They turned left on to the main road and headed back in the direction of Kyrenia. A sign for Karsiyaka flashed by and then one for Lapta. Here, the black car turned right. They drove a few yards up the hill and then swung into the drive of a small hotel. The sun had not filtered through the pine trees here, so Os reached into the back seat for his overcoat.

Os assumed, from the state of the building, that it was no longer used for tourists; the place had a neglected air about it and there were no cars in the car park beside their own. He followed the large man, in his incongruous dinner-suit, into the building.

The caretaker was waiting in the foyer; in silence and single file they went up the stairs to the first floor. The caretaker crossed over to the fourth door on the right and then, with his key already in his hand, unlocked it. Os stepped into the home of a Russian croupier.

Considering the cubic space was limited, she lived very neatly. The wardrobe could not contain all her clothes, so some hung from hangers over its door. But the bed was made and the dressing table was tidy. Os pushed the wardrobe door further open. A collection of black evening clothes hung alongside several casual dresses and blouses; underneath was an extensive selection of evening shoes.

Several bottles of perfume were grouped on the dressing table. Os pulled open the top drawer. Inside, folded neatly, were piles of underwear, bras and matching knickers, along with bustiers and suspender belts. In the drawer underneath lay an extensive collection of silk nighties, both long and short Instinctively, he pushed his hand underneath and touched paper, a large brown envelope. His stomach tensed He drew out photos of a beautiful woman.

Os flashed the top photo at the caretaker. "Is this Natalia?"

The middle-aged man squinted and then nodded. Os flicked through the ten professional-looking pictures. Natalia was a stunning woman, tall and slim, with long blonde hair. In some photos it was piled up in a knot on her head, and in others she wore it loose. Os wondered whether she had had the photos taken here in Northern Cyprus or back home in Russia Had her lover commissioned them or had she other plans? Whatever the case, he now knew what she looked like. Os slipped them back into the envelope. A sudden thought occurred to him. He pulled back the duvet on the double bed and was not surprised to see that, instead of regulation hotel cotton, the sheets were red satin.

The small en-suite bathroom had the appearance of a beauty shop. The shelves above the sink were stacked with expensive looking jars and bottles, and on a chair by the shower, a wash-bag overflowed with a selection of make-up. Apart from an absence of any personal documents, there was nothing to suggest that Natalia had gone anywhere at all. Os turned to the caretaker.

"When did you last see her?"

The man pursed his lips. "Yesterday evening. She went out on her own. About seven o'clock."

"Was she met by anyone? Was there a car outside?"

"I don't know - I didn't take much notice," he grimaced, "I was watching a football match on the TV in my office, wasn't I. My door was open, so I saw that she wasn't dressed up like she often is when she goes out." The caretaker glanced at the man in the black suit, perhaps aware that he was talking too much.

"You mean when she's not working, she goes out to meet someone on a regular basis?" Os asked.

The caretaker shook his head, his unshaven cheeks quivering. His eyes settled on a distant spot. "I've no idea. I'm not their keeper."

There was going to be little point questioning the man in front of one of Salinsky's men. If necessary, he could return another time and talk to him on his own. But it was beginning to look as if Molly was wrong about her brother-in-law's relationship with the woman who owned this room. From her personal belongings, it would not appear that she was having a serious relationship with someone who just worked in a computer shop. Os had no idea what croupiers earned, but, whatever the salary was, he doubted that she could afford to live like this without serious financial help. This woman had a benefactor, who had a lot more money than someone like Jamil Emral.

Os smiled. "I hope I won't need to bother you again." As he walked down the stairs back to his car, he heard footsteps behind him, then a voice talking in Russian. The black suit was presumably reporting back to Salinsky.

Chapter Three

As expected, he found Fikri in the canteen, reading the paper with two empty coffee cups by his side. He did not look up until Os pulled out a chair and sat down.

"Oh hello, Sir. I'm just having a short break."

Os could see how short the break had been by the cigarette stubs heaped in the ashtray. "How did you get on?"

Fikri folded his newspaper and set it aside. "Jamil has worked at the computer shop for the last three years. Before that he worked for the electricity board. I spoke to the boss; Jamil is the only outsider working for him, the other two are family. He said that Jamil was a good worker until recently, when he started to have a lot of time off."

Os leaned on the table then feeling its stickiness quickly sat back. "For what reasons?"

"Bad back. You know the usual thing, Sir."

Os smiled at Fikri's critical tone. The sergeant had a reputation for having time off himself. "So what was his job exactly?"

"He went to customers' homes to set up the internet and help them with their new computers."

Os told Fikri about his visit to the Casino and later at the workers' hostel.

"So you don't think this Natalia was Jamil's girlfriend?"

Os narrowed his eyes as he thought back over the recent events. "It's difficult to imagine. The manager and Natalia's friend, Alexandra, seemed adamant that Jamil was not her boyfriend, but they did admit that he was a punter there. However, from what I saw, she's in a totally different league to him. She's obviously got a man looking after her, but it's someone with money." Os shook his head. "No, I think Jamil probably just fancied her, otherwise why not introduce her to his brother and sister in law. He would have wanted to show off a beautiful girl like that."

"You still don't think that he was shot by mistake - the killer thinking he was someone else?" Fikri asked.

Os thought over the question as he scanned the canteen, busy with police officers smoking and chatting around the white plastic-topped tables. "It's possible," he answered. "But he was riding his own motorbike, following the road he always took back to his father's house, and he wasn't wearing a helmet. It's coming up to a full moon -so, even at night there would have been good visibility." Suddenly noticing the clock on the canteen wall, Os stood up. "All we can do is keep digging into his background. We'll both go back to his workplace tomorrow and ask more questions, then talk to his father. We need to find out as much as we can about Jamil Emral; there will be more to him than we know at the moment. Shop workers, unless they are involved in something very shady, don't usually get murdered. I'll see you in my office at eight tomorrow. By the way, what did you find out about the Half Moon?"

"They both own it, Sir. Her money probably bought it, but there were two signatures on the form registered."

When Os reached the canteen door, he turned, and as expected, Fikri was helping himself to another coffee, already puffing on a fresh cigarette. It seemed that although the sergeant's shift had come to an end, he did not choose to go home.

An hour later, Os strode into the bar area of the Colony Hotel. Zelfa was already sitting on one of the sofas, flicking through a newspaper, a glass of white wine on the coffee table in front of her. Not for the first time it occurred to him that this beautiful woman, in her blue trouser-suit and high heels, would never be taken for a police officer.

Noting that she already had a full drink in front of her, he ordered from the bar then sat down opposite her.

She smiled, indicating her wine glass. "With the day I've had, I didn't much feel like coffee. What have you been up to?"

Os told her about his visit to the Casino. "She definitely has a boyfriend, but I can't see it being Jamil. So we're no closer to finding a motive for his murder. What about you?"

"Visiting brothels!" She grimaced and suddenly she looked ten years younger and vulnerable, a girl just venturing out on her career. "It's probably punishment for screwing up on the last case."

Os laughed. She was probably right. "At least he didn't demote you back to sergeant like he promised." The boss had been more than fair with Zelfa. If she hadn't behaved so rashly and put herself and another policeman in a situation where they were both taken hostage, that policeman would still be alive today.

Os changed the subject. "So what's he got you doing?"

She took a sip of her wine, her big brown eyes, twinkling. "You're looking at the new police liaison officer between the government and the brothels. Did you know there was a politician whose job it is to make sure they all run smoothly?"

The waiter put Os's glass on the table next to a bowl of nuts. Os watched him return to the bar before asking, "What do you mean?"

"The number of brothels is increasing, so his responsibility is to make sure that everything runs smoothly, monthly health checks for the girls and no major problems with the punters."

He scanned her face. "So what's your job exactly?"

"I've got a list of the houses and I check that everything is running properly- make sure, as best I can, that the only girls working are the ones with paperwork and up to date medical records." She shrugged, "As you can imagine, it's impossible to know whether they have anyone there illegally, unless we pull the places apart, and the government obviously doesn't want us to do that - they get too much money from the system".

Os felt a sudden sense of shame. "This is all fairly new you know; the country's changed so much. Ten years ago there were only a handful of casinos and brothels, but now they're allowed to spring up everywhere."

"Brothels have always been a problem, but casinos were one thing we didn't have to bother with in Istanbul," Zelfa said.

Irritated with his country's government, he answered, "I know! Turkey couldn't control the gaming world, so they made it illegal - and Northern Cyprus welcomed them with open arms. The number of gambling houses is increasing every year, as is the associated crime." He threw back his wine and then held up his empty glass to catch the waiter's attention.

Zelfa twisted her glass stem, watching the pale yellow liquid circle the bowl. "Strangely, I found my first day more interesting than I expected. And I'm sure I'll get better protection for the women than a male police officer would." When Os did not rise to the criticism, she added, "Quite a few of them can't speak Turkish except for the odd word, you know".

Os slipped some notes on to the waiter's tray, then picking up his fresh wineglass asked, "Where are they from?"

"Mostly from the old Soviet areas, you know Kazakhstan, Azerbaijan, Uzbekistan. They come here for a minimum of eighteen months, and if they work hard, and cause no trouble, they go home with a big bonus - more than they could earn in years at home."

"And if they don't like the work?" Os asked.

"Then they're sent home early with nothing."

"And what's the minister like, the one you're liaising with?"

"I haven't met him yet. I'm driving over to Nicosia to see him tomorrow morning." She became suddenly interested in the state of her polished nails. "But I wanted your opinion first. "Do you think I should go back to Istanbul?"

He took in her shiny, shoulder-length hair and beautiful face and suddenly knew that he would miss her if she did.

"Is that you want to do?"

She shrugged. "I'm not sure. I know I've been lucky that I'm still in a job, but I've made a real mess of things, haven't I? The station must hold it against me. Rauf Yucel was one of their own and it was because of me that he died." The coquette in her had gone. She sat, shoulders slumped, miserable. "To be honest, I find it difficult walking into the station sometimes and I hate going to the cafeteria." She attempted to smile. "I just know that people are talking about me."

Tears formed in her eyes; she fumbled in her bag for a tissue and blew her nose. Os looked away. But, he could not tell her that she was imagining things. Several officers had already criticised her to him, though of course he had not responded. Losing one of their own was not something that could be forgiven easily.

Instead, he answered, "If you leave, it will be like you're running away. They'll get over it, people always do."

She sighed, her eyes not meeting his. "I suppose, if I went back to Istanbul now, it would always haunt me. I'd always feel that I'd failed here."

The bar was filling up with people calling in from work or on the start of a night out. Although he had never drunk in this bar before, it was obviously one of the many glitzy establishments that had sprung up in the last few years. He could understand why she had chosen the venue; the comfortable sofas, in yellow brocade, were grouped far enough away from each other so that conversations could not be overheard.

Bizarrely, he wondered whether Rose would like it. In the ten months that they had lived together, they had chosen to spend most evenings at home, occasionally going out to eat at a local restaurant or visiting friends. Perhaps, he should have made more of an effort to show her his country, encouraging her to love it as much as he did. Not that she disliked Northern Cyprus; since they had split up, she had remained here, still living in the house her aunt had left her, outside the hill village of Karaman.

Zelfa spoke. "So, who have you got working with you on

this case?"

Os grinned. "Fikri, one of the sergeants. I thought my days with him were over, but he's just told me that his wife wants him to keep working. They're helping their daughter buy a house."

The tension in her face was easing. "What about Sener? I thought he was your favourite?"

"He is. But he's putting in for his assistant inspector's ticket, so he's on a course in Yenicekoy until Wednesday."

"Yenicekoy?"

"The police training takes place there. It's not far from Famagusta. He'll split his time between the training centre and here over the next six months. What about you?"

She tilted her head so that her dark silky hair spread out over her right shoulder, a look of puzzlement on her face.

He clarified "Where did you train? I've never asked."

"I did four years at the Acadamy in Ankara. Didn't you do the same, or is it different over here."

Os knew that anyone wanting to become a police officer with rank attended the Acadamy. Each year, the Turkish government paid for five Turkish Cypriots to register for the course. It was assumed by everyone, that it was the quickest way to get on. He shook his head. "I didn't decide to become a policeman until I finished my law degree in Istanbul. So I trained on the job."

"You've done well then, Chief Inspector," she grinned.

He thought how sexy she looked, now that she had relaxed. She leant back into the sofa, her shapely legs crossed, swinging one high-heeled shoe.

"It's been harder," he replied. "I've had to prove myself more but I'd had enough being a full time student. I also couldn't accept the other students being so much younger than me."

She threw back her head and laughed. "You sound as if you're fifty. Shall we have another drink?"

Sometime later they stood outside the hotel, sheltering from the light drizzle illuminated by the yellow street lights. She pulled up the fur collar of her coat and looked up at him.

"Are you sure you don't want to come home and eat? I've got some steaks in the fridge; it would only take me a minute to throw something together."

Os hesitated before shaking his head. "Thanks, another time. I need to write up some case notes. But try not to worry, the other thing will pass." He reached out and squeezed her arm. "I'll see you in the morning. Are you alright getting home?"

She grinned. "I'm a policewoman, or have you forgotten. I'll see you tomorrow." Putting up an umbrella, she hurried off into the night.

As Os cut through the empty back-streets, the rain became heavier. Wanting to protect his soft, brown leather jacket, he broke into a trot, but by the time he reached his apartment, he was soaked. As he stood dripping in the middle of the living area, the cold hit him. There had been no fire for over twenty four hours and there was a strong smell of damp. A sense of loneliness overpowered him and he thought back to Zelfa's offer of dinner. If she had been a man, he would not have hesitated, but he would be a fool not to be aware that there was something sizzling between them, and the last thing he needed, at this moment, was for his life to become more complicated. Rose still buzzed in and out of his head and he shared an office with Zelfa, for God's sake. He hung his jacket over a chair then went into the bedroom and changed his damp shirt for a thick sweater.

To Os's amazement, Fikri was already in the entrance hall when he arrived the next morning. As soon as he saw the chief inspector, the elderly sergeant extinguished his cigarette in the sand bucket and hurried towards him, his slack face unusually animated.

"A Mr. Emral from Karalangalou was attacked in his home, sometime during the night. A neighbour found him unconscious on the floor this morning."

Os could feel his sergeant's excitement. "Is he related?"

"I don't know yet, Sir. I was told about it ten minutes ago

when I arrived. He's been sent to hospital and a couple of constables have gone out to the house but that's all I know."

"Let's get moving then. We'll take your car."

Os removed several newspapers from the passenger seat and flicked on the siren. Fikri, seemingly energised by the scream, reversed the car and shot out on to the road.

It took less than ten minutes to find the address they had been given. A police car was already parked outside the small bungalow which was set on its own small patch of scrubland. Both men strode up the path flanked by a rusting motorbike and the remains of a couple of bent wooden chairs. A uniformed policeman stood in the open doorway. Os recognised the constable as one of the new young men who had recently joined the station.

"We've not long sent Mr. Emral off in an ambulance, Sir. Constable Kolac's gone with him to Kyrenia hospital. The old man's concussed · someone's given him a good going over." The young constable jerked his head, indicating the inside of the house. "And it's a real mess here, Sir. Every drawer and cupboard has been turned out." He stepped aside, allowing the two newcomers to enter the house.

The constable was right: the house was a mess, though Os suspected that it was not all due to the break-in. It was to be expected, two men living together, one of them an old man. He placed the traditional Turkish sofa back upright; there were deep slashes in the upholstery and its straw stuffing was strewn across the stone-flagged floor. A picture lay on its side, the back prised off and the glass smashed. A sideboard still occupied the back wall, but all the drawers had been removed and the contents scattered. Os turned to the young constable hovering by the door.

"Is the rest of the house like this?"

"Yes, Sir! Every room."

"And how did they get in, that's presuming that there were more than one?"

"There's no forced entry, Sir. The old man must have opened the door. Maybe he knew them."

"And we've no idea when this happened?"

The constable shook his head. "The neighbour called in

to see him this morning and found the door unlocked. He said he was keeping an eye on Emral after his son's death."

"So this neighbour rang for the ambulance?"

The constable nodded. "He's very upset, as you can imagine, Sir. He said they've been neighbours for years. We let him go back to his house, but we told him not to go anywhere else, until he'd been questioned properly."

"Good. When the other officers get here, you can start questioning the neighbours. Find out, who was the last person to see Emral and what state of mind he was in. He'd only just lost his son, but was he worried about anything else? He might have confided something to someone. The break-in, of course, could have been speculative." Os pulled a face at the state of the room. "But I can't see why someone should go to the trouble. Nothing here gives any impression that there's money to be had." Os rehung a faded print of Kyrenia back on the wall. "You can leave the immediate neighbour to me."

The constable pulled out his notebook and scribbled down his instructions. Fikri watched from the doorway, a lit cigarette in his hand.

"Ring the station, Sergeant and get another five men down here. I want the house and garden searched thoroughly," Os ordered. "Whatever they were looking for, they probably found, but we'll double check."

Perhaps it was Os's sharp tone that made Fikri straighten.

"What are we searching for, Sir?" the younger constable asked.

"I've no idea yet. Are you aware that, the man murdered two days ago, was his son?"

The young constable's mouth dropped. "Out in Ozonkoy?"

"That's the one."

The constable flapped his hand. " I forgot to tell you, Sir! Another son's been here. He just missed the ambulance, so we sent him down to the hospital. The neighbour rang him when he found Emral unconscious."

Os's eyes narrowed. "He must have driven fast."

"He wanted to come inside and see what damage had been done to the house, but I wouldn't let him. I told him

42

that it was a crime scene."

Os nodded his approval.

The young man flushed. "He didn't like it, Sir. He seemed quite angry. But there were two of us and we are the police."

Os resisted a smile. "You are indeed. I'll go and talk to him later. I have a feeling that he's not being totally honest with us."

The constable frowned. "Why's that Sir?"

Os examined the keen, honest face. "His brother was shot dead, then his father is attacked and the house broken into. He might not be directly involved, but I'm sure he's a good idea what's going on. There was a possibility that he had been murdered by mistake, but now, with this...," Os waved his hand at the debris around him, "It's too much of a coincidence."

He walked back into the room, his mobile phone in his hand.

"You take over here, Sergeant. When the men arrive, I want the house and garden turned over. I'm going next door first, and then on to the hospital. Ring me if you have anything to report." In case Fikri decided to light up another cigarette, he added, "You two can start immediately".

Os threw one last glance around the soulless living area and walked to the front door. As he went down the path, he smiled as he heard Fikri issuing orders to the constable.

The door opened to his knock. The woman on the doorstep showed no surprise at the police badge, but indicated that Os should come in. A middle-aged man, presumably her husband, was sitting at the kitchen table, a newspaper open in front of him. He stood up, grinding his cigarette out in the centre of an overflowing ashtray. Os held up his hand.

"Please, stay where you are. I've just called in to ask you a few questions. I know that you've already talked to the constable, but I just need to get a few things sorted out in my own mind." Os pulled out the other kitchen chair and sat down. "If we could start from the beginning... What time did you find Mr. Emral?"

The man looked across at his wife, his expression full of uncertainty.

"It was about eight o'clock I think, Dear," she answered. "We'd had our breakfast and we were talking about Mr. Emral before you left for work." She turned to Os. "You know how difficult it would be for him living on his own. His wife died years ago and he and Jamil have lived together ever since." She pursed her lips. "Mehmet's married of course to an English woman. Maybe Mr. Emral can go and live with them when he gets back from the hospital."

His wife's explanation seemed to galvanize her husband into talkativeness. "Yes, I only meant to call in for a few minutes. I'm late now of course. The policeman said I had to ring work, tell them that I would be very late and that I had to give a statement."

"Yes. That is normal procedure," Os answered. "Now tell me everything you saw. Think carefully now."

The man narrowed his eyes, as if picturing the scene in his head. "I went up the path and knocked on the door. I knocked twice but he didn't answer."

"And everything looked as usual, outside? Did it?"

The man considered this. "I didn't really notice, but if it had been different I would have noticed, wouldn't I?"

Not necessarily, Os thought, but he chose not to break the man's train of thought.

"When he didn't answer the second time, I was worried. Mr. Emral always gets up early and often the door is open – he likes visitors."

"So then?"

The man shrugged. "So then I turned the handle. I was going to just step inside and call out to him, to make sure that he was okay," he added, perhaps worried that the policeman would think that he had entered without permission. "I saw the mess immediately and knew something had happened. I went straight into the house and found him on the floor. The back of his head bleeding - I could see because he was lying face down. But he was still breathing. I called out his name, but he didn't answer. That's when I phoned the police."

"On your phone here?"Os asked, wondering whether he had left the house again. The assailant might still have been in the house when the neighbour had knocked.

The neighbour shook his head. "I used his. I didn't want to leave him on his own, so I stayed there until the police and the ambulance arrived."

And you saw or heard no one?"

He shook his head. "The ambulance was here very quickly - and the police. I didn't have to wait long."

"The constable said that you had spoken to him the night before? How had he seemed?"

"Very subdued. He's taken the death of his son very badly. Well you would, wouldn't you? You don't expect your children to die before you do."

Os did not answer. He had a sudden flash of Rose in the hospital bed, telling him that she had lost their baby. He knew how he had felt then; how much worse it must be if you had spent years living with a son, helping to create his personality and future.

"But he didn't give any indication that he was worried about anything else?"

The man pursed his lips, his skin settling into deep lines on either side of his face. "No, we only talked about his son."

"And what did you both think of Jamil?"

The wife answered immediately. "He was a nice lad. We've known both boys since they were children."

"Were either of them ever in trouble?" Os asked.

She shrugged her plump shoulders. "No more than any others. They sometimes missed school. I don't think either of them found school easy. But they were never in trouble with the police."

"I got Jamil his job at the electricity board. I've worked there for years so when an apprenticeship came up, I put in a good word for him. ' There was an understandable boast in the man's voice. "Good jobs are hard to find for the young ones nowadays, especially when you haven't got any decent qualifications."

"So he'd worked there for how long?"

"Eight years. Then he left to work for a computer shop. But he did all those other jobs on the side as well."

"Zafer!" His wife spoke sharply.

Her husband grinned sheepishly. "I don't think it matters now he's dead." He turned back to Os. "He used to do private jobs for people. He even started working for the foreigners and they pay a lot more. I know he was saving the money he earned - he wanted to buy his own house."

"We've been told that he started to take time off in this job - any idea why?"

Annoyance flashed across the man's face. "He was working on the side, wasn't he! You know what these young ones are like, money's so important to them. He wasn't a bad lad, just wanted the things we've worked all our lives for- now."

Os turned to the wife. "And did he have a girlfriend? Did he ever bring girlfriends back to the house?"

She wrinkled her nose. "He used to. He was a good-looking boy, girls were always after him. But I haven't seen anyone with him for the last year. We've often talked about it...," she nodded at her husband. "We'd have thought he would be like his brother and want to get married."

Os moved on to another subject. "Have there been burglaries around here before?"

"No," the man answered. "I don't know any houses that have been broken into in this area, but it's starting to happen isn't it!"

"What burglaries?" Os asked, interested in the man's opinion on the changing culture of the country.

He nodded. "We always used to be able to leave our doors unlocked, but not anymore."

Os took his card out of his pocket and placed it on the table. "We think that there might be more to this than a straight burglary. So, if you do think of anything different that you might have seen or heard recently, give me a ring. We've finished with you for now, so if you want to go into work...."

The man picked up the card and studied it, seemingly in no hurry to leave. Os opened the front door and went out on to the covered veranda.

The young constable stood a short distance down the road, talking to a woman. Os considered joining them, then decided against it. Fikri would call him if there was anything important, and meanwhile he needed to talk to Mehmet Emral.

Chapter Four

Mehmet was hunched over his father's hospital bedside, the older man's hand clutched in his own. As Os pushed open the door, Mehmet turned. His face was pale and there were bags under his eyes.

Os remained standing at the door. "How is he?""

"Can I help you?" A nurse stood behind him.

Os flashed his badge then pointed, indicating that it was the man in the chair he wanted to talk to, not the one in the bed.

Despite her youth, she appeared to have no problem protecting her patient. "It would be better if you both left. Mr. Emral needs quiet."

Outside, Os said, "I'm sorry about your father".

Pain clouded Mehmet's eyes as he stared at the opposite wall. "They say there's a good chance that he'll pull through, but he'll lose his memory. He'll never be the same again."

The annoyance Os had previously felt towards this man faded, and he softened his tone. "What's going on here, Mehmet? First your brother's murdered, and now your father's been attacked. The two events are obviously connected. You must have some idea why someone thought it worth their while to break into your father's house?"

Mehmet's face blanked. "He was my brother, but I didn't know everything about him." Anger tipped his voice. "Did you find that woman, the Russian that Molly said Jamil was friends with?"

It was an interesting word friend; it could mean so much or so little. Os raised his eyebrow."His girlfriend?"

Mehmet gave a quick shake of his head. "I've no idea how serious it was; we never met her."

"I did speak to a friend of hers and it looks as if you're right. She said that it was impossible for croupiers to have relationships with any of the punters. It's a sackable offence."

Mehmet's tone dipped. "So you didn't see Natalia?"

"She didn't turn up for work and she wasn't in her room. No one knows where she is, or if they do, they're not saying."

Mehmet grabbed Os's arm. "You've got to find her. She could be in danger."

Os looked down at his arm and Mehmet removed his hand. "Why do you say that?"

Mehmet paused, as if making an effort to calm himself. "I'm probably not thinking straight, but my brother has been killed and my father attacked; now you say this Natalia hasn't turned up for work."

"Shouldn't you be more worried about yourself and your wife?"

Again Mehmet took a few moments to answer. "We've got nothing to do with what's happened. Why should we be in danger?"

Exasperation tightened his stomach. "I'm sure your father thought the same, and look what happened to him. You're keeping something back from me, Mehmet, and putting yourself and your wife in danger. Think about that," Os said coldly, "If you come to your senses, give me a ring". Without waiting for an answer, he turned and strode along the corridor, down the stairs, and out to his car.

As soon as Os stepped into the station, the duty sergeant called out that Superintendent Atak wanted to see him. Irritation flicked through his stomach as he walked through the corridor and knocked on Atak's secretary's door.

She was seated at her computer. Despite her new, and more glamorous hair-style, her face was set in the same rigid lines that had always been part of her unapproachable persona. She appeared to have difficulty tearing her eyes away from her screen and when she spoke her tone was cold. "He's expecting you, Chief Inspector."

Os pulled open the adjoining door to find that the superintendent had company. A policeman, whose uniform looked tailor-made, turned from his position by the window to stare at him.

The superintendent's voice was more formal than usual. "Good morning, Osman. I'd like to introduce you to our new assistant superintendent. Ismail has just arrived from Ankara."

The policeman towered over Os as he held out a long, bony hand.

"Chief Inspector Zahir is one of our finest officers," Superintendent Atak gushed. "He's just solved a most complicated crime down in the Karpas."

Ismail's thin mouth twisted into a smile. "Congratulations, Chief Inspector. I believe you've just been promoted."

Os took it as a statement rather than a question.

The commander waved a beefy arm, indicating that Os should sit down. "Tell us how the case is progressing. I heard that the father of the dead man was attacked in his home last night? What do you make of it?"

Os paused, always surprised by how quickly his boss got to hear things.

"Start from the beginning, Osman," Atak encouraged, "Ismail might be able to come up with some fresh ideas."

Os stared at this new, enthusiastic commander then noticed that the assistant superintendent had taken out a notebook and pen. Suddenly uneasy but having no option, he related the events to both men. "On Sunday morning the station received an anonymous phone call - a fatal accident involving a man on a motorbike, outside the village of Ozonkoy. Sergeant Derya identified the body as being the brother of a restauranteur in the village. We both went to the house, then the sergeant took the brother to identify the corpse." Os paused as the secretary came in with a tray of coffee cups.

The assistant superintendent looked up from his note

making, but did not put down his pen. "Carry on, Chief Inspector; I'm beginning to find this fascinating."

For such a tall man his voice was unnaturally high. Os focused on being as succinct as possible."However, as soon as the body was prepared for burial, fresh evidence came to light. The doctor changed his statement of accidental death to murder. There had been a great deal of blood congealed around the head and face, tying in with the fact that he had not been wearing a helmet. But, once the body had been washed, the doctor discovered the bullet still lodged in the back of the skull. I'm waiting for clarification from the lab, but it could be Russian."

The assistant superintendent's eyes widened. "That's very observant of you, Chief Inspector."

Os chose not mention his six month secondment in the States and the two- week course he had done there on the firearms that different countries used. There was something about this man - the less he knew about him, the better.

"The sister-in-law thought that Jamil had been seeing a Russian croupier from the Ruby Royal Casino. She hadn't turned up for work yesterday and wasn't in the hostel. Judging by the opulence of her room, I'd say someone's been spending a lot of money on her."

The assistant superintendent smirked.

" Jamil Emral was only an electrician. Alright he was doing extra work on top of his day job, but I doubt that he could afford the things she has in her room." Os finished his coffee. "Her friend, and the manager of the Casino, were both adamant that she would not be having a relationship with one of the punters. I showed them a photo of Emral and neither of them said that they recognised him."

"Well they wouldn't, would they, since it's supposed to be illegal for a Turkish Cypriot to gamble in one of those places," the superintendent interrupted.

"I was about to ring the Casino to see if she's turned up today," Os continued.

The assistant superintendent leant forward, his elbows on his knees and his fingers steepled together. "No such thing as coincidences eh, Chief Inspector?"

Os was forcing a smile when his mobile rang. Fikri's voice seemed unnaturally loud.

"We've found money in the outside oven of Emral's house, Sir."

"How much?" Os asked, already on his feet.

"I haven't counted it yet, Sir. I rang you first, but it looks like a lot."

"I'm coming over now. Keep the men searching; there might be something else." He snapped his phone shut, aware that both men were staring at him. He repeated Fikri's news.

The superintendent beamed. Again, there was the unusual experience of being washed in the man's approval.

"Excellent, Osman. You appear to be making real progress with this one."

Os glanced into the cold eyes of the assistant superintendent.

"Chief Inspector," Ismail nodded in a form of dismissal.

Os strode down the corridor, excitement tempered by a sense of foreboding. Despite the commander's support, he could not shake off the cloud of negativity. He and the assistant superintendent had taken an instant dislike to each other.

Chapter Five

Fikri stood in the doorway, a package under his arm, his usually dour face alight with animation. Os followed him into the house, where he placed both the package and another object on the table.

"Eighty thousand lira, Sir, and five hundred and forty pounds in English money. And a gun."

Os flicked open the dirty waxed cloth to reveal a well-oiled regulation Turkish army pistol. "Interesting! Check the number. I doubt that it's the one he used during national service. It's probably stolen. Show me where you found all this."

Fikri led the way out to the back of the house. He pointed at an old outside oven. "It was wedged inside that. Constable Hasan found the money and the gun behind a piece of wood. "

Constable Hasan was watching them as he raked under the bushes. Os held up a hand in greeting. The young man grinned back.

"Was nothing found in the house?" he asked Fikri.

" There might have been before the break-in. But we've searched everywhere. I'd say this must be what they were looking for, Sir."

They were standing on a patch of land, perhaps ninety square yards. Two rusting bicycles had been dumped next to a discarded washing machine. Several faded shirts were pegged to a sagging line.

Os went back into the house. "I'll take these back to the station. If the money's not stolen, why was it hidden here instead of lying in a bank account?" The answer was not in his sergeant's eyes. "There's more to Jamil Emral than we first imagined. Keep the men at it for another hour, and then if nothing else turns up, lock up and come back to the station."

With a sense of relief at leaving a house that smelled of dirty clothes and sweat, Os walked outside to his car.

Zelfa was at her desk when Os walked into their office. Os leant against the edge of his desk. "We've found a huge wad of money at the house. The serial numbers are being checked now."

Zelfa put down her pen. "Do you think Jamil Emral was a thief then?"

Os shrugged. "I don't know yet. What are you up to?"

She rested her head against the wall. "I've just got back from checking out another brothel near the airport."

"No problems?"

She shrugged. "The girls had to be got out of bed, so you can imagine that they weren't thrilled."

"How did they react to you?"

"Avoided eye contact and I couldn't blame them; it's not exactly dignified passing over documents that say you're clear of any sexual diseases. I didn't take it personally - with the reputation police have around brothels, I'd behave the same as them."

She looked very pretty this morning in a red jumper, her shiny dark hair twisted into a knot at the back of her head. "How did the manager cope with you being a woman?"

For the first time, Zelfa grinned. "I don't think he was too happy."

Os laughed. "No bribes then, like free use of the girls?"

"Interestingly, they did offer me a big bottle of perfume. I was tempted."

Os raised his eyebrows. Her grin widened. "Two of the heavies stayed in the room the whole time I was there, presumably to stop the women from being indiscreet. I took

54

a constable with me, a big, strapping man, but even then I had to kick up a fuss as we were three girls short. I made them go and fetch them." She chewed on her lip, marking her lipstick- the same shade as her jumper. "We inspected the place afterwards · very depressing. The lights are on a permanent dim, to hide the dirt I suppose." She paused and then asked, "Didn't you say that you once did this job?"

"Only for a month and I was just a sergeant, working under an inspector. We concentrated on the brothels along the border, places that attracted the Greek Cypriots."

"And were you offered anything?" she asked, her smile not quite reaching her eyes.

"Of course! Free use of the women."

"You weren't tempted?"

"No!"

"I'm pleased to hear it." He thought he heard relief in her voice. "I'm not sure many officers here would say the same."

His own uncertainty was evident in his tone. "The police force isn't that corrupt."

She looked back at him, but said nothing.

He changed the subject. "Have you met the new assistant superintendent yet?"

"I didn't know that we were getting one."

So it was not common knowledge yet. "He's from Ankara. I'll be interested to hear what you think of him."

"What's his name?"

"Ismail."

"I don't think I've heard of him." She grinned. "I can tell that you don't like him."

Os shook his head. "I'm off to talk to anyone who knows the Russian croupier, Natalia. I only called in to drop off the money. She's still not turned up for work and no one admits to knowing where she is."

"Are you free Thursday night?"

Os turned back from the doorway. "Yes. Why?"

"I was going to cook for you. About eight if that's okay?"

Her eyes were on his and suddenly he was answering. "That would be good. I'll look forward to it."

He walked out to his car, oblivious to anyone he passed, conflicting emotions raging inside him. Was it really just a simple invite to dinner from a colleague? He did not think so. He suddenly thought of Rose and felt the familiar pain in his chest. But that relationship was over, finished.

The sign for Karalangalou flashed by. The bank that he had always used when he had lived in Karaman, was coming up on the right. The parking area in front was clear, so he pulled over.

As he ripped the queue number from the machine, he saw that Carrie, the American wife of his friend Aka, was already at the counter. He hesitated, considered walking out, and then stood his ground. He was being stupid. He needed to pay his utility bills and take out some money; if he left now, he would only have to come back another time.

Carrie turned to leave and saw him immediately. A wide smile stretched across her vibrant, freckled face. "Os, how lovely to see you. I was going to tell Aka to ring you tonight. Why don't you come round for supper on Thursday?"

Feeling like a rabbit caught in the glare of headlights, he answered, "That would have been lovely but I've already got something on".

Hazel-coloured eyes searched his face. His number flashed up on the screen above the counter; he held up his ticket apologetically.

"What about tonight then," she spoke quickly. "We're not doing anything. We were just going to have kebabs."

The bank teller cleared her throat.

"That would be lovely," Os answered. He pushed his bills across the counter.

"Seven-thirty do you? Will you have finished work by then?"

"I'll be there." She flashed another smile and then swung out of the bank. Through the window he watched her climb into her old Fiat and drive away.

A few minutes later he was back in his own car and on the road again. The idea of a home-cooked meal was good, as long as Carrie did not bring up the subject of Rose. Aka was his old school-friend, but Carrie and Rose had remained friends. If only Carrie would not go on about her. The year-long relationship was over and he did not need to be reminded. He concentrated on the road ahead.

He saw the turning to Lapta village as he flashed by. He braked, reversed, and seconds later he was on the road that led up to Natalia's hostel. As he pulled up, the caretaker appeared in the doorway.

Os crunched across the gravel. "Is Natalia back yet?" he called.

The older man did not reply. For a moment, Os thought that she had returned, and that he was protecting her. But then the caretaker shook his head. "No. She's not come back."

"I'm going up to have another look at her room." Os held out his hand. "If you could give me the keys!"

The caretaker hesitated. Was he going to telephone the Casino to get their advice? But then he shrugged and went into his office. Os took the proffered key and made for the stairs.

Instead of unlocking Natalia's door, he knocked on the adjoining one. Alexandra, the woman he had interviewed the day before, opened her door. Her eyes deadened as soon as she recognised her visitor.

So that there could be no misunderstandings, he flashed his badge. "Can I come in, please?"

Like the caretaker, she hesitated and then stepped back. He entered a room that was identical to Natalia's in size and layout, but her possessions could not have been more different. Clothes hung from the cupboard doors, but they were of a much cheaper quality than her friend's. The dressing table was also covered with cosmetics although they were of the type that could be found on the shelves of any supermarket. A thin blanket, with the name of the hotel printed along the edge, covered the single bed.

Os leant against the window and indicated, with a flourish of his hand, that she should sit down. She obeyed him. She was Russian, so she was schooled in doing exactly what the police told her to do.

"How long have you known Natalia?" he asked.

"We at same school. We best friends," she answered in her stilted Turkish.

"So you decided to come over to Northern Cyprus together."

"There was advert in paper. They wanted women to work in casinos here - all kinds of jobs. We are croupiers."

"They offered you training?"

"We already croupiers in Russia, but me and Natalia, we wanted change. The pay is better here. The sun is hotter too. But now we either work or sleep."

Her tone made Os ask," So you wished you'd stayed at home?"

She pursed her lips, which in the privacy of her own room, were devoid of the thick lipstick that she had worn at work. Now that she was in jeans and a jumper, she looked much younger than he had initially thought; he doubted that she was even twenty years old. "Sometimes. But they take passports. They think they can treat you how they want. We work each day longer hours than in Russia."

Os frowned. "Presumably they're not forcing you to stay here?"

She shook her head and her blonde ponytail swished from side to side. "No, but they say we lose money for bringing us here. You must work a year first."

"And you haven't done that yet."

To his surprise, she nodded. "But now Natalia does not go home. She in love." Immediately she put her hand to her mouth and her eyes widened.

"That's what I wanted to talk to you about," Os replied.

Alexandra shook her head so fiercely that her pony-tail whipped across her face. "I should not say that."

He softened his voice. "I don't mean Natalia any harm, you know. I am, however, concerned that she's gone missing, especially when a man, she might have been close to, has been murdered. I want to make sure that she's safe."

A shadow passed across her eyes. "I do not know where she is."

"She was meeting her boyfriend on her day off. What plans did she have?"

Alexandra shrugged. "He usually comes here. He take her for meal, but they always go back to her room."

Os was surprised that she actually blushed. "He was married then! If it's nct Jamil Emral, who is it? One of the other punters, or does he work at the Casino?"

Alexandra looked tired, as if the pressure of keeping a secret was suddenly too much. His name Ersin Kucuk . He manager at Casino."

Os remembered how confident the other manager, Salinsky, had been when he had said that Natalia could not be having a relationship with one of the punters. Os had assumed that it was because of the house-rules. But actually it was because he knew that his colleague, Kucuk, had claimed her.

"How long has this been going on?"

"A year. As soon as he saw her. She very beautiful, Natalia."

"Is she in love with Kucuk?"

Alexandra became engrossed in the gold ring on her little finger, twisting it round and round. "No. She likes him," she added defensively, "but not love him."

But, only a few minutes before, she had said that Natalia was in love. Was she making mistakes with her poor knowledge of Turkish?"Why's that?"

Alexandra shook her head. "Kucuk buys her expensive things. She can have anything she wants."

"Is he a good man? You must know him quite well." Os added before she could deny an opinion. "He's your boss."

"He knows I am Natalia's friend, so he nice to me too. But other people in Casino say he has very bad temper. He get rid of many people."

"And she's never stayed away overnight with him before. Never gone to a hotel?"

"No. As you say, he married man."

Os watched her closely. "Have you seen Mr. Kucuk since Natalia went missing?"

Again she shook her pony-tail.

Os fought his exasperation. "You must have some idea where Natalia has gone? Are you telling me that she wasn't two-timing Kucuk? Who could blame her? He's married himself."

Weariness had returned to her voice. "No one else, only Mr. Kucuk."

She was still playing with her ring; she was lying. He took the photo of Jamil out of his pocket and held it out to her. "Have another good look," he invited. "Are you sure you've never seen him with Natalia? Is this the man that Natalia's in love with? You're not going to get into trouble if you say anything. In fact," his voice became cold, "If you don't tell us the truth, you will be in trouble – you could end up in jail".

Her cheeks flushed. "Why pick on me? There are many girls here you could talk to."

"Don't you care about her at all?"Os snapped. "If she was a good friend of the murdered man, then her life could be in danger too."

"I talk no more. She come back soon and then she tell you."

He fastened her skittering blue eyes with his own. "I just hope that it won't be too late to help her, Alexandra. I know that you're scared, but you could help. You've still got my card?"

She nodded.

"If you decide to be sensible, then ring me. I could arrest you for holding back information and I might yet. Think about it. The longer you wait, the worse it could be for Natalia. She could be in serious danger."

Alexandra's eyes brimmed with tears. "I say nothing," she repeated.

Os crossed to the door. He had a bad feeling in his gut about Natalia and he knew that he wouldn't feel differently until he saw her alive and well.

Chapter Six

The girl on the desk recognised him immediately. After a brief phone conversation, in Russian, she gave an insincere smile and, in halting Turkish, she told Os that he could go straight up to the manager's office. As the door of the lift slid closed, he wondered if he was about to meet Ersin Kucuk.

But it was Petrov Salinsky who, as the lift doors opened, got to his feet. As Os crossed the room, Salinsky came out from behind his desk and held out his hand.

"I didn't expect to see you again so soon," he said. "Please," he waved towards the sofas, "Can I provide a drink of any kind?"

"No thank you. This won't take long." As if to reinforce the point, Os remained standing. "I believe that Natalia is having a relationship with your colleague, Ersin Kucuk."

Salinsky smiled. Os guessed that, having spent what was probably a great deal of money on his teeth, he made a regular point of showing them off.

"I've heard that you've been talking to Alexandra today. These girls make more of things than we men." He splayed out his manicured hands. "He's fond of the girl, I'm sure, but the relationship is not serious. He's a married man with children, Chief Inspector. Mr. Kucuk does not confide in me, as far as personal matters go, but I can say with confidence, that it is nothing more than a sexual fling."

"And where is Mr. Kucuk now? I obviously need to talk to

him. I'd hoped to meet him here at work."

"He's in Istanbul. He left yesterday and won't be back until Thursday night."

"And his business there?" Os persisted.

"Mr. Kucuk is in overall charge here, though the three of us are listed as managers. It is him though who has all the dealings with the owner - a Turkish businessman from Istanbul. Mr. Kucuk goes over there once a month, to keep him up to date."

"And might Natalia have gone with him this time, to keep him company?"

Salinsky pursed his thick lips and shook his head. "I'd say definitely not. The talks are intensive and Natalia would have informed me beforehand that she would be missing her shift."

Os watched the man pluck a cigarette from a silver box and light it. After a couple of drags, he appeared to remember his manners and pushed the box towards Os. Os declined.

"I have no idea whether to believe you or not, Mr. Salinsky. You could have told me all this when I came yesterday, but instead, I've had to make a return trip, wasting valuable time. I'd like the number of Mr. Kucuk's cellphone, now please, and then I'd like you to ring him for me."

For the first time the Russian looked surprised.

"He's used to calls from you, whereas he might decide not to answer mine."

Salinsky shrugged and pressed a button on his desk phone. From where he was standing, Os could hear the dialling tone, but no one on the other end picked it up. The call connected into the answering message.

"When you get this, Ersin, give me a ring. It's urgent." Salinsky muttered. Then he replaced the receiver and looked up at the policeman.

Os moved his mouth into a smile. "Thank you, Mr. Salinsky. If you speak to him first, which I'm sure you will do, then please inform him how important it is that he rings me. Discovering the whereabouts of Natalia is paramount. Now, if you could give me his mobile phone number and directions to his house, I'll let you get on with your work."

"Why do you want to know where he lives? I told you, he's in Istanbul. I'm not lying."

"I'm sure you're not, but I still need to speak to his wife."

Salinsky pushed back his chair. "What about? You're not going to tell her about Natalia are you?"

Os sighed. "This is a murder inquiry, Mr Salinsky. I don't go out of my way to cause problems between husband and wife, but when someone's been murdered, and a possible friend goes missing, I must put sensitivities aside. If I could only find out the whereabouts of Natalia, then perhaps visiting Mrs. Kucuk would not be so necessary, but until I do...."

"Let me try him again," Salinsky said.

Os crossed over to the floor to ceiling, glass window and looked down into the road. From where he was standing, he could hear the dialling tone and then the answering machine. He looked back at Salinsky and the manager shook his head.

Os turned off the engine. The house was set back in its grounds, behind a ten foot high, metal gate. It had been easy to find. Although there were several enormous houses on the main road, this was the only one painted green. It was not a soft green, which might have been attractive, but a dark green with dark blue shutters. He wondered, as he had done many times, about some people's need to live on a main road. If Os had this kind of money, he would live by the sea or up in the hills, somewhere that was private and away from the noise of passing traffic. He left his car and walked across to the gates. Pressing the button of the intercom, he waited.

He had expected a man's voice, not the gentle female who answered. Os flashed his badge at the camera, and a few moments later the gate swung open. A woman stood at the front door, waiting for him to cross the large expanse of gravel. She looked to be in her thirties, an attractive dark-haired woman, holding the hand of a little boy.

"Mrs. Kucuk?" he called, as he reached the bottom of the

stone steps.

She nodded, her eyes wary as Os joined her.

"I'm urgently trying to get in touch with your husband. I'm hoping that you can help me."

"He's in Istanbul for a few days." She bent down and whispered in the little boy's ear. He nodded and toddled back into the house. Os could hear the sound of a cartoon playing on a TV. She continued to stand in the doorway.

"I'd like a few words if that's possible," he persisted.

She hesitated, perhaps undecided whether she would have to invite him inside.

He made the decision for her, pushing the door further open with his right hand and smiling to soften the action. "This will only take a few minutes."

Again she nodded, but her brown eyes were clouded with anxiety. Os stepped into a large hallway, from which a wide marble staircase spiralled up to the first floor. Through an open doorway he could see the flashing TV screen. He followed her into a spacious kitchen opposite that was not so dissimilar in size to the living area of his apartment. An elderly woman, in an apron, was standing at the sink, peeling potatoes.

"Could you please keep an eye on, Hassam, Mum. This policeman wants to talk to me about Ersin."

The older woman nodded and shuffled past them, but not before Os saw her pursed lips. Her daughter might have married into money, but it did not mean that she approved of her son-in-law.

Attempting to appear less intimidating, Os pulled out a kitchen chair and sat down. He was surrounded by an ostentatious display of money, which in his view, was not partnered with taste. The bright red and black glossy kitchen units, like the exterior of the house, were showy and vulgar. With obvious reluctance, she sat down opposite him.

"When did your husband leave for Istanbul?"

"This morning. He caught the eight-thirty flight from Ercan."

"And you are expecting him back when?"

Her voice was so low that he had to lean forward.

"Thursday. He normally catches the last flight."

"Do you know the purpose of his trip?"

"He goes every couple of months, but it is usually just for the day. He's staying longer this time because the owner is building a hotel and casino in the Karpas. Ersin has been put in charge of it."

Os heard her pride. Did she know about her husband's relationship with another woman, or perhaps she accepted his dalliances, as part of the price she paid to be married to someone with so much money.

"I need to speak to him urgently. He's not in any trouble," he assured her. "It's to do with one of his staff, a Natalia Sakalova. She's gone missing and we think she's linked to a murder inquiry. I've already spoken to the manager on duty today, but your husband's not answering his phone."

Mrs. Kucuk's heavily made-up eyes widened. Whatever she had assumed the police wanted, it was not this.

"I'd like you to try and contact him now." Os continued. "Miss Sakalova's life could be in danger and I can't risk waiting until he returns to talk to him."

She stared at Os for a few moments, as if trying to make sense of what he had said. She then crossed over to the phone on the kitchen wall, and pressed in a number. Again he listened to a distant phone ringing, and then the answering machine clicked into place. She left a message, asking her husband to ring her, and then she replaced the receiver and turned back to Os.

"He must be in a meeting. I'll ring again in an hour."

Os took out a card and slipped it on the table. "I'd appreciate it if you could keep on trying to get hold of him. When you do, tell him to contact me immediately, and at any time. I'm sure he'll understand the importance of my request. The Casino has given me his mobile number, but I'm sure you'll be more successful in reaching him. I assume he'll ring you later on tonight."

She did not answer, but she did pick up his card. He left her there and let himself out. As he walked the short distance back to his car, he wondered whether he would hear from Kucuk in the next few hours. Perhaps the news would be nothing more than he had decided to take Natalia with him after all.

Chapter Seven

Os poured himself another brandy and declined the offer of a cigarette from his old school friend, Aka. He felt more relaxed than he had done for a while. All evening, he had expected Cassie to talk about Rose, but her name had not been mentioned. Now, perversely, he wondered whether Rose had met someone else. She was a very attractive woman; there would be plenty of men interested in her. His stomach clenched and before he could stop himself, he asked, "How's Rose?"

Cassie stopped clearing away the dishes and looked at him. "She's fine. I saw her yesterday - we've started Turkish cookery lessons together."

"Oh," was all he could manage.

Cassie grinned. "She's learning Turkish as well. She's got a Turkish teacher who goes up to the house twice a week."

"So she's obviously intending to stay here." He attempted a grin. "You'll be telling me next that she's selling her apartment in Liverpool."

Did he sound bitter? A few months ago they had spent two weeks in Liverpool while she put her apartment up for rent. At the time he had wanted her to sell it. How long ago that now seemed.

Her eyes searched his briefly before she answered, "No, she's holding on to it. She doesn't want to take the risk of not being able to afford a place back in England, if eventually she does decide to go back."

This was the same answer Rose had given Os months ago. And, in many ways he understood. So many expats were trapped here in Northern Cyprus because they had sold their houses in Britain and now, because prices here had not kept up, they could not afford to return. He decided to move away from such a difficult topic, and it seemed, for once, that Cassie was not interested in talking about her friend. Instead the rest of the evening was spent watching football on the TV.

His eyes kept straying to his mobile phone, as if willing it to ring. Kucuk must have had his message by now. Why was he not returning his call? At eleven, Os excused himself, and taking the short flight of stairs down to his own apartment, went straight to bed.

Zelfa, was already at her desk when he walked into their office. There was no welcome smile as he hung up his leather coat and sat down behind his desk. "Coffee?" He noticed that her desk was clear and she was twiddling with her pen, a habit she had when she was worried.

"What's wrong?" he asked after he had finished.

She pushed her hair behind her right ear, and attempted a smile. "I don't know, maybe I'm being silly, but I've been thinking about it all night."

"People still making comments?"

"No. Nothing to do with that. It's the brothel I went into yesterday afternoon. A much smarter establishment this time."

"Whereabouts?"

"Not far from the large roundabout, just before you go into Nicosia. There're two of them, almost side by side. I went to check up on them both at the same time." Os watched anxiety flit across her beautiful face. "The first one only had five girls working there. They were all from the Balkans – a couple of them were quite old. I wouldn't have thought that they had much longer in the job." She paused, perhaps recalling the scene. "I was in and out in an hour. The man in charge there obviously wanted me out as quickly as possible; he had all the girls out of their rooms and down to meet me within minutes. Everything seemed to be in order.

And then I went next door. It was like walking into a first-class hotel. There were a couple of minders in the usual black suits and a beautiful, middle-aged woman on the desk. I was shown straight into the boss's office, coffee and charm in abundance. Initially, it was a welcome change after some of the negativity I've been getting."

"Initially?" Os's eyebrows shot up. "Did he try to buy you off?"

"Nothing like that. When the girls came in, he stood by the door, all casual, having the odd joke with them."

Os sat back in his chair, surprised how long it was taking her to explain: she was normally so efficient with her words. She had not been herself since the incident in the Karpas, less confident. A knock interrupted them and the porter entered with their coffees. Zelfa waited.

"There were no problems with the documentation as far as I could see. These were beautiful young girls from the Balkans and Russia. And they had an energy about them that was missing from the older ones next door."

Still Os waited.

Perhaps sensing his impatience, she hurried on. "I must have seen eight girls. Then the ninth one held out her papers and whispered something."

Now Os leaned across his desk.

"I didn't hear what it was the first time. She spoke in Turkish, but her accent was terrible. So I asked her to repeat herself. Her eyes seemed haunted but she leaned towards me and whispered again: 'Something very bad here'. I could see that the manager was looking straight back at us." Zelfa pulled her beautiful features into a grimace. "Then he called across at her to hurry up - that there were other girls who wanted to get back to their beds."

"So what happened then?"

"She left the room and I carried on checking the other girls' papers."

"And how was the manager with you afterwards?" Os asked.

"Just the same as before - very professional. Neither of us mentioned her." Zelfa shrugged. "Maybe he didn't notice anything and I'm making more of it than necessary."

"What do you think she was trying to tell you? I suppose she was there voluntarily?"

"Her papers were correct, as far as I could make out. And I didn't want to draw attention to her by calling her back to ask her what she meant. Not then anyway, with him able to listen in to everything she said.

She stared moodily into her coffee. "But I'll have to go back and find out what she meant. Maybe she didn't realise what she was letting herself into when she signed up. Often they don't, you know. The adverts use the word hostess, but once they're here, and find out that it's actually prostitution they've applied for, they're in an impossible situation. The brothel keeps their passports and they have to pay back the fare for their passage here. How can they do that if they don't work? The men who run these places are not easy to deal with."

"Do you want me to come with you?" Os asked.

"Thanks, but I'll take the sergeant with me – he's bigger." She grinned, and pushed her coffee cup away, as if signalling an end to the subject. "I'm probably worrying about nothing." Her brown eyes suddenly turned impish. "By the way, I've found out why Assistant Superintendent Ismail is here."

Os sat back again in his chair. "Go on."

"He's been sent over from Ankara to sort out the overspending here." She paused. "Apparently, Kyrenia station is overstaffed by two inspectors, as well as other ranks."

Shocking as the news was, he really was not surprised. The government had been forced to make redundancies in other areas of the civil service; now it was the turn of the police. Something drastic had to be done to reduce the country's debt. "So, have you heard which one of us has to go?" he asked.

"Not yet. Only that, because I'm paid by Istanbul, it won't be me." Her tone changed. "It's not going to be good here. He'll go through every rank, even counting the porters. He'll then make his recommendations."

Despite the inevitability, the situation was disturbing. "Turkey's had enough of Northern Cyprus's spending; they've been bankrolling our inflated civil service for years. They're obviously tired of our inability to make any changes and have decided to take action themselves." Os narrowed his eyes. "How did you find out?"

"I rang a couple of friends in Istanbul, yesterday. They'd certainly heard of him. Apparently, Assistant Superintendent Ismail has quite a reputation in the force over there. This is his specialty - human resource assessments in individual stations. If he thinks that there are too many staff..."She grimaced again. "His recommendations are usually carried out." Os said nothing. She continued. "He put his head in here last night just as I was about to go home."

Os's stomach muscles clenched. "Who was he looking for, you or me?"

She smiled, though there was no humour reflected in her eyes. "He didn't mention you at all. He said that he had been told that I was still in the building. He wanted to take me for a drink...., 'being as we are both from Istanbul'. Apparently he was born there."

"And did you?" Os asked. "Go for a drink?" There was something disturbing about her socializing with the man he had met only briefly, and decided immediately, that he did not like.

She scanned his face before she answered. "No, I didn't."

Before he could comment further, the phone rang. As he listened to the voice at the other end, he wondered irrationally whether the man had been eavesdropping. He forced some respectability into his tone.

"Yes Sir. Four o'clock this afternoon." Os replaced the receiver and glanced across at his office mate. "Talk of the devil." He forced a laugh though it sounded harsh even to his own ears. "How paradoxical! Only a few months ago,

I was thinking of retraining. Now I've decided not to be a lawyer and stay here, I might have to change my mind again."

He suddenly realised that he had been so engrossed in the case for the last twenty-four hours, that, apart from Fikri, he had not had a proper conversation with anyone. "Is all this common knowledge in the station?"

"You can't keep anything quiet for long, can you? It would have been better coming from Kemal himself though."

It was strange to hear the boss called by his first name; Zelfa was the only one who did so. But she was right, and the fact surprised him. Superintendent Atak ran a tight ship; Os would have expected him to have made an announcement and warned them somehow that they were all going to be observed, with the idea that they could lose their jobs. And it would not just be Kyrenia that had been singled out; if they were overstaffed, then it would be the same for all the police stations in Northern Cyprus. This meant of course that, instead of individuals being moved across to another station, there would be mass redundancies.

"I forgot to tell you. Sergeant Rafiker called in earlier. He wants to see you."

Os felt a slight uplifting of mood. "Sener? Is he back?"

"He said that he would be in the canteen."

Os pushed back his chair. "I'll go down and see him. I'll catch you later."

Now Os shared an office with Zelfa, he and Sener tended to use the canteen as a meeting place. He strode down the corridor looking forward to the sergeant's news.

Sener was sitting on his own, an empty cup and an open newspaper in front of him. He stood up as Os approached. "Let me get you a coffee, Sir."

Os pulled out a chair and watched as his friend walked over to the self-service counter. When he came back, Os asked, "How was the course?"

"Difficult. But I'm managing. There's a lot of reading around the subject. I tried to get as much as I could done there. I'll have little chance now I'm home." Despite being only thirty four, Sener was the father of five children, the youngest under a year old.

"And the others on the course? What are they like?"

"Five of us are going through on this round. They seem alright. Obviously, I'm the only one from Kyrenia; the others come from Nicosia, Guzelyert and Iskele." Sener grimaced."But it's all probably a waste of time. I've heard they're going to get rid of two inspectors here, so they're not likely to promote me, are they?"

The news had spread already. Os gave the only answer possible. "Things change, Sener. Get through the course first."

"That's if they don't make me redundant beforehand. Rumour has it that we are five sergeants over-staffed." Despite Sener's flippant tone, his brow furrowed.

"You seem to know more about what's going on here than me."

"I had a couple of phone calls when I was driving back. And last night, the phone didn't stop. Fatma wasn't pleased, I can tell you." Sener winced at the memory. "After the fourth call, she screamed that if I was not going to help around the house, after being away for a week, I could get back in the car and go back to Iskele." He waved his hand at their surroundings. "Look at them all. There's not much work going to get done, today, that's for sure."

For the first time, Os took in what he had initially assumed was just the usual gathering of people in the canteen. But now he could see that it was different. For a start, at this time in the morning, there were far more people here than there should be. Everyone's body language was also different than usual. People were not sitting back in their chairs, talking and laughing, instead they were bunched forward, their voices lowered as if they did not want anyone to hear what they were saying.

"I've got an appointment with the new assistant superintendent at four this afternoon," Os told him.

Sener raised thick eyebrows. "You must be one of the first then, Sir. Perhaps they're starting from the top and working down."

"Have you seen him yet, the new man?" Os asked.

"No Sir. Have you?"

"Only briefly. He was in the superintendent's office, when I went in to give my report. I'll have a better idea after I've been in today." He decided not to mention his first impression. "But whatever's happening here, I've got a murder to solve. I haven't the time to sit around wondering whether I'm going to be out of a job."

"Do you need my help, Sir?" Sener leaned across the table. "I'm not assigned to anything else at the moment and I'd love to get involved."

Os kept his voice bland. "I've got Fikri with me; they won't give me another sergeant. He was on duty when the body was found. He actually lives in the village where the shooting took place."

"In Ozonkoy?"

Os grinned. "I'll tell you where we're up to, in case you find that you've got time on your hands."

Chapter Eight

"Parts of it make no sense at all," Os said, having explained everything from the moment the body had been found. "For instance, why was he shot with a standard issue, Russian army rifle? The brother denies knowing anything. They were twins for God's sake." Os brimmed over with exasperation. "I thought twins confided in each other. If, Jamil was involved in something illegal, then Mehmet would know. Mehmet even says that he and his wife, Molly, never met his brother's Russian girlfriend. If that's true, why would a man in his late twenties not introduce a girlfriend to his twin brother? Molly mentioned her, but Mehmet said that she was just a friend. And having seen Natalia's room, I'm inclined to believe him. But now she's missing. Are we talking co-incidence here, or is Molly telling the truth?" Os tutted. "And I still haven't heard from Kucuk."

"The Casino manager?" Sener asked.

Os snatched up his ringing phone. "Ah." He gave the thumbs up. "I was expecting a call from you last night, Sir. You're saying that Natalia Sakalova is not with you? You are absolutely sure about this, Mr. Kucuk?"

Sener leaned forward.

"If you're flying back on Thursday evening, I'd like to talk to you on Friday morning," Os told the manager. "I can come to your house or the Casino or, if you'd rather, we can talk down at the station. Whatever is convenient for you." Os raised an eyebrow at Sener. "So, I'll see you at the station at 10am. I'll look forward to it." Os snapped his phone closed.

"So he didn't want us on his turf. What a surprise," Sener remarked. "Do you think he was telling the truth, Sir- about the girl?"

Os walked over to the counter to pick up two more coffees, turning over the conversation in his head. Kucuk sounded worried; it had been there in his voice. But that did not mean that the manager was lying; if Natalia was not with him, he would be concerned about her disappearing. His wife might have been on the phone, asking questions, or there could be problems with the business in Istanbul. Or all three.

He placed the two fresh cups on the table. "Perhaps he'll put her on the plane today, and she'll turn up at work, as if nothing has happened. Can you check whether both their names were on the flight to Istanbul, yesterday?"

"Of course, Sir. Where do you go from here?"

"I need to get a better picture of Jamil's personality and lifestyle. Let's meet in my office in half an hour. Bring Fikri with you."

"Good morning, Os. No doubt you've heard the news?"

Os looked up to see, Inspector Sahim frowning down at him.

"Can I join you?"

Os was about to say that he was working when the inspector sat down. "Congratulations," he said, instead. "I heard about your baby boy."

Sener finished his coffee and left.

Sahim smiled, then his face fell back into its gloomy folds. "My first. I was there when Handon gave birth. It's my first day back at work. Not a good one either; two of us to go, I've heard, and any number of sergeants. And Mustafa and I have been moved out of our office."

This was news.

Sahim mimicked what Os guessed had been Superintendent Atak's instructions. "The new assistant superintendent needed an office."

Os nodded sympathetically. Sahim shared a prime room on the first floor, looking out towards the mountains. Os had always hankered after it himself. So now it was assigned to the important newcomer.

"Where have they moved you to?" He attempted to think of where there was space.

The frown deepened. "They're giving us one of the storerooms. It'll take a week at least to empty it, so we're working on the hoof. I should have stayed off longer."

Os was suddenly glad of his small office, with its two narrow windows with no view. Although it now had aircon, it was too small to be attractive to anyone more senior than himself. "Who told you about the cutbacks, Sahim?"

"Everyone is talking about it. And this morning, Mustafa asked Superintendent Atak if the news was true."

"What did he say?" Os was intrigued to hear the boss's slant on events.

"Apparently he looked guilty or embarrassed; Mustafa wasn't sure which. He just said that it was out of his hands. This assistant superintendent is in complete charge of staff reorganization. Atak was not even allowed to let us know that it was going to happen."

"It's not like him, sitting back and letting someone else take over."

Sahim pulled a face. "The orders are coming from Istanbul, so he probably doesn't have any choice. Maybe his own job is being looked at."

Os said nothing. Sahim was a good man, as far as he knew, but he had no intention of confiding in him. After working in Kyrenia station for nearly eighteen months, Sener and Zelfa were the only two people he chose to be totally honest with.

Os was sitting in his chair, staring at his crime board, when Sener and Fikri arrived. Os grinned as both men glanced at the other empty desk. "Inspector Ure's gone out."

Both men perched their backsides on it.

"I've heard they're giving big pay-outs to people who

want to retire early," Fikri said, his small eyes, bright.

Os examined his elderly sergeant. There was an energy around him that was not usually present. "Who told you that?"

Fikri waved his pudgy hand in the air. "It's all around the station, Sir. The word is that a quarter of the workforce has got to go and there'll be big hand-outs. The unions will kick up otherwise."

Os doubted that Fikri's information was true. "I thought you had to continue working so that you could put a deposit down for your daughter's house."

Fikri smiled slyly. "But if they give me a big pay-off, she can have that, can't she!"

Os refrained from saying that it was a little early to be making such decisions. Instead, he said, "Well, let's get on with this. We're missing something. Everyone we've talked to is lying." Os pointed at the photos on the crime board, ignoring Fikri's disappointed expression. "Jamil was close to three people, his brother Mehmet, his wife, Molly and his father. We're assuming that the assault on him is linked to his son's death. Then there is also Natalia Sakalova. We've not been able to talk to her yet, and we don't even know for definite if she had any kind of relationship with Jamil - apart from a professional one. And if they didn't, then why did Jamil pretend otherwise?"

Fikri slid further back on Zelfa's table so that his thick legs dangled. "Like we said before, Sir - Jamil might have thought that they would be impressed by a glamorous girlfriend. He might have been jealous that his twin brother was married, and running his own business, even if it wasn't a very successful one."

"Perhaps. We need to remember though that this was a good-looking man, who, according to his father's neighbour, was popular with the women. Jamil also appeared to have built up a nice little electrical business, alongside his main job. Fikri, I need you to go back to this neighbour and ask if Jamil ever talked about a new girlfriend, especially a Russian one." He paused. "Nothing from the constable at the hospital, I suppose."

Fikri shook his head. "I spoke to him just before, Sir. Mr. Emral is still unconscious."

"As soon as he comes round, go and question him. I want to know exactly what happened, what he heard and saw. And if he will admit to knowing about the money hidden in the outside oven. If we knew where it came from, then we might be able to move forward with this."

"Could it be nothing more than payment for the extra work he's been doing?" Sener suggested. "Or stolen."

Os grimaced. "It's a lot of money in both lira and Sterling; it would take some saving. And no one has reported a theft. It doesn't mean that it hasn't been, of course, just that it's not been reported."

The three men were silent as they considered this option.

"Sener, I want you to check out the father - any past criminal record - was he still working? Certainly, the state of his house gives no suggestion at all that either he or his son had any surplus money."

"You say Jamil was a gambler, Sir," Sener interrupted. "Was he a successful one? Has anyone from the Casino admitted to him playing there, and if so, did he throw money around?"

Os smiled. "It was good to have him back on the team, even if it was temporary. Fikri was pedestrian - carrying out orders, but very rarely saying anything that challenged.

"I'll ask again, but I don't think this money was accumulated through gambling - I think Salinsky would've have admitted knowing him if he'd won huge amounts; it's too easy to check up on."

"What do you make of Salinsky, Sir?" Fikri asked.

"He's cagey, as I would expect him to be. He was very convincing when he said that there was no link between Natalia and Jamil. He knew all along that Kucuk and Natalia were an item - he admitted it the second time I went back there."

Fikri unbuttoned his straining jacket. "Anything more from Kucuk, Sir?" Fikri asked.

"He rang this morning from Istanbul. He says he's there on his own. If he's lying, she'll be back today and into work." Os grimaced. "I'd like it to be a lie, but somehow I think he's telling the truth." Os turned back to the board. "And then there's Natalia's friend, Alexandra. They came to Northern Cyprus together and are very close friends. But I'm certain she's lying about something, I'm just not sure exactly what. She's admitted that Natalia is having an affair with Kucuk, but denies knowing anything about Jamil."

"They go back quite a way don't they, Sir? I'd think that they would tell each other most things," Fikri added. "Women do."

Os suppressed a grin. Fikri had never given the impression of knowing much about women.

"Unless she was ashamed of her friend's behaviour," Sener interrupted.

Os felt the buzz. Even Fikri, who could be so dour, was thinking creatively. "Go on," he encouraged them.

"Well if Natalia's been screwing Kucuk for months in the bedroom next door to her, other people in the hostel will know as well. You can't keep things like that quiet in such a small community. Alexandra wouldn't want other people to know that Natalia was also having sex with another man somewhere else."

Os nodded. "We don't know what kind of person this Natalia is other than she's good at her job. Fikri, give the Casino a ring. Speak to Salinsky if he's on duty. Find out if Natalia is back, and if not, whether the Casino is still holding her passport. If they have got it, then she can't have gone to Istanbul and we can put out an alert for a missing person. But if she's at work, we'll get down there straight away and interview her."

Os waited for Fikri to pick up his cigarette and matches and leave the room before he directed the next question at Sener. "Alexandra must be worried about her - unless she already knows where she is, of course."

"Alexandra won't trust us - we could be in the pay of the Casino," Sener answered. He paused then asked, "You definitely think that Jamil's death is linked to Natalia and the Casino, Sir?"

Os stared at his board. "Jamil was involved in something and, at this moment, that seems the most likely to me. Which brings us back to the beginning. His brother Mehmet is lying to us."

Zelpha's desk phone began to ring. Os indicated with a nod that Sener should answer.

"Chief Inspector Zahir's office. Sergeant Rafiker speaking."

Sener took out his pen and pad. "She's not here at the moment. Can I give her a message?" He scribbled down a few words and numbers then replaced the receiver.

"Anything important?" Os asked.

"It was the morgue, Sir. A prostitute was brought in this morning. A suicide! Inspector Ure is listed as the liaison officer, so they were just informing her as a formality."

Os pointed at a sheet of paper taped to the wall. "Her mobile number is there, if you haven't got it. I'll go and check on Fikri."

Fikri was down the corridor, talking on his phone. When he saw Os, he brought the conversation swiftly to an end and stuffed the mobile into his trouser pocket.

"Anything I should know about?" Os called.

Fikri's eyes hooded. "Not really, Sir. I was just telling my wife about the pay-offs."

"And did you manage to get through to the Casino with all these other important calls that you had to make?"

"Yes, Sir. Natalia's not turned up and they say they still don't know where she is."

"Who did you speak to?"

"The manager." Fikri took a pad from his jacket pocket and referred to his notes. "It wasn't the Salinsky you mentioned, Sir. This man's name was Erdener."

This was the third manager, not one that Os had met. "Tell me how the conversation went, exactly."

"I said I was the police and asked for Salinsky. The woman on the end of the phone said that he wasn't on duty and did I want to speak to the other manager, a Mr. Erdener."

"So two Turkish and one Russian," Os mused.

"Sir?"

Os glanced sideways at his sergeant, irritated by his dullness. "Managers, Fikri. Go on. What happened next?"

"I was put through very quickly; I only had to wait a couple of minutes. I asked if Natalia Sakalova was back in work. When he said no, I asked him if he knew where she was and he said no again. Then I asked about the passport and he had to go and look in the safe. It was there with the others. So I rang off."

Os opened his office door and indicated that Fikri should go in ahead of him. Sener was standing by the crime board. The office suddenly became crowded. But, unlike Inspector Sahim, at least he had one.

Os joined him at the crime board and circled Natalia's name in red pen. "I've got a bad feeling about her. I hope we don't find her dead somewhere."

"You don't think she could be the murderer, do you Sir?"

Os stared at Fikri's bulbous face, attempting to read whether he was joking or not.

Fikri spoke defensively. "Why not?"

Os modified his tone. "What are you thinking?"

Fikri slid back on to Zelfa's table, spreading his thick thighs. The trouser material was stretched tight and Os realised that his sergeant had put on considerable weight recently.

"I'm just taking on board what you're always saying, Sir. That we shouldn't go for the obvious. She and Kucuk are an item. She's obviously into power and money if she's with him, so why would she have any kind of involvement with another man who had neither of those. It doesn't make sense. It's much more likely that Kucuk got her to shoot the electrician."

Os caught Sener's eye but his sergeant stared blandly back.

"Well we don't know anything about her, Sir." Sener's voice was dubious.

"Come on then. I'm interested to hear why either of you think Kucuk wanted Jamil dead?"

"Maybe Jamil stole that money from the Casino. Kucuk would want to make an example of him. And if he took it from her table, then she might want revenge. You know what these Russians are like!"

Again, Os's eyes slid over to those of Sener. He sighed. "Okay. Both of you go and talk to the neighbours. See if Jamil mentioned Natalia. Then go to the Casino and find out what you can about Jamil's gambling habits and the other croupiers' opinions of Natalia. Pick up her passport while you're there." He waited for their nods. "And go home afterwards. I'll meet you down in the canteen at 8.30 tomorrow morning and you can tell me what you've got."

"What are you going to do, Sir?" Sener asked.

"I'm going to visit the brother and his wife again. See if I can find out why they're lying. And then at four, I've got my meeting with the assistant superintendent." Os stopped himself from pulling a face. Fikri would think nothing of repeating, what his inspector had said or done to anyone who shared the same numerous coffee breaks. Os picked up his keys. "Ring me if you are unsure of anything. Otherwise I'll see you in the morning."

Chapter Nine

Molly was in the restaurant kitchen. Os detected her fear when she glanced across, but on recognizing him, her face immediately blanked. He sat down at the counter dividing the kitchen from the restaurant.

Her face was sullen. "Mehmet's not here. He's gone to see his father in hospital."

Os was all concern. "How is Mehmet? It can't be easy for him, losing his twin brother, and now his father has been attacked, probably by the same people."

She picked up an onion and peeled off the brown skin, blinking rapidly. "He's managing. He won't be home for at least a couple of hours. So, if you want to come back later, I'll tell him that you've been."

Os smiled at her. "Now that I'm here, I can talk to you just as easily. Any chance of a coffee?"

He watched her while she unwillingly reached for a mug and spooned in instant coffee. "You see I'm having some difficulty with this case and it would help if I knew more about Jamil as a person. How long have you known him?"

She continued to busy herself. Os was about to repeat the question when she answered.

"Almost as long as Mehmet. Three years."

"I know this might not seem relevant, Molly, but I need you to tell me about the early times, how you and Mehmet met and how this . . . .," Os waved his hand at his surroundings, "....started".

She pulled a handkerchief out of her jeans pocket but kept it balled in her hand. "I can't see how it's relevant to Jamil's death, but I met Mehmet on holiday here in a club. I'd split up from my first husband, divorced." The kettle clicked off. Carefully, she poured boiling water into the mug and then added milk.

Os wondered how different she might have been in those days. She had been crying again today; her eyes were bloodshot and her face blotchy. There were deep lines around her mouth and the corner of her eyes, aging her.

He thanked her as she pushed the coffee mug towards him. "So you stayed and married him?"

She bit her lip and her eyes swam. "Not exactly. I went back to England and we kept in touch. We'd already talked about how great it would be to start our own place." She blew her nose. She seemed to be forcing herself to go on. "Mehmet worked in a bar, you see, so he knew how things were done. And I'd always enjoyed cooking. I used to do dinners for my first husband's business clients."

"So you met Mehmet's brother at the same time?"

She nodded. "They were very close. I couldn't tell them apart, visually, in the beginning but they had very different personalities."

"In what way?"

She shrugged and for the first time, Os noticed what she was wearing. Perhaps it was because she was cleaning, but he could only describe her as drab. Her jeans were baggy at the knees and her thick jumper was shapeless. Both garments looked as if they should be thrown out. Her hair also needed washing. The death of her brother- in-law had reduced her to quite a state.

"Mehmet wanted to settle down with me immediately." Her eyes darted to those of Os, then away. "I thought, you know, with me being so much older, that he would not bother when I went back to England. But he caught a plane over a month later, and asked me to marry him." Her voice trembled. "Jamil would never have done that; he was a real ladies' man. He had a different woman every month then."

"And now? Was he interested in marrying anyone before he died? The Russian girl, Natalia perhaps?"

To his surprise she turned her back on him. After a few seconds, she blew her nose, then crossed over to the sink and ran the tap. Her voice was muffled as she said, "I made a mistake about her, I realise now. It was a joke about her being his girlfriend. She would never have been interested in him. Why should she be? She must meet all kinds of wealthy men in her job."

"You're sure about this?" Os willed her to turn round so that he could see her face. But she did not oblige.

"Of course. Anyway the croupiers can't have relationships with the punters, can they, or they lose their jobs."

How many times had he heard that? And why had she changed her mind about Natalia? "So this is your business?" he said instead.

"It was my money that bought it, but legally I put it in both our names. Mehmet would have put money into it if he could."

Perhaps there was still some love there between them. Os looked around at the tired- looking interior of the restaurant. "I hope it works out for you."

"It's the hardest thing I've ever done."

Os was tempted to ask if running a business was more difficult than marrying a Turkish Cypriot, but knew that the answer had no relevance to the case. Instead he said, "Do you really not know what Jamil was involved in".

"Nothing, as far as I know."

"I'll treat anything you say in confidence, Molly," Os persisted. "I'll find out in the end. I always do. You might think that you're helping his reputation but all that's happened, is that his father has been attacked. I'm not trying to frighten you, but whoever did kill Jamil and attack his father might decide to come here. It's not finished. We've found a great deal of money hidden in the garden, far more than I would have expected. Was Jamil into drugs, Molly?"

She hesitated for a second. At last, would she tell him what she knew? But then she shook her head. "He liked a

drink and he smoked, but I'm sure there was nothing else."
She frowned. "How much money did you find?"

"I can't say yet. But a lot."

She shook her head, as if the movement would add strength to her denial. "He wasn't a thief."

Os watched her through narrowed eyes. "How do you know, Molly? You say you knew him well, but you didn't know about the money. How could he possibly have saved so much?"

"He used to do jobs for the ex-pat community. It must be from that."

Os shook his head. "I don't think so. Some of it might have been, but not all of it." Os climbed off his stool. "Have a think about what I've said. Whoever killed Jamil is a dangerous man. You have to think about your husband. The murderer was looking for something when he broke into Jamil's house – presumably the money we found. He might come here looking for it."

Pain flashed across her face but he brushed any guilt aside. Until the murderer was caught, these two were vulnerable, and the sooner they realised it the better.

"I expect you to ring me, Molly. If you don't want your husband to know, then I'll do my best to keep any information between us. But I need your help if we're to stop the murderer before he or she does any more damage to your family.

Chapter Ten

Sheet rain bounced off the roof of the car. Water splashed over his shoes as Os dashed across the road. He pulled open the driver's door and then sat for a few moments as huge raindrops exploded on the windscreen. More than ever, he was sure that she was keeping something back. Was she foolish enough to think that she was protecting Jamil's reputation? Perhaps it was not Jamil she was protecting, but her own husband. If Mehmet was involved, then her behaviour would make sense. It would also explain the tension between them.

Os drummed his fingers on the steering wheel. If the brothers had been in a money-making scam, then it was interesting that Mehmet had chosen not to spend any of it on the restaurant, especially as Molly had implied that her husband wished he could contribute financially to the business. If Mehmet was now financially independent, then could he be thinking of leaving her? It would certainly make sense of the atmosphere between husband and wife. Os slid the key into the ignition. Perhaps he was allowing his imagination to run away with him but, nevertheless, he would get Sener to check out Mehmet's finances in the morning.

Miniature rivers snaked across the empty road. It appeared that both humans and animals had all taken refuge somewhere dry. This was one of the problems with winter: the drains could not cope, so floods were a regular occurrence. He turned on the ignition.

By the time he arrived back at the station, he was late for his appointment. He found himself suddenly anxious as he strode into the police station.

The duty sergeant called out, "The new assistant super has been looking for you, Sir. He told me to ring him as soon as you came in."

Os grimaced. "Thank you. I'm on my way up there now." He lengthened his stride. It was four fifteen and he was fifteen minutes late.

The response to his knock was immediate. Os pushed open the door and found himself in a room that had changed dramatically since it had been occupied by the previous two inspectors. Assistant Superintendent Ismail appeared to have replaced all the furniture. A highly polished desk, as large as the one in the superintendent's office, took centre-stage, and the man himself was sitting, ram-rod straight, in a high- backed chair.

"Ah, Chief Inspector. At last!"

His fine teeth were stretched into a smile that did not reach his eyes. He waved at the solitary chair opposite him. "Please."

As Os sat down, he decided that everything about Ismail seemed thin: his body, his black hair that stretched thinly across his skull, his lips and his tapering fingers that tapped impatiently on the shiny desk. His suit jacket was tailor-made, the material French or British; this man spent serious money to look good. What a contrast, Os thought, to the superintendent, who saw clothing as a mere necessity; fashion had no interest for Superintendent Atak. Ismail leaned back in his leather, padded chair. "As you know, I've been sent over from Turkey to implement cuts to the police force. I'll be based in Kyrenia, so I'll start here." He paused, as if expecting questions, but when Os did not respond, he continued. "I've also decided that I'll have a better insight if I line-manage some of the officers here. As you can appreciate, the politicians in Ankara require written reports of my progress."

So the station gossip was true, Os thought; redundancies were on the way. Was he to be the first?

"I picked you as one of my team because you interest me."

Os kept his voice bland. "Why's that, Sir?"

Ismail showed his teeth. "Your meteoric rise. You must have friends in high places. Certainly you have the full backing of Superintendent Atak."

"I think you'll find that my promotion was straightforward, Assistant Superintendent."

Ismail held up both hands. A thick gold ring glinted on his little finger. "I'm not intending to cause offence; I'm merely making an observation. I have no doubt at all that you're an excellent officer."

For some reason Os did not feel comforted by these words.

"I understand that you trained in this country." Ismail drummed long fingers on the file in front of him. "I'm surprised, that an officer of your abilities didn't choose to take the opportunity of the superior training in the Ankara Police Academy. You'll have been aware that the Turkish government makes six places available for Northern Cyprus every year. With the quality of your degree you would have been easily eligible."

Os explained that, after having done three years completing a law degree in Istanbul, he had preferred to train on the job.

Ismail pressed his fingertips together. "I can see that, yes." His voice suggested that he did not. "But, enough of your background for now. How is your case coming along? Have you any idea who murdered this……," he opened the file and his thin lips formed the words, "Jamil Emral?"

Os suddenly realised that the folder on Ismail's desk was his file. A ball of insecurity unravelled in his stomach. Was he going to be the one made redundant? He focused on the question.

"No Sir, not yet. It's a strange case."

"And the girlfriend, have you found her?"

"No, Sir, though we don't know that she is the girlfriend; she's having a long- term relationship with her boss in the Casino. Of course that does not rule out a liaison with the electrician as well. Ersin Kucuk, the chief manager of the Casino, says she's not in Istanbul with him. My two sergeants are at the Casino now, collecting her passport and making enquiries about her. She has become a priority in the case."

"You don't think that she is the murderer?" Ismail asked.

Os shook his head. "She could be a key to the puzzle though. I've just come back from talking to the sister-in-law, Molly. She's now retracted her statement that Natalia was a girlfriend."

Ismail's eyes narrowed. "Why would she do that?"

"An interesting question, Sir," Os answered blandly. No doubt we'll learn the answer when we find Natalia. I just hope that she's still alive."

Ismail's phone rang. Os watched him straighten, and his previously, slightly accusing tone, became deferential.

"One moment, Sir. I've someone in my office who is just going."

Os did not need a second telling. As he reached the door, Ismail called out, "We'll talk again soon. Let me know immediately if anything happens and, Chief Inspector, go easy on the Casino. We don't need a lawsuit accusing us of harassment."

Os closed the door and strode back down the corridor. It was not until he was seated behind his own desk that he realised that he had ignored several people on his way. He picked up the phone to order coffee and then put it down. If Zelfa had been here he would have ranted to her, but, as she wasn't, he would go home.

Mentally, he ran through the list of friends who would be up for a drink. Aka was the one he would prefer over everyone else, but he was mindful that he should not be too demanding of his friend; he did not want to fall out with Cassie. And he knew he was drinking too much; perhaps he should stay in. Sighing at the prospect of a night alone in his draughty apartment, he reached for his leather coat and went out into the corridor, shutting the office door behind him. The phone rang as he was climbing into his car.

"Yes, Zelfa. What can I do for you?"

Chapter Eleven

The only noise was the clicking of Zelfa's heels as they both strode along the grey, subterranean corridors. Maybe she felt like he always did when he visited the morgue, depressed.

Os nodded at the clerk who was sitting in his office. "Katja Baich?"

The clerk jerked his grizzled face to the left. "Room two."

"Pathologist?"

"Dr. Gok."

Os's spirits lifted a fraction. He pushed open a door and held it for Zelfa to go through. Dr. Gok was standing at the sink scrubbing her hands.

"Inspectors!" she greeted, as she reached for a paper towel. "I think you've had a wasted journey. She committed suicide - I've found nothing to imply violence."

Throwing the ball of paper into the bin, she crossed over to the central table and pulled back the white sheet. The three of them stared down at the body of a young woman. Zelfa made a hissing sound.

"Are you absolutely sure?" She asked, her eyes locked on to the once-pretty face of the corpse.

"Yes." The pathologist's voice was devoid of its usual warmth. "In my professional opinion, this woman took an overdose of sleeping tablets herself." She touched the alabaster face. "There's no bruising around the mouth, or anywhere else on the body to suggest force. I've already spoken to her doctor; he's been prescribing her these tablets for months. Presumably, she's saved them up and then took them all at once. It suggests that she's been planning it for a while."

Os breathed in the strong floral scent that he always associated with the pathologist. She had once admitted to him that she wore it as a barrier between her and the dead. "Can I have the contact number of her doctor; we'd better have a word with him."

Dr. Gok's tone was instantly warmer. "Of course, Chief Inspector Zahir."She scribbled down the details and passed them to him.

"If there is nothing else you can tell us, we'll get out of your way, then," Zelfa said.

The pathologist nodded coldly at the female inspector.

"What will happen to the body?" Os asked.

She sighed. "We'll send it for burial here, I suppose, unless her family can collect her soon. We haven't the facilities here to keep the body for long; space is at a premium, I'm afraid. If we were in the States, we could have sent her ashes back home, but in this country, where there is no cremation...." the American pathologist held out manicured hands.

Os thanked her. A life disposed of, and did anyone really care? He caught up with Zelfa in the corridor.

"Why is that damn woman so superior?" she snarled. "I noticed that she simpers over you though."

Os chose to ignore Zelfa's question. "Do you want me to come with you to see this doctor?"

Her shoulders sank a few inches and her eyes softened. "Do you mind?"

"Not at all. We're here now. We'll go on to the nightclub afterwards."

There was relief in her thanks. They walked in silence back to the car.

The doctor's practice was in an up-market residential area of Nicosia. A polished brass plate stated that this was the surgery of Dr. Yilmaz, a specialist in gynaecology. Zelfa pushed open the glass doors and they both walked into a spacious reception area. White leather sofas were clustered around glass tables on which lifestyle magazines were scattered. A water dispenser and an expensive-looking coffee machine stood next to a tray, stacked with china cups, milk and sugar. A brassy, over made-up receptionist peered at them, frowning at the unexpected intrusion. Os flashed his badge.

"We'd like to speak to Dr. Yilmaz please."

The frown deepened. "Could I ask what it's about?" She indicated the two women sitting on separate sofas. "As you can see he's very busy."

"I'm sure he'll make time for us," Zelfa snapped. "Tell him that we're here to talk about Katja Baich."

There was no sign of recognition as she considered the name. However, she attempted a polite smile. "As soon as he is finished with his present patient, I'll let him know you are here. Can I get you a coffee?"

They shook their heads. Os sat down on a leather chair while Zelfa paced the room. Both women eyed them over their magazines. Yimaz was obviously doing very well to be able to afford such elegant surroundings. Whether that was because of his skill, or because his wealthy clientele needed to be impressed by the appearance of his surgery, it was impossible to know.

At that moment the receptionist's phone buzzed. She listened to the caller and then stood up and went through the door behind her. A few seconds later she returned and smiled professionally at Os.

"Dr. Yilmaz will see you now, if you'd like to follow me." She led the way out into the corridor, and then after knocking, opened the main door into the doctor's office.

The doctor was already on his feet, coming out from behind his desk, his hand outstretched. Os was clasped in a firm hand-shake. He then shook Zelfa's hand before waving them to two armchairs. His handsome, middle-aged face was settled into an expression of concern.

"My secretary said that you were here about Katja Baich?" He shook his head. "Terrible news, terrible news." His eyes widened as Zelfa placed a small recorder on the edge of his desk."

"I'm sure you won't mind, Doctor. It's so much more accurate than taking notes."

Perhaps it was her tone that decided him; so instead of demurring, he forced a smile. "How can I help?"

"Your patient, Katja Baich." Zelfa said. "We'd like to know as much of her background as possible please."

The door opened again and the receptionist handed him a buff folder. He opened it and scanned the contents.

"The pathologist, Dr. Gok has already spoken to you about her?" Zelfa's tone sharpened, as if irritated by the doctor's attempt to play for time. Having been informed that one of his patient's had died, he would have already made it his business to know everything in that file.

"Yes of course." He spread out beautifully manicured hands. "You'll understand that I don't make public that side of my business." He smiled again, this time with more confidence. "The government needed qualified doctors to check the medical health of these girls, and I see it as my contribution to charity."

"One that you get paid very well for," Zelfa snapped.

The doctor opened his mouth to protest, but Zelfa did not give him the opportunity. "We're interested in the pills that killed her. Were they the same ones that you were prescribing?"

The doctor glanced down at the folder,flicked through a couple of the sheets, then looked up, his eyes not quite meeting those of either officer.

"I believe they were, though I can't understand how she managed to get so many of them. They're a brand that I prescribe for a lot of the girls. Most of them have difficulty sleeping."

He shrugged as if the reason was obvious. But Zelfa had the bit between her teeth.

"Why, Doctor?" she persisted. "Why do you find it necessary to prescribe these tablets indiscriminately?"

Alarm chased across his face. "I didn't say that. I'm paid to go once a month to check on the girls in these so-called..... nightclubs." His nose twitched as he said the words. "So any prescription lasts a month. I assure you, it's not irregular! You must be aware how unhappy some of these girls are, doing what they do. I can't change the system; I can only ease the problems."

Zelfa's tone became less strident. "So, how long had you been prescribing these tablets to Katja?"

"Six months."

"And you say that you use the same prescription for all the girls who have difficulty sleeping."

Perhaps realizing where this train of questioning was going, the doctor's face lightened. "Yes. It would have been easy, I suppose, to get tablets from someone else. I did try to ease her off them a couple of months ago, but she burst into tears in front of me, and said she couldn't manage without them." He suddenly frowned. "In fact, over the last three months, I would say she was far more nervous and pale. She did ask if I could make the tablets stronger as they weren't working as well."

Os cut in. "Have you any idea why? Had something happened to her?"

"She didn't say." Perhaps thinking he needed to explain himself he added, "I haven't the time to counsel them. The prime reason for me seeing the girls is to give them an internal. The government pays me to keep sexual diseases to a minimum. Fifteen minutes is allotted to each girl - anything else I can do to help them is a service I personally provide."

Os noticed Zelfa's lip curl. "So you had no idea whether she was depressed or considering suicide?"

"Of course not!"

"Well you can only hope that the courts don't consider this negligence on your part, Doctor," Zelfa snapped. "You wouldn't want the gravy train that provides all this," Zelfa waved her hand at the plush surroundings, "to disappear, would you?"

The doctor reached into his desk drawer and took out a gold lighter and a packet of cigarettes. Both officers watched him as, shakily, he put a cigarette to his lips and lit it. Os looked at Zelfa and she nodded. They both stood up.

"Thank you for your valuable time, Doctor," Os said. "We'll see ourselves out."

Chapter Twelve

"What a smarmy bastard," Zelfa said, as she clipped in her safety belt. "When he said that thing about charity work, I had difficulty not leaning over and slapping him."

"Well, I'm glad you resisted," Os grinned. "Next stop - the club where she worked?"

Zelfa nodded and turned on the car headlights. The heavy traffic had died down, so Zelfa had no problems slipping into the main traffic leading out of the city. A wind had stirred up, brushing pieces of rubbish across the road in front of them. The lights were in their favour, and in a few minutes, they had reached the large roundabout, with roads leading off to Famagusta and Kyrenia. Zelfa took neither route. Instead she turned left, passing the large shops that specialised in bathrooms and kitchens. A few yards on, she pulled into a car park and turned off the engine.

She looked across at Os. "Have you been here before?"

He peered out at the smoked glass and stainless steel structure that was lit by soft red down-lights. "No this place looks new. Very plush."

Zelfa checked her face in the mirror and then opened her car door. "Ready?"

He nodded.

"Celik knows me, so I'll lead it," she said.

He grinned. "I wasn't expecting anything else. I'm right behind you."

She attempted a smile, though it hovered uneasily around her lipstick-coated mouth. "Thanks."

Then she was out of the car, slamming the door shut. Os caught up with her, as she pushed the glass door open and stepped into a foyer area.

Two large men, in evening dress, stood like sentinels just inside the door. A middle-aged woman, in an expensive-looking, dark red suit, greeted them politely, but eyed them suspiciously. Zelfa, strode up to the black, veneered desk and flashed her badge.

"Mr. Celik please!"

The receptionist's eyes flickered, but she kept her smile and picked up the phone. Os turned. The two men had both folded their arms, the black suiting straining over their thick arms. Os smiled at them, but they merely stared back, reminding, him of two oversized toads.

A door opened, and a man, also dressed in evening suit, stepped into the foyer, but any similarity to the bouncers stopped there. This man was slighter, and to Os's practised eye, his suit looked tailor-made. He held out a manicured hand to Zelfa and flashed perfectly-formed, over-white teeth at her, while his eyes darted across to Os, "Inspector Ure. What can I do for you?"

Zelfa raised an eyebrow. "Katja Baich?"

The skin around the manager's eyes tightened. "Perhaps, we would be more comfortable discussing this in my office."Zelfa nodded. He turned and they followed him.

A tall black woman, in a tight-fitting, black sequin dress, stood microphone in hand, filling the small lounge with her husky voice. A couple were at the bar, deep in conversation, the man's hand resting proprietorially on the woman's thigh. Two other couples sat on different sofas, seemingly absorbed in each other's company, the soft lighting and background music providing adequate privacy. The manager walked quickly as if to protect his clientele from prying eyes. He pushed open a door to the left of the bar, allowing the two officers to go in before him.

Os sat down in one of the leather-upholstered chairs and looked around at the comfortable surroundings. Despite the recession that had hit most of Europe, this establishment did not seem to have suffered.

The manager slid into his own swivel chair, and, after first offering them cigarettes from a silver case, helped himself to one.

"Katja Baich," Zelfa said. "We'd like you to tell us what happened. From the beginning!"

The manager lit a cigarette, pulling on it a few times, his eyes narrowing against the smoke. Anxiety tugged at his eyes, despite his attempt to appear relaxed. "She was discovered by one of the girls in the hostel where the majority of my workers live. She'd gone into Katja's bedroom to get something." He shrugged, as if to imply he had no idea what. "She couldn't find it so tried to wake Katja up. But she couldn't. She then ran down to the porter who rang me. I went over there, and when I saw the state she was in, I rang the police."

"Describe what you saw when you walked into her room," Zelfa said.

Mr. Celik pursed his lips and shook his head from side to side. "The porter and this girl, Viktoriya her name is, were both waiting for me. Viktoriya was crying. Katja was lying on the bed in the evening dress she had worn for work." He spread out his hands, "That's all."

"And you had no idea that she was so unhappy that she should take her own life?" Zelfa asked incredulously. "Was there a boyfriend?"

His mouth tightened. "Whatever you might think, Inspector, the girls here are very well looked after, and well paid. If you don't believe me, go into some of the other nightclubs. There's no trouble here, I make sure of that." He adjusted his tone. "As far as I know, she didn't have any male friends. I keep a close eye on my girls – it's the only way I can be sure that they're safe."

Os believed him.

Despite, Zelfa's insecurity in the car, she now appeared to be holding her own. "That might be so, but I still want to see her room and talk to the girl who found her. Viktoriya, I think you said her name was."

The manager's eyes narrowed. "Why? The medical profession have confirmed that Katja committed suicide. Very sad, but I'd have thought that was the end of it."

Zelfa stood up. "Perhaps, but I prefer to do things my way. If you could give me the address of the hostel, I'll get over there now."

Celik gripped the arms of his chair. "As you wish. But I don't want Viktoriya upset. I need her working tonight and she'll want to. We're not a charity; if she doesn't work, she'll not be paid." He paused, as if an idea had just come to him. "Why don't you come back here in a couple of hours when she's on duty? You can use this office if you want."

Zelfa shook her head. "No. I'd like to get on with it now and then go home myself. The police force is not so different, and I'm not on overtime."

Perhaps it was the expression on Zelfa's face, but the manager stood up and went to the door. "I'll get someone to go with you. It's a difficult place to find."

"Okay," Zelfa answered. "But I'll speak to her on my own."

He left the room, leaving his office door open.

Zelfa lowered her voice. "I need to go there on my own. She's more likely to open up to me as a woman. Let me drop you off at your parents' house and I'll pick you up afterwards."

"Are you sure?"

She nodded, her eyes darting to the open door. "Maybe I'm mistaken. Perhaps she did take her own life, but I've got to be sure in my own mind. I should have acted straight away when she told me something was wrong."

"I think you're being too hard on yourself."

Zelfa blew out a mouthful of air. "She asked for help and I just left her there. I owe it to her now."

"You're sure that you don't want me to come and wait outside?"

"No. I'll pick you up afterwards." She attempted a smile. "I'll treat you to a meal on the way home - I owe you that."

"You ready?" The manager stood in the doorway. "We'll go this way."

He pulled back a curtain and then turned the key in the

hidden door. Cold air hit them as they walked out into the car park.

"I'll get a taxi," Os said to Zelfa. "Can you remember how to get there?"

She was about to protest then closed her mouth. Os had no desire for any of these people to discover where his parents lived, and she understood this.

She nodded. "I doubt that I'll be longer than an hour or so. I'll ring you if there are any problems."

A taxi appeared and Os flagged it down. "See you later, Inspector. Good luck."He gave the driver his parents' address and then took out his phone and keyed in their home number.

Chapter Thirteen

His mother opened the door, her eyes sparkling. He pulled her into a hug; she had put on the extra pounds that she had lost only six months ago, when his father had been so ill.

"What a night, close the door and come in."

He followed her into the sitting room; his father stood up from his usual chair by the fire.

"Good to see you, Son. Are you staying the night?"

Os sat down next to him. "No. I'm working. I came over with a colleague to do some interviews. She's going to pick me up from here later."

"That nice Zelfa?"

Os noted his mother's eagerness. "Yes. But how are you two keeping? How's work now you're part-time, Dad?"

His father grinned. "I should have done it years ago. I've time to read the paper, meet your uncle for coffee and a game of backgammon....." He reached out and patted Os's hand. Os squeezed it, delighted that his father appeared so much stronger and like his old self.

"Do you think you'll give up altogether?"

The older man shook his head. "I want to keep my hand in. Drinking coffee is fine for an hour or two, but I wouldn't want to spend my days there - like your uncle does."

Os was reassured. His father's older brother had retired when he was fifty, and now did very little but sit in his local coffee shop gossiping, and playing backgammon with whoever could be persuaded to join him. From what his father had told him in the past, his aunt was happy that he was out of the house.

His mother placed an engraved brass tray on the small table between them. Os picked up his coffee cup and helped himself to a piece of Turkish delight.

"Have you eaten, Os? Or should I make you something?" she asked.

"He held up his hand. "No, I'm fine, thanks. I'm stopping for something to eat on the way home."

"With Zelfa?" his mother asked.

He kept his voice neutral. "It just saves us both cooking something when we get back, and it gives us an opportunity to talk over the case we're working on. I've got to go back into the office afterwards to write up a report," he lied.

"Has she got a boyfriend here? She's such a pretty girl and so nice. And you're such a good looking man. Everyone says so."

Os laughed. "I've no idea if she's got a boyfriend, Mother. She's only a work colleague."

His mother grunted. She sat down in her rocking chair and folded her hands in her skirt. Os realised that her still-pretty face looked smug.

"What?" he asked.

"Your sister-in-law is pregnant!"

"That's wonderful.' He spoke with enthusiasm, but something tugged at his chest. His brother was the younger by two years, but he had been married, as far as Os knew, happily, for three years, and now they were expecting a child. And what was Os doing with his life: a string of failed relationships, the last one having been the most painful.

"We spoke to both of them this morning, didn't we, Father? They seemed very excited."

"Are they coming home at all?" Os tried to remember when they had been here last: over eighteen months ago, he decided.

The pleasure in his mother's face, faded a little. "Not at the moment. Levant's working too hard, but when I say anything, he gets cross. The Americans don't have as many holidays as us, I know, but I miss him."

Os felt a flash of annoyance at his brother. Admittedly he was doing well in Chicago, working for Bosch, but his carefree attitude to his family was the opposite, to that of his own. He could never go abroad and leave his parents again, especially now they were so much more vulnerable.

"I'll give him a ring," Os promised.

As if sensing his mood, his mother said," I bumped into Asli yesterday, in the shop down the road. She was looking very well. She asked after you. She's teaching now, here in Nicosia. She'd love to hear from you."

"How's Rose?" His father asked.

Os saw his mother pull a face, "I don't know," he answered. "I haven't seen her since I moved out six months ago. Aka's wife, Cassie and Rose are still friends. I believe she's not thinking of going back to Liverpool just yet."

His mother tutted. "What you need is a nice Turkish Cypriot girl, one who has the same values as you and will make you happy."

"Mother," his father interrupted. "It's not for us to interfere with Os's life. Whoever he chooses is fine." The ringing of the phone brought an end to the conversation.

As she hurried into the hall to answer it, both men looked at each other, their eyebrows raised. Then they both laughed. "That's your mother. She means well."

Os knew that, but it did not stop him from feeling infuriated when she tried to interfere. He suspected that was one of the reasons why his brother had left for the States in the first place. Certainly, his mother's outspoken views had not helped his own relationship with Rose. Rose could have met her halfway of course, but she had found his mother too controlling; her way of coping had been to visit only occasionally and she had only rarely invited them to her house.

"How are you really, Son? I can see that you're not happy. Is there anything between you and this policewoman we've met?"

His father's intuition always surprised him. He was about to deny it, then answered, "I like her, yes. But not only do I work with her, I also share an office." He grinned. "Not a good combination."

His father drummed the arm of his chair with his long fingers. "But if you really care for her, then would it not be worth the risk? She seemed a nice girl and I worry about you. Do you still care about Rose? You never told us why you moved out?"

Again the questions took him by surprise and, for the first time, he found that he wanted to answer them. "I don't know what I feel. I try not to think about her at all - there's no point. She never wanted to marry me."

His father watched him. Os wondered whether the rawness he felt showed.

"She loved you though; I always saw that in her face when you were both here."

Os stared at his father. "Maybe, but it wasn't enough for her." His father said nothing, so he felt obliged to continue. "Her parents were divorced and her sister was married twice unsuccessfully." Os paused, "Rose is also divorced." He looked his father in the eyes. "She said she loved me, but she wouldn't commit herself totally. I don't think she ever really wanted children."

His father nodded, his eyes fixed on those of his son. "Ahhh. That's different. You could perhaps manage without marriage - though I'm not sure your mother would cope very well." He grinned briefly before his face settled into a more serious expression. "But not having children is a different thing. You and your brother have given us so much joy. I think that if you sacrificed having children to please her, it would always be between you." His father shook his head "You'll find someone that will make you happy, Son. You deserve a good woman."

Os turned away, sudden tears pricking at the back of his eyes. A photo of a woman filled the TV screen. Instinct made him lean forward and turn up the sound. He was right: the news reader was explaining how Katja Baich, a Russian hostess, had killed herself. Thirty seconds had been allotted to her death before the newsreader moved on to other events. Father and son watched in companionable silence while Os's mother could be heard, still on the phone to her sister.

The doorbell rang.

"I'll get it," his mother called.

Os stood up, and then bent over to kiss his father's head. "I'll see you soon, Dad. Maybe we could go hunting one Sunday?"

His father nodded, pleasure flooding his lined face. Zelfa had stepped into the hallway and was talking to his mother. Os joined them.

"Are you sure you both don't want anything before you go? It's no trouble," his mother asked again.

"No thank you," Os answered firmly. Neither of us wants to be late back. We've both got a lot of work on."

"Thank you anyway, Mrs Zahir. It's very kind of you to offer." Zelfa smiled down at the older woman.

Os took the opportunity to kiss his mother, and with his hand on Zelfa's arm, nudged her back to the front door.

As soon as they were in the car, and Zelfa had turned on the engine, he asked, "Well how did it go?"

Chapter Fourteen

"I spoke to the woman who found her, Viktoriya. She was quite open - I felt as if she was, anyway." Zelfa paused, as she waited for a car to pass, before pulling out into the traffic. "She's known Katja Baich for a couple of years. They both started in the nightclub, roughly at the same time." Zelfa glanced across at him and he noticed that her eyes glittered. "She still can't believe that Katja took her own life. Apparently, Katja's got three children back in Russia staying with their grandparents. She used to send most of her money back every month for them - she even took up cleaning at the club so that the oldest boy could have extra music lessons. Viktoriya said that Katja was always boasting how good he was at the violin."

"What does she think really happened then?"

Zelfa shook her head. "She doesn't know. She even admitted that Katja asked her for some sleeping tablets last week- said that she had lost hers. And Katja had been very upset about something for about two weeks. But she wouldn't talk about it to anyone as far as Viktoriya knew. She'd repeatedly asked Katja if there was something wrong at home - with the children or her parents - but Katja always said no."

"She could have just been exhausted," Os considered. "If she was working as a hostess all night and then getting up in the morning to clean the club, it couldn't have been easy."

"I suggested that," Zelfa said. "She agreed that Katja was always tired but the boss did give her the easier jobs, cleaning his office and the lounge area. Katja always boasted that she knew how to play him." She glanced across at him again. "Still up for stopping at that restaurant?"

"Of course."

Os stared out into the night as he wondered about the life of these girls. Katja might have thought that she could use sex to manipulate men, but if Zelfa's instincts were accurate, she had not managed to get everyone on to her side. And there was still the question of whether she had been murdered.

The black outlines of the mountains soared above their car, while below, on the plain, the lights of Nicosia twinkled. Occasionally the headlights of a car came towards them and then flashed by, but otherwise the road was quiet. January was not a month that attracted tourists and the majority of locals would have arrived home from work by now.

The black sky was studded with the usual array of stars. It was one of the things that visitors always remarked on: the fantastic clear night skies of Northern Cyprus. Tonight the moon was just a white crescent on its journey to becoming full.

Zelfa pulled into the car park of a roadside restaurant. The gravel crunched under their feet as they crossed over to the entrance of the large log cabin. Light glowed through the red curtains, while coloured-glass lanterns were strung under the eaves. Os opened the door and then stood aside for Zelfa. He followed her into a large oblong room that was half-full of diners. Zelfa chose an empty table near one of the open fires. She settled herself on the padded seat, leaned back against the highly varnished pine-panelled wall, and smiled. "I love this place. It reminds me of when I used to go skiing as a child back in Turkey. A lot of the lodges up in the mountains are built like this."

Os looked around at the multi-coloured Turkish rugs scattered on the wooden floors and walls. Several log fires burned in circular grates positioned down the centre of the room. Behind a long hardwood bar, a couple of men polished glasses. Rows of glasses and a huge selection of bottles, glistened in the electric light. Behind them, through an open door, was the kitchen.

"I haven't been back here since you and I had that meeting with the superintendent in August. We were outside then of course, but I've always wanted to know what it was like in winter." She grinned. "It's just as cosy as I remembered it."

The waiter arrived and they ordered the house speciality, meze and lamb chops. Two beers were placed in front of them.

"A lot has happened since then," Os answered and then regretted it.

In six months, his life had changed beyond recognition, but there were aspects which he had no desire to discuss. He remembered that Zelfa had, in this very restaurant in the summer, attempted to get him to talk about Rose. There had been difficulties between them then. In fact, if he was honest with himself, the cracks in their relationship had begun to appear when they had returned from their visit to England last July. But, now that relationship was finished, and he was not going to admit to Zelfa the details. He took a sip of beer, very aware that Zelfa was waiting for him to explain.

Instead he said, "I wonder how long it will be before the new assistant super decides who has to go."

She answered immediately. "Kemal won't let it be you. He values you far too much. You've got the best record for solving crimes in the station."

Os smiled grimly. "It seems that the super has no say in all this. I get the feeling that Ismail just doesn't like me."

She wrinkled her nose. "He's only met you twice."

"Well, they'd better decide soon who's going because no work is being done. I was down in the canteen this morning and it was packed with officers talking about it. My sergeant, Fikri has thought of nothing else, I'm sure."

"What would you do if you were made redundant?" she suddenly asked.

He had already thought this through although the decision saddened him. "Do what I was thinking of some months ago, go into law." His mouth twitched. "My parents would be delighted."

The waiter slid several saucers on to their table and then removed the cloth covering the hot pitta bread, puffed up to the size of a football. Zelfa tore off a piece and dug into a bowl of fresh yoghurt. Os speared a toasted chunk of haloumi cheese, chewing slowly, enjoying the salty texture.

For a while neither of them spoke as they worked their way through the various dishes spread out in front of them. The quality of mezes varied enormously, depending on the restaurant, and this particular one was average. Os eyed the bowl of pickled vegetables and decided that his stomach might not appreciate the acidity. Instead he chose a chunk of freshly cooked beetroot.

"How is your mother?" he finally asked.

Her eyes immediately clouded. "She's deteriorating. She needs most things doing for her now. And the worst thing is that the carer we employed has just given in her notice. She's got family problems, something to do with her daughter. So she's going home."

He was immediately concerned. "What will you do?"

"I've contacted the agency the carer worked for and they're going to find someone else. I'll have to go back to interview whoever it is though." She pulled a face and then gave a rueful smile. "I don't trust anyone else. Especially with me being over here. I want to make sure that whoever we take on is right for my mother." She sighed. "You're lucky, you don't have this problem."

Os thought about his own parents. There would be a time when they would need looking after, but she was right, it was different for him. Even when his father had his heart attack, the extended family all helped out.

Os's phone vibrated on the table.

"Yes Sener?"

"I thought you'd want to know, Sir that Natalia still hasn't shown up for work and I've got her passport. I've questioned the people who worked with her again, but nobody's admitted to knowing anything."

"And the neighbours?" Os asked.

"Again, nothing that we don't already know about."

"And the father?"

Sener sighed, the sound echoing down the line. "He'll be lucky if he comes round. And actually, it might be better if he doesn't; the doctors think that he'll be a vegetable if he survives." Sener paused and then added, "Finance have also confirmed that the money is not listed as stolen."

Os stared at the dark red rug hanging on the wall behind Zelfa. "It's looking like it could be another murder then. Thank you, Sener for that. I'll see you tomorrow."

Zelfa dropped him off by his front door. He considered inviting her in for a drink, but then decided against it. He could have done with the company, but the conversation with his mother had unnerved him. Rose had swum into his subconscious a few times that evening. He had been successful in pushing the image of her long red hair and elfin-shaped face away, but nevertheless it was disturbing. Zelfa had not appeared in a rush to get home, whiling the engine and keeping him in conversation. Finally he had wished her good-night and had climbed the steps to his front door.

He had slept fitfully, but was in the canteen for 8.30 am. Fikri was already there, the newspaper, and a couple of cigarette stubs in the ashtray in front of him. He folded his paper as Os approached.

"Morning, Sir. Sener sends his apologies. The new assistant superintendent wanted him for a meeting this morning."

Os sighed. No doubt Sener would be put on another case and he would be left again with Fikri. And since it seemed Fikri was already planning his own redundancy, it was unlikely that Os would have his full attention.

Os forced enthusiasm into his tone. "We'll get off then. I know you've already been to Jamil's workplace, but I'd like to see it myself. You drive."

Fikri was a much more cautious driver than Sener. Os relaxed back into his seat and fastened the seat-belt.

"So tell me about yesterday," Os said.

"It was difficult getting anyone to talk, actually, Sir. We must have interviewed ten people from the Casino, but not one of them mentioned her relationship with the boss. When we did bring it up, it was obvious they knew about it, but wouldn't admit to knowing anything about it. With them all living in such close proximity, it would be difficult to keep anything a secret for long."

"Did you get a feeling for Kucuk?"

"We asked questions about him, of course. No one told us anything new. I made a point of asking each one of them what he was like as a boss, and you couldn't have got more uncommitted answers. Their faces seemed to go blank when you mentioned his name. They're all scared of him, I'd say."

"Even more than the other two bosses?"

"Well he's the chief isn't he?" Fikri thought for a few seconds. "I'd say yes."

"And the neighbour, what did he have to say?"

"Nothing new. He repeated the fact that he got Jamil his first job. But then Jamil decided to take up the work with the internet company. He was on more money there. He was fond of what he called 'the lad'. But maybe a little irritated that he packed in the job he got for him."

"And Natalia? Had Jamil talked about her?"

Sener shook his head. "We asked all the neighbours and they all said the same. Jamil used to always have a woman until recently. And, if anyone ever asked, all he did was laugh and tap his nose."

The traffic was light and already they were in the middle of town. Fikri turned left and then right into Tin Pan Alley. The street had taken its name from the contents of the shops. Locals came here if they wanted something in metal: pans, garden utensils, parts of cars and bikes, as well as numerous other items, were displayed. Several blacksmiths stood over their braziers, hammering pieces of hot iron into various shapes. The street-scene looked as if it had not changed in fifty years.

"It's just along here, Sir."

Os followed Fikri until they were both standing in front of the window of a small shop. The words Internet Services and Computers, were stencilled in white across the glass. Os pushed open the door and they both stepped inside.

A man and two women looked across at them expectantly and then, perhaps recognizing Fikri, their faces fell. The owner, a man in his fifties, walked over to them. Os flashed his badge.

"I'm Chief Inspector Zahir, Mr. Kasif. I'm aware that you've already talked to my sergeant about Jamil Emral, but there are aspects that I'd like to go over again, if you don't mind."

Kasif nodded wearily. "You'd better come into my office."

Both policemen followed him across the small shop-floor. Five computers, of different styles and makes, were on display, as well as leaflets describing the services of the internet provider. The two women, one in her early twenties and another the same age as the owner, watched them with identical dark brown eyes.

The owner passed through a doorway at the back and into a small office. Several old computers were stacked on the floor and there was one on the desk, its back removed.

Os turned to Fikri. "Perhaps, you could go and talk to the two women, Sergeant."

Fikri nodded, leaving Os to take the only other chair.

"How long did Jamil Emral work for you, Sir?"

Kasif's face clouded. "Five years. I took him on because I'm a friend of his father." His mouth tugged at the corners. "He was a bright boy, interested in computers. I've got my wife and daughter working for me, but it's useful to have another man. We have to go out to the houses and set things up, and sometimes there are problems, so we have to go back. I wouldn't want my daughter doing it. She's fluent in English and German, so I need her here; quite a few of our customers are foreign, so sometimes she did come with us to translate. Jamil could speak some English, but that was all."

Os noted the pride in his voice and suddenly found himself wondering what it must be like to have watched your child grow up into an adult and then be proud of their achievements.

"So your daughter worked a great deal with Jamil?"

"I'd hoped that something would happen between them. I know my daughter was very fond of him, but he was not interested in that way." Kasif fixed Os with saddened eyes. "As far as he was concerned, they were just friends."

"Tell me exactly what he did for you, Mr. Kasif?"

Kasif reached for a packet of cigarettes, tapped one out for himself and offered the packet to Os. Os shook his head. "My wife and daughter managed most things in the shop. As I said, my daughter was very good with the foreigners. My wife also handles the accounts. Jamil and I were the ones who went out to houses. We're in competition with four other internet providers in this area, but we were doing okay. We're reliable and we offer a good back-up service. If the customer is having problems with the internet, our contract promises help within twenty four hours." He waved his hand at his surroundings. "We also fix computers. I taught Jamil and he was a quick learner. In the end, I even sent him to Turkey on a week's course." He smiled ruefully. "Perhaps I was still hoping that he would become my son-in-law and eventually take over the business."

Os smiled sympathetically at a man whom he had taken an instant liking to. "You appear to have done a lot for your friend's son. Did he repay it with loyalty?"

Annoyance flashed across the owner's face. "For a long time, yes. But over the last year he's taken time off - increasingly so, I'm afraid. Trouble with his back, he said. He blamed it on a fall he had when he started working for me. He climbed up to the roof of a house to install the server and then slipped." He shook his head, his mouth pursed. "He seemed okay at the time, but then it started to cause him problems. To be honest with you, I was going to have to talk to him about it. He'd certainly changed over the last year. He often seemed tired, and as I say, taking a lot of time off. It was affecting my business."

"He never confided in you, told you what was going on in his life. Was he worried about anything, money, women, friends?"

Again the owner shook his head. "He'd stopped talking to me – properly that is." He held out his hands, palms up. "I did ask him a couple of times if anything was wrong, but he made it obvious he didn't want to talk."

Os stood up and placed his card amidst the mess on the desk. "Okay. If you think of anything that might help us discover why he died, let me know."

Back in the shop, Fikri had also finished his questioning. He stood apart from the two women reading the shop flyers on internet services. They both walked to the door and then Os stopped.

"I don't suppose that Jamil had a personal area? He didn't have his own desk or anything?"

Kasif's wife answered. "His locker is in the toilets. I don't know if he used it, but if you want to have a look? Come, I'll show you."

Os and Fikri followed her past her husband's workroom to the back of the building. The area was big enough for a toilet, sink and a couple of steel lockers, one of which was locked.

"Have you a key?" Os asked her.

She shook her head. "Jamil had the only key to his."

Os turned to Fikri who had also crowded into the area. "Get a locksmith - there must be several in the street outside."

Os waited in the main shop, aware that he was being watched by the family as they invented tasks for themselves. A few minutes later, Fikri returned, a man in a long brown apron right behind him, dangling a bunch of keys. Fikri led him through the shop into the back-room. Os remained where he was; the area was barely big enough for two people, never mind three.

It took the professional a couple of minutes, and then the two of them were back. Fikri passed over the contents of the locker.

"Pay him, Sergeant and get a receipt," Os said.

He unfolded the jumper. Inside lay a watch and an exercise book. Kasif came to stand by Os.

"What have you got there?" he asked.

Os discarded the jumper then flicked through the pages of the exercise book. "It seems that Jamil was doing jobs on the side. I doubt this is how you usually keep track of your accounts." He handed it to Kasif. "What do you make of it?"

Kasif turned the pages, his face flushing - list after list of names and addresses, with amounts of money printed in columns.

"You're right. Some of these are my customers. Or they used to be. I haven't seen some of them for months. Now I know why." He ran a nail-bitten finger down a page. "See the ones that are marked in red? Well they are my customers or were. The other names I don't know about."

Os took back the book and sat down. Jamil appeared to have been very well organised; dates were listed, alongside names, addresses and amounts of money paid in Turkish lira or English pounds.

"I should have known he was doing this. I wouldn't have wanted to believe it though with everything I've done for him," Kasif said bitterly. "I treated him like my son."

Os took in the pain in Kasif's eyes and spoke gently. "I'm afraid I've seen this sort of thing many times, Sir. But then I'm in a job where you tend to see the worst in people, as well as the best."

Kasif said nothing.

"Thank you for your co-operation anyway. We might be in touch again. Could I ask you to photocopy these pages for me before I go?"

Kasif nodded and walked over to the machine. Os watched him photocopy each page twice, one for Os and one for himself. A few minutes later he handed the book and paper back to Os.

Os nodded at the two women and then walked out into the street. Fikri was outside.

"I think a small celebration is in order. We'll walk down to the Savoy Hotel and have a coffee." He grinned as Fikri's eyes widened. "You've not been in before then? Me neither. We'll have a look at their casino while we're there. "

Chapter Fifteen

Os led the way down the middle of Pan Alley and then turned left on to the High Street. He stepped into the road in order to pass two well-dressed young women staring into a shop window. Kyrenia had an inordinate number of gold and silver jewellery shops, intended for the Turkish mainland tourists who came to gamble. Other windows displayed bales of high quality wools, silks and satins, which in a few days could be transformed by tailors into suits or other garments. Shoes, designer leather bags, and clothes hung from shop awnings next to pharmacies and small grocery shops. For some reason he found himself contrasting it to the high streets of small towns in Britain. There, all the shops seemed similar, but here in Kyrenia, was individuality, along with a sense of chaos.

A couple of minutes later he stepped through the door of the Savoy Casino. Os chose not to flash his card at the large man in the dark suit who stood just inside. Instead, they passed through into a room full of gaming tables, the walls lined with slot machines. It appeared to be a much smaller operation to the one at Ruby Royal Casino. Although it was not yet midday, there were already customers, twenty odd people, who chose to spend their morning pitting their wits against the odds. Os and Fikri crossed the thick purple carpet towards the hotel foyer. Apart from the practised eyes of two more suited individuals, no one else took any notice of them.

The hotel foyer opened up into a lounge. Everywhere was

purple and gold, the furniture modelled on the Ottoman era. Os grinned as he chose an enormous armchair, upholstered in black and gold velvet. He ordered two coffees.

His sergeant lowered himself on the end of a sofa, uncomfortable in his well-worn brown suit and scuffed shoes.

"Not your kind of place?"

Fikri grimaced. "I hope you're paying, Sir. I don't think my wife would be too keen to hear that I'd been spending my wages in such a fancy place." He shuffled his wide bottom from side to side. "I don't know about you, but I don't even find these seats very comfortable."

Os laughed. "All in the sake of research, Sergeant. Now what did you discover back there?"

Fikri decided that the most comfortable position for him was to lean forward, his shirt buttons straining over his stomach. He gave a kind of leer. "If you ask my opinion, I think the daughter was sweet on Jamil. She couldn't say anything bad about him. But her mother was different. She went on about how much time he'd had off and how her husband was having to do everything." Fikri leaned against the gilt-painted wooden arm. "I watched her when we found the book in his locker. She was furious."

"I'm not surprised." Os opened the exercise book again and flicked through the neatly compiled lists. "We're going to have to talk to everyone of these people. "He handed the photo-copied sheets to Fikri. "Have a closer look at these and we'll see what's the best way to divide them."

"Presumably we're going to get help with this, Sir?"

"I'm sure you'll persuade a couple of constables to give you a hand." Os continued to stare at the neat handwriting of the dead man. "Now let's see. It looks like he divided the accounts in the order that people took him on. With some, he's only visited once."

Fikri gave a low whistle. "He earned a lot from a man called Joe Hains. With a name like that, he must be English. Over the last nine months he's clocked in over two thousand pounds."

"Turkish lira?" Os asked.

"No, Sir. Definitely English pounds."

Os flicked through the pages until he came to the list Fikri was referring to. "Your maths is good, Fikri. "Does the total amount of money marked down here equate with the amount that was found in Jamil's garden?"

A waiter, carrying a tray piled with coffee pots and cups, approached the table. While Fikri scribbled down numbers, Os took in his surroundings. Three men, in dark business suits, talked into their phones or worked on their laptops. A couple of women gossiped on one of the brocade sofas, a large pot of tea in front of them. The rest of the room was empty. Either business was not good or the majority of the people staying in the hotel were gamblers and were still sleeping after a night on the tables. It was an interesting interior, but not to Os's taste. Despite its opulence, he preferred the comfort of soft sofas and chairs. But he was sure that it would appeal to a lot of the Turkish tourists who liked to fly over for a long weekend, gamble a little and shop. He sipped his excellent coffee, then turned back to the list of names.

He would obviously start with Joe Hains. The house was listed as one of those that edged the sea at Lower Lapta. To have a property like that, he would need a great deal of money. Os keyed in Sener's number. The sergeant picked up on the second ring.

"What are you doing?"

"Some work for the assistant super, Sir."

"Ismail?" Os asked dully.

"Yes, Sir," Sener said patiently as if there was more than one.

"Can you get on the internet in the next few minutes?"

"I'm on it now, Sir."

"Good. Look up a Mr. Joe Hains for me. I'd imagine that his original domicile was the UK but he now lives in Lower Lapta. He supplied our Jamil with a lot of work over the last year," Os explained. "I'm going to call on him in half an hour and I'd like to know, if possible, who I'm dealing with."

"I'll ring you back, Sir."

Fikri looked up from the sheaf of papers. "There's less here than the amount we found in the oven, Sir. About twenty thousand lira short."

"That's interesting. He's been so meticulous in keeping a log - why not enter the last twenty thousand?"

"Unless he stole it, Sir. These accounts are for the jobs he's done for people. He wouldn't write the amount down if that was the case, would he? He could have found it in someone's house when he was working there and decided to take it. Some of these foreigners have money that they don't want to put into the bank. I once heard of an Englishman in Bogaz who was supposed to have kept forty thousand pounds hidden in a false air vent."

Os pursed his lips. "It's certainly an idea."

"So that's the motive, Sir?" Fikri said with obvious satisfaction. "He stole from someone he was doing work for, they missed the money immediately, and when they confronted him, he denied it. So they killed him."

"Well it's the best anyone's come up with so far, Fikri."

The sergeant grinned at receiving such rare praise.

"So, are we looking for someone who had a reason for not keeping that kind of money in the bank? Os finished his coffee. "It could be Casino money of course."

Fikri put down his cup. "What do you mean, Sir?"

"If there really was some kind of relationship between Jamil and Natalia, it doesn't have to have been romantic. They could have been stealing from the Casino. I've no idea how of course; I would imagine that all casinos keep everything very tight."

"He was killed with a Russian bullet, Sir. Lots of Russians working in the casinos."

Os smiled. It was so rare for Fikri to show real enthusiasm, but it was there in his voice now. "It would be good for you to retire, having solved this case. Something to tell the grandchildren about "

Fikri nodded and Os imagined his brain whirring with the possibilities.

"Okay. This is how we'll do it. I'll go and visit Hains, and the rest of the people that follow on from him in the book, and you do the first half."

Os smiled as Fikri's eyes widened in alarm. "Get some men to help you. We want to know how they heard about Jamil and what kind of conversations they had with him. He spoke English well. You need to get a sense of what they felt about him - any resentment. Or if they go the other way and sing his praises too much." Os waved at a waiter, who a few minutes later brought a small wooden box containing the bill. Os placed some notes inside and stood up. "Ask them if they lost any money while you're there." Os raised his eyebrows. "Ready? You need to drop me off at the station so I can get my car."

For once, Fikri seemed disinclined to remain where he was. The lounge of the Savoy Hotel was not the station canteen.

It had started to drizzle by the time they were back on the street. Os was glad he had thought to wear the long raincoat he had bought in a department store in Liverpool when he had been there in the summer, a summer where it had rained most days. He strode back up the hill, dodging numerous umbrellas, with Fikri trailing behind.

As soon as they were in the car, Os turned up the heating. Quickly the air became impregnated with the smell of fusty damp wool. Fikri lit a cigarette then held it clamped between his teeth as he changed gear. Os pushed himself against the door to avoid an overspill of the car's full ashtray.

"If anything interesting comes up, ring me. I'm interviewing Kucuk at ten in the morning, so shall we say 8.30 tomorrow in the canteen?" When Fikri nodded, Os added, "Depending on what he has to say, we'll decide whether we ask the commander to authorise a national search for her."

Fikri turned into a side-street, past bungalows where the paint was peeling, and where metal chairs and swings stood empty in the gardens. Logs were stacked neatly on covered terraces. With the winter rain, rough grass had sprouted, and geraniums and other flowers flourished in pots. For some reason, he thought of England again and its cultivated gardens. The wealthier Turkish Cypriots, and of course some of the ex- pat community, had irrigation systems, but whether that was right in a country where every year there was a water shortage, Os was unsure; certainly it was one of Sener's favourite topics when he chose to get on his soapbox about such things.

Perhaps, because of the fine drizzle, there were few people about. Smoke drifted up from chimneys and evaporated into the damp air. A couple of dogs sat miserably at the entrance to their kennel, their length of chain twisted snake-like by their paws. Perversely, he liked this time of year; there were very few tourists, so everywhere was quieter.

But the one thing he did not enjoy in winter was his apartment. It had been pleasantly cool when he had rented it in August, but now, in January, it was just cold and damp. The lack of any kind of heating meant that you had to surround yourself with mobile gas fires. When he did sell his apartment in Nicosia and buy somewhere in this area, the first thing he would install would be central heating.

Fikri pulled into the police car park. Os opened the door, desperate for fresh air, then strode to his own car and climbed in. He took a few seconds to select a Leonard Cohen CD before he fastened his seat belt and turned on the engine.

Chapter Sixteen

He drove up through the streets behind the station that led up to the bypass. The majority of people living here, in low-budget accommodation on the edge of town, were Turkish or Turkish Cypriots. The area was well-serviced, with small supermarkets displaying piles of fruit and vegetables on trestle tables outside. Like any part of Northern Cyprus, there was an abundance of hairdressers offering both hair and beauty treatments; Turkish and Cypriot women, especially the younger generation, put great store by their appearance.

As he reached the junction, the lights changed to green. Os turned right on to the bypass that, after many years of financial mishandling, had finally been completed. Millions of Turkish lira had been wasted on this relatively short stretch of road, which enabled the traveller to avoid the congested ones of Kyrenia. He was unsure how many construction companies had started work, and then for what were quoted as financial reasons, had not finished. But, after what must be five years, there was a stretch of road that cut through the base of the mountain range, offering the most amazing views of both sea and mountains.

Today the road was almost deserted. Os kept his speed steady, while he took in the countryside. Below, to his right, the sea appeared grey, matching the sky. A couple of tankers could be seen on the horizon, but the morning ferry to Mersin, would have left several hours ago. Normally there were a few sailing boats cutting up the coast, but perhaps the dampness of the day had been a deterrent. He passed two concrete structures on his left, houses that had been started, but now, presumably for lack of money, had been left to disintegrate. The country was blighted with such structures, ever since the fatal time leading up to 2004. It had been assumed by the majority that peace would finally come to the island, and that, after thirty years, the borders between North and South would be removed. The Turkish Cypriots had agreed to the Annan Plan, but it was the Greek Cypriots, whose refusal to accept had been rewarded by their entry into the EU along with Greece.

But for those few hopeful years, it seemed that anyone with any entrepreneurial ambitions, could put themselves up as builders. Many had become very rich. Foreigners had flocked in to buy holiday homes of varying quality. But now it was obvious to all but a few politicians that peace was unattainable, the interest in buying property had died and many builders had gone bankrupt.

The bypass swept down to meet the road that hugged the coastline. The sign, welcoming travellers to the village of Alsancak, flashed by. Os turned down his music as the village of Lapta came into view. He glanced at his watch as hunger gnawed his stomach. He swung across the road and pulled into a small car park.

A narrow stone path led down to a circular building which was constructed in timber and glass. A promontory of rock stretched out in front of it, below which the sea crashed. Wooden tables and chairs were stacked together on a makeshift patio Os pulled open the rickety, panelled door and stepped inside. Apart from the owner, the place was empty.

The middle-aged man looked up from clearing a table, and grinned. "Osman! How are you?" He crossed over and the two men shook hands. "I'm okay, Kemal. I've come for one of your fine pizzas."

"About time. I can't remember when I last saw you. It must be last summer."

Os grinned sheepishly. "Well a lot's happened to me since then."

Kemal's eyes narrowed. "I've heard. You've split up from Rose. Another woman?"

Os shook his head. "No. It just wasn't working."

Kemal crossed over to the narrow counter that divided his kitchen area from where customers sat and ate. "I was surprised when I heard, I have to say. I thought that you two would end up together, you know, get married and have children. The whole hit."

Os shrugged his shoulders, attempting to look unconcerned. He liked Kemal, and had known him for years, but he was not going to open his heart to him. He doubted if he would understand anyway, Kemal had been married to a Turkish Cypriot for years and had three children with her. He might flirt with the occasional tourist in his restaurant, but Os doubted that Kemal would take it any further. Os found himself envying his friend.

"How's the family?" he asked.

Kemal rolled his eyes. "Good, but expensive!"

"Well, I'll have one of your specials and a bottle of mineral water to go with it."

"Not a beer?" Kemal grinned.

Os shook his head. "No. I'm on my way to visit one of your neighbours. I need to keep a clear head."

Kemal slapped a ball of dough on to a flour-dusted board and expertly rolled it into a thin circle. He then heaped on tomato paste, then cheese, olives and thick slices of sausage. With a flick of his wrist, Kemal slipped a wooden pallet underneath the dough and slid it into the hole of the clay oven.

"Who?" he asked at last.

"An Englishman, Joe Hains. Do you know him?"

Kemal's eyes narrowed. "I know him in that he likes his pizza, and so comes here now and then."

"You know where he lives?"

"Sure. Carry on down this road and it's the big, light-blue house on the right, overlooking the sea. You can't miss it. It's got big steel gates, which have never been open in all the times I've passed by, so you'll have to ring the bell. I've heard he's got dogs."

Os examined his friend's face, which had suddenly developed a shuttered look. "So what's your impression of him?"

"He likes his privacy. I don't think he's got a woman. He's always with two other men at least, and they're always the same ones. I think they must be his minders. They look like it anyway."

"Big men?" Os asked.

Kemal suddenly laughed. "You just know, don't you. They're certainly not his friends - you can tell from the body language. And if he comes in with someone else, the other two sit at another table."

"No women then?"

"I don't think he's interested. Don't ask me why I think that, it's just a feeling."

"Gay?"

"Maybe. But he doesn't behave like other gay men who come in here. And there are a few."

Kemal placed a bottle of mineral water and a glass on the counter. Os picked them up and went to sit at a table by the fire in the centre of the round room. He removed his raincoat and folded it neatly on the chair next to him. He liked this place in winter. The salt-smeared windows faced the sea, but inside, the rickety, wooden chairs and tables and the Turkish woollen rugs on the stone floor, gave a cosy ambiance. It helped of course that the pizzas were always excellent. Os leaned forward, picked up a log and stacked it on the fire. Flames shot up into the brass chimney.

"I don't suppose you know where he got his money from, or how long he's lived here, do you?"

Kemal turned back from the oven. "He doesn't talk to me, not properly. He orders his food, maybe makes some remark about football because I once told him I support Manchester United, but that's it." Kemal pulled a face. "And funnily enough, he's not the kind of man that I feel I want to know more about. I prefer to keep it that way?"

Os stared at his friend. A big part of why this pizzeria continued to survive, when so many did not, was because of Kemal's personality. He was interested in everyone, knew their names, and if they were regulars, he made it his business to find out about them and their families. Os watched him turn back to the oven, slip the wooden pallet under the cooked pizza and flip it on to a round serving board. He then walked over to Os's table and placed it in front of his friend. At that moment the door opened again and a couple walked in. Os could have sworn that Kemal breathed a sigh of relief.

As he listened to Kemal greeting the man and woman in a way that suggested they were regular customers, he started to eat. The couple seated themselves on high stools at the counter and chatted while Kemal cooked.

His pizza was perfect, the base thin and crisp and the topping full of flavour. He and Rose had come here at least once a month, sometimes twice. Most of the time they had sat outside, listening to the waves crash against the cliffs below and the cicadas chirping from the protection of the undergrowth. Rose had always been enthralled by the night skies here in Northern Cyprus, quickly learning the names of the different planets and stars. He had never been interested in astronomy before he had met Rose, but now, even with her gone, he found himself looking for the obvious markers.

The rain had stopped and the sun pierced the grey sky with slivers of yellow light. Already the sea colour had lightened, though it was a long way from the turquoise-blue of the summer months.

He pulled the vibrating phone out of his pocket and checked the number of the incoming call. "Have you found out anything, Sener?"

"Sorry it took me so long getting back to you, Sir. I kept being interrupted. I'm afraid I haven't been able to find out much at all."

Os plucked a piece of salami from the pizza and popped it in his mouth. "That's not necessarily a bad thing."

"Hains has lived here for five years; his previous address was London."

"Any form?" Os asked.

"No convictions Sir. But it appears that he was accused of

supplying drugs in Birmingham some years ago. The case was dismissed through lack of evidence."

Os compared this information with what Kemal had said about the Englishman and his two minders. "Any further leads on how he made his money?"

"He's just listed here as a businessman. It doesn't say what kind of business though."

Os stared out at the lush greenery on the other side of the window. "Thanks, Sener. It was worth a look. What are you doing for Assistant Superintendent Ismail anyway?"

There was pause at the other end of the phone. For a moment Os thought the line had gone dead; when Sener finally answered, his voice was thick with embarrassment.

"He's asked me to research a list of officers. He wants their age, qualifications, whether they are outstanding or indifferent police officers etc. etc."

"Oh," was all Os could think of to answer. It was likely that Os himself was being researched, but there was no way that he was going to embarrass his sergeant by asking. Instead he said, "So, how long do you think you're going to be tied up with that?"

Sener's misery appeared to have increased. "I don't know, Sir. Why, do you need me on the case?"

"It would be useful, but there's not much we can do about it at the moment. Get that done and then I'll see what I can do."

Os heard the flatness in his own voice. If Ismail had chosen Sener to do his research, then he probably had further plans for such a promising officer. Sener's computer skills were recognised throughout the station and Os's decision to start him on the inspector training had been greeted favourably by all his fellow officers. Sener was considered to be intelligent and hard working, and he had made his way up the ranks.

There was still a third of his pizza left, but Os had lost his appetite. He stared gloomily at the fire. If anyone was going to research his past history, he would prefer it to be Sener, but it was what Ismail was going to do with the information that concerned him. He slipped some notes under his plate, stood up and shrugged on his raincoat.

Kemal broke off his conversation with the newcomers, to frown at Os. "I thought you were hungry?"

"I've got to dash. I won't leave it so long next time though."

Possibly, because of the two other diners, Kemal only raised his eyebrows. "Good luck this afternoon."

Os grinned and crossed over to the door. As he pushed it open, a gust of wind nearly wrenched the timber and glass structure out of his hand. He pulled it closed behind him and then trekked back up to his car.

Now he knew the colour of the outside walls of the house, it was easy to find. He left his car on the wide kerb and walked across the road. A bell in an iron plate, was fastened into the stone wall. The speaker crackled into life. "Yes? Can I help you?"

The language was English, though spoken with a strong accent. Os held his badge up to the camera pointing down at him. "I'm Inspector Zahir, from Kyrenia Police Station. I'd like to speak to Mr. Hains."

There was a pause, then the voice said, "What about?"

Os's voice tightened. "I'd prefer to talk to him if that's alright with you."

Again there was another pause as if the request was being considered. Then there was a click and the steel gate began to open. A tall, broad-shouldered man, in jeans and a tight fitting T-shirt, walked down the steps of the house and came towards him.

"Mr. Hains?" Os called.

The man shook his head. "No, he's inside." He waited for Os to reach him, and then he turned on his heel and retraced his steps.

Although he would have painted the house a different colour, probably white, the setting was wonderful. Many houses were advertised with a sea view, but no one could argue the truth of this position. All there was to separate the house from the sea, was a large swimming pool. At the end of a private jetty was a motor launch. The house was surrounded by what looked like an imitation lawn. A high wall ran around three-quarters of the property, over which only the roofs of the neighbouring properties could be seen. But unusually for Northern Cyprus, Mr. Hains had thought it necessary to install CCTV.

A short slim man appeared in the doorway. Os guessed that he was in his fifties, but as Os got closer, he was struck by the smoothness of the man's face. He either had very good skin or had undergone a face-lift of some sort, perhaps the bags under his eyes removed, or the skin under his chin, tightened. Joe Hains did not smile, but his expression was not unfriendly. He held out his hand. Os took it and despite its smoothness, he felt the strength there.

"I'm sorry to bother you. We're making routine calls on anyone who employed Jamil Emral in the last six months. You possibly know that he was killed on Saturday night."

Hains's line-free eyes widened. "Killed?"

"I'm sorry." Os could see nothing but shock in the man's face. "I thought you would have read it in the papers. He was killed on Saturday night on his way home from his brother's restaurant. But I'd prefer it if we could discuss this inside."

"Of course." Hains stood back to allow Os into a large hallway. "We'll go in here."

Three large, white-leather sofas, two armchairs, a huge, long-haired rug and an enormous TV screen above an imitation fire, did not fill the room they entered. Several large pieces of modern art hung on the cream-painted walls, while one wall, all smoked-grey glass, overlooked the swimming pool. Despite it being January, the pool was full of water. But the biggest draw was the sea beyond. Os had to drag his eyes away from the white-tipped waves, and the motor launch that bobbed up and down at the end of a jetty. He turned round to find Hains watching him.

"You've a lovely house, Mr. Hains," Os said.

"Thank you. I like it. But you said that Jamil was dead. How did that happen?"

"He was shot."

Hains shook his head several times. "Why would anyone want to do that?"

"At the moment, we've no idea, I'm afraid - we're just

trying to build up a picture. Could you tell him what your dealings with him were?"

Hains took the armchair, and indicated with a wave of his hand, that Os should also take a seat. "He was just a bloody good electrician. I've got a few properties that I rent out." He shook his closely cropped head, as if not quite believing what he had just been told. "Jamil installed my internet and TV system. He left me his card. He said that he had all the qualifications of an electrician, so if there was ever anything I needed doing, to ring him. He was obviously building up a little sideline, which was fine by me." Hains shrugged. "His English was excellent and he always did a good job. He also never overcharged, not like some of them here." Hains flicked open a silver box and helped himself to a thin, black cigarette. "I liked him. I'm sorry to hear that he's dead." He took a few moments to light, and then draw on the cigarette. "How did you know about me by the way?"

"He kept a book of his accounts. You appeared to use him more than anyone else, so you were first on my list?"

"My apartments are all above board, Inspector. I pay tax on them all."

Os held up a placatory hand. "Please, don't misunderstand my visit here. I'm only interested in finding out why and who killed Jamil. I was hoping that you could shed some light on it. When did you last see him?"

Hains frowned as he gave this question some thought. "Probably about a week ago. He came around to collect some money I owed him."

"Could I ask how much you gave him this time?" Os asked.

Hains made a hissing noise. "Jamil didn't give receipts. I know that I paid in Sterling; he preferred that to Turkish lira. He said that it was more stable. Perhaps, two hundred pounds or thereabouts."

"A strange request for a man like Jamil, wouldn't you say? He would only have had to change it into lira himself?"

"I didn't know him that well, I'm afraid. I've no idea what he did with his money. Maybe gambled it away. I know he was interested in gambling; it was one of the things we talked about."

"You're a gambler yourself, Sir?"

Hains opened his mouth and gave a bark of a laugh. "It a mug's game. I've never been interested personally, though I know a little about it. I'm not one to throw hard-earned money away"

"Did you ever get the impression that he was in any kind of trouble?"

Hains tapped the cigarette ash into a glass bowl. "He seemed a perfectly ordinary, hard working man to me. We weren't friends, we just passed the time of day - nothing more, Inspector."

"Then I won't take up any of more of your time, Mr. Hains. If you do think of anything, however small, please ring me." Os passed him one of his cards. "Is Northern Cyprus your permanent residence now, Sir?"

"Yes. I bought this place first and used it as a holiday home and then I decided to retire. I used to run a security firm in the UK." He grinned. "I did well."

"And here? Besides your properties that you rent out - are you involved in anything else?"

Hains smiled. "Apart from collecting the rents every month? No. I'm in the lucky position of not having to work any more. I recommend it Inspector."

Chapter Seventeen

He certainly had done well for himself, thought Os as he walked back to his car. While he fastened his seat belt, he looked back at the gates which had automatically closed behind him. He could understand Kemal's view of Hains, but today the Englishman had gone out of his way to be helpful and he had appeared in no rush for Os to leave. Despite the fact that there seemed no female presence, the man obviously had good taste. If he had been in security in the UK, then it explained why he had chosen to protect his property here, even though he was living in a country where some people still chose to leave their houses and cars unlocked. Nevertheless, before Os turned on the engine, he keyed a number into his phone.

"Osman, how are you?"

Os grinned at his colleague's cheeriness. "Good. I'm glad to hear that they are treating you well down at the customs office. Just a quick call. I want you to look into an Englishman called Joe Hains. Anything at all on him. When he first arrived here, how many times he's been out of the country since, and anything else you've got on him."

"No chit chat?" his friend teased. "Okay, I'll get back to you? When you're next in Nicosia let me know and we'll meet up. I hardly know you, now that you're across in Kyrenia."

Os glanced down at the list of accounts that Jamil had so carefully compiled. The next two houses were up in the sprawling, hill-village of Lapta. He turned the car around and went back the way he had come.

Not far down the road, he turned right. Here, the road widened, and the surface became pothole-free as it swept up into the hills. Os knew this improvement was down to the local mayor, who was renowned for his efficiency. Lapta's streets were always clean and any council business ran as efficiently as was possible for a settlement in a country that was shunned by the majority of the world.

The number of houses hugging the roadside, increased as he neared the village. He turned left at a T junction, and passed a blacksmith sitting in the front of his workshop hammering out a piece of red-hot iron. A young child, engrossed in a similar task, but using much smaller tools, played nearby.

He drove through the main street thronged with small shops; clothes hung from awnings, while shoes and boots, some in their boxes, lined the pavement tables. Cafés were tucked in between these places of merchandise, but today the coffee drinkers were either at home or inside, avoiding the inclement weather. Indeed the streets were quiet, with the occasional pedestrian hurrying by. A roundabout, with a statue in the middle, came into view. Os turned right, and then a sharp left pulling up behind a small truck.

Os looked up at the decaying frontage. The outside of the house was faded pink, with the plaster cracked and missing in places. A first-floor balcony ran the length of the front of the house, from which a cascade of geraniums poked out between the wrought-iron railings. From the open front door, a TV blared out into the street. A torrent of water cascaded down from the roof guttering; it hit the pavement, splaying out, then rushing down the street, carrying mud and debris with it.

Mindful of his shoes, Os stepped over the fast-flowing stream and rang the bell. Seconds later, a large man wearing a coat, filled the doorway. Os flashed his badge. "Yes?"

Irritation showed in his broad face, much of which was covered in white facial hair.

"Mr. Taner?"

"Yes?"

"I'd like to have a few words with you about Jamil Emral. I believe that he's done some work for you in the house."

The look of irritation was replaced by one of interest. He stroked his long moustaches with a calloused hand. "I read about it in the papers."

"Can I come in for a minute? I can see you were on your way out, but I don't think this will take long."

He went back into the room and turned off the TV. "I don't see how I can help - I barely knew the man. He was recommended to me by a neighbour, the German up the road."

Os looked about the flagstoned room and decided that he would stand. The area was a combination of both kitchen and dining area, and the smell of garlic and tomatoes was overpowering. An empty plate, congealed with red sauce, remained on the oilskin-covered table. But it was the top of the dresser that caught Os's eye. Several dead rabbits, their brown fur matted in blood, were heaped on top of a plastic sheet. Memories of winter Sundays spent hunting with his father, flashed through his head.

"Someone brought them in for me in work this morning," Taner explained. "I'll skin them when I get back tonight." He gave a semi-toothless grin. "You like rabbit, Chief Inspector? You can have one if you want."

Os held up his hand. "Thank you, but no. I live on my own, so I'm not up to much in the way of cooking. I'm here to ask you what kind of work, Jemil Emral did for you?"

"I used him first to put in the internet." Taner lifted both hands, then dropped them to his side. "Not for me, you understand. I have no interest. But my two sons say they needed it for work in school. I don't know what's wrong with books, but there you are; I'm just old-fashioned I suppose. Emral told me that he was an electrician, so I had him doing a couple of other jobs." Taner scratched his hairy cheek. "The papers said that he was shot?"

"Yes, extraordinary, isn't it? I don't suppose you've any idea why, have you?"

"Alarm filled his bloodshot eyes. "You don't think I did it, do you?"

Os stared at him, taking in the heavy coat which he had now unbuttoned to reveal a thick woollen shirt and denim trousers. His heavy-soled shoes were stained with what looked like oil. "Of course not, I'm just trying to find as much about him as I can. Did you ever talk, about personal things?"

Taner glanced at his watch. "A little, I suppose. I did ask him why he was doing two jobs. He said that he wanted to get married, eventually."

"Did he mention the girl's name?" Os asked.

Taner shook his head, his moustaches swaying from side to side. "Why would he? It wouldn't be anyone I knew. I was just interested in why he worked so hard. I did it myself and that's why I ended up with my own olive-oil factory. I admire hard work." He glanced at his watch again. "Look, do you mind if I go now? I said I would be back by two. I've got a farmer coming in with a truck full of olives; I don't want to miss him."

Os handed him his card. "Just one more thing. You said that you'd been told about him by a neighbour. I don't suppose it was a Mr. Berghaus was it?"

"Yes." He jerked his head to the left. "He lives just up the road. The one with the tree outside."

"You've been very helpful. If you can think of anything else, anything at all then, I'd be very interested."

Taner nodded, called goodbye to whoever was upstairs and then led the way out into the street.

"Bloody weather," he growled at the cascading water. "I suppose I'll have to get up on to the roof when this stops. Roll on the spring, I hate this time of year." He heaved himself into his truck, and in seconds was roaring off down the road. Os pulled up his raincoat collar and decided to walk.

The house that Taner had described was smaller than the one he had just been in, and if the outside was anything to go by, was in a much better structural state. Os tugged at a shiny brass bell, and then stood back and looked more carefully at his surroundings. The tree that Taner had referred to, was a small olive tree growing in a large terracotta pot. A section of the front door had been removed and replaced with a stained-glass picture of a garden scene. The wooden window frames were well cared for, as was the stonework of the house.

The door opened and Os found himself looking at an elderly man dressed in a thick jumper and corduroy trousers.

"Am I talking to Mr. Berghaus?" Os asked in English.

"Y-e-s? How can I help you?"

Os took out his badge. "I'd like to have a few words with you. Are you all right talking in English? My German is not so good."

The man nodded and stood aside.

Fifteen minutes later Os left without discovering anything further about Jamil's activities than he had already unearthed. His work for Berghaus apparently had been exemplary and the man was more than happy to recommend him to his neighbours.

Chapter Eighteen

The late afternoon sun was attempting to break through the clouds as he drove up the hill towards Karaman. As the road swung through the village of Edremit, the hillside village came into view. The tumble of old, whitewashed houses, clung to the mountainside, glowing as if a paintbrush had danced around their edges with gold. If he could have asked Fikri to do this interview, he would have, but his sergeant's English was poor and very few of the expats bothered to become fluent in the language of the country they had decided to make their own. This visit, like the last one, would probably not bring anything new. The same things about Jemal were being repeated, that he was hard working and talented, pleasant and able to communicate in different languages. He had told most people that he was saving up, either to start his own business or to get married.

Starting up his own business made sense. He was obviously ambitious, but if there was any truth in his getting married, who was the lucky woman? If they could find Natalia, maybe she would explain things. Apart from her, there was no other woman that anyone had linked him to.

He felt his stomach tug as the Treasure Restaurant came into view. Instinctively he looked left to the road that led down to Rose's house, but there was no one about. He pressed down on the accelerator and the car surged up the last steep section of mountain road. Memories of numerous walks with Rose's dog, Tramps, filled his head. They had been tremendously happy days living with Rose, that was until she became pregnant and everything went wrong. But the relationship had been doomed from the beginning. There was nothing to be done, other than what he was already doing, and that was to move on.

The sun had now dipped behind the mountain. Some houses showed occupancy, with lights glowing behind curtains, and smoke drifting up through chimneys. It was an unusual village. The cottages were all made of local stone and all of them were in reasonable repair. As far as he knew, there were only foreigners living here. Consequently it was not like the average Cypriot village; there were no rusting piles of metal in the gardens and it was obvious that the inhabitants took great care in the appearance of their properties.

The road opened out into a small square. Os inched into a space between two vehicles and turned off the engine. He stared across at the familiar site of the Greek church. He had been inside it once with Rose, to look at the collection of icons that were stored there. Unlike many of the churches on the island, inhabitants of the village looked after it; they even used it occasionally for services at Christmas and for classical concerts. On New Year's Eve, the bell-rope hung down over the outside wall so that villagers could bring in the New Year with its chimes. An electric lamp glowed by the blue wooden door, reminding him that up here in the mountain village, dusk always came earlier. Os buttoned up his raincoat and got out.

The house backed on to the square. As soon as he looked up at the green- shuttered windows, he suspected that he was going to be unlucky. Nevertheless, he stepped over the cobbles to the front door.

A pile of timber was stacked neatly against the wall, and an outside lamp glowed. Os rang the doorbell. He might be lucky. The windows of some of these houses were ill-fitting. So, in the winter months, the occupants chose warmth over light. He waited a few seconds, then rang the bell again, using the light to study his list. He was right, there was no telephone number written against the name. He stepped back into the street and took a last look up at the building.

"They're in England at the moment."

An elderly woman with a large dog stood staring at him. He must have looked puzzled because she repeated herself. "The Ellsons are in England. They're back in a few days, I think."

The dog was now sniffing at Os's crotch. He pushed its muzzle away, but the animal was insistent. The woman, oblivious to her pet's anti-social behaviour peered at him.

"Don't I know you?" She spoke in English with a Welsh accent.

Os remembered he and Rose had passed her on their numerous walks, a friend of Rose's aunt, an eccentric woman - always with a stout walking stick - who chose to wear long skirts and heavy boots, even in summer.

"Have you a telephone number for them in England?" Os asked.

She was frowning, as if trying to remember where she had seen him before. "No, I'm not that friendly. Try in the pub. People often leave their number there if they're going to be away."

"Thank you." Os pushed the dog away and walked back down the hill. She called the dog and, to Os's relief, he trotted back to his owner.

He passed through the familiar narrow lanes, lined by whitewashed houses and the village shop, now closed, until he came to the pub. Os had never been in here before. He and Rose had eaten in the village restaurant a few times, but an English pub in Cyprus was not somewhere either of them had any wish to frequent. It was a side of the expat community that puzzled him. If he lived in England, he certainly would not be seeking out traditional Turkish coffee houses; he would have become involved in the local community and made sure he learned the language. Not that he had any desire to live in England; it was far too cold and damp and overcrowded.

He unlatched the door and stepped in. At the opposite

side of the room, across the flagstoned floor, was a long wooden bar. A large mirror reflected the glasses and numerous bottles. But they were all a blur as he gazed at the woman sitting perched on a stool. Tramps bounded over and leaped up at him. Although genuinely pleased to see the dog, it was an opportunity to busy himself. He crouched down and fondled the dog's ears before glancing back up at Rose.

She walked over to him. Though near enough to smell her perfume, he chose not to kiss her cheeks in the Cypriot way. The dog kept close to his legs, constantly nudging his hand with his wet nose.

"He's missed you," she said. She wore a bright green jumper that brought out the red highlights in her curly long hair. She indicated the walking stick propped up against the bar. "We've been over to Ilgaz and back, along the mountain path."

He immediately pictured the route the two of them had often taken whenever he had a day off, a two-hour round-trip along the old road cut into the mountainside, with fantastic views of the sea and the settlements on the flat below. There had been a time when you could have driven between the two villages, but that was before the track collapsed after heavy rain. He and Rose would eat lunch in the garden of a small restaurant there, a contented dog lying under the table.

"Would you like a drink?" she asked.

He declined with some regret. "I can't, I'm on duty."

He turned to the barman and flashed his badge. "I believe you have the contact number for the Ellsons. I've been told they're in England at the moment."

The barman frowned. "Is their house okay?"

"There's no trouble. I just need to talk to them."

The barman took a mug from a glass shelf and rooted inside. Seconds later he placed a piece of paper on the bar. He waited while Os scribbled the number in his book, then reversed the action.

As soon as the barman moved off to serve a customer, Rose asked, "How are you?"

His voice was brusque, even to his own ears. "Fine, busy."

Her eyes widened, perhaps shocked by his tone. "I hear about you from Cassie "

"All good, I hope," was all he could think of saying.

"Did she tell you that I was learning Turkish? I thought I'd better if I'm going to stay here."

He noticed how her eyes sparkled and how her skin had a rosy bloom. In fact, she looked fabulous; maybe living on her own was suiting her. "I thought you might go back to Liverpool," he said.

She shook her head and her red curls danced. "No. I really like it here. Not so much the really hot weather, but why would I want to go back to rainy, cold winters? I went to my sister's for two weeks over Christmas and I couldn't wait to get back."

He noticed that she no longer used the word 'home' when she was talking about England. He suddenly wanted to pull up a chair and sit next to her, close enough to smell her once-familiar perfume and touch her hair and skin.

Instead he said, "I've got to go, I'm working." Something flickered across her eyes, but he hardened his heart. "It was nice seeing you."

She leaned across and kissed his cheek. "You could always call in at the house," she said softly, placing her hand on Tramps' head. "We both miss you."

He nodded and then walked quickly to the door. In that short time night had fallen outside.

It was only when he was sitting back in his car that he realised that his heart was pounding. He pulled the seat belt across his chest, but continued to sit there, angry with himself. She was nothing to him now; she had decided that she didn't want him, so what was he doing, allowing his emotions to flare up like this. It was over: despite her invitation to visit, there was no point going back. He pulled out his phone and keyed in Fikri's number.

"How are you doing, Sergeant?"

Fikri sounded tired. "Nothing at this end at all, Sir. Not of any interest anyway. Everyone we've spoken to so far says the same thing about him, hard working, pleasant, could speak a couple of languages, always wanted his money in cash, good at his job…"

Os sighed. "Yup! It's the same here. How many more have you on your list?"

"About ten, I think, Sir."

"Well do what you can and finish the rest off in the morning. I'm talking to Kucuk as soon as he arrives back from Istanbul, so I'll ring you after I've finished with him. But, if by any chance you do find out anything of interest, my phone will be on all evening."

"Okay, Sir."

Os started the engine and pushed in a CD. The gravelly tones of Leonard Cohen suited his mood perfectly. As the words of *Suzanne* filled the car, he drove through the narrow streets down the mountain. The last song of the CD was finishing as he pulled into the car park of Kyrenia Hospital.

Visitors with overflowing bags crowded the corridors. Rose had gone with him to visit his uncle in hospital once and had been horrified to find that relatives were expected to feed the patients. "We don't have your NHS," he had told her.

"But what happens if someone doesn't have any relatives? Do they starve?"

He had not been sure. "The relatives of other patients help out," he'd guessed. It had always been like that in Turkey, and in Greece, as far as he knew, people just got on with it.

There was another man in Mr. Emral's bed. Os froze in the doorway. Did he now have a second death? A nurse tapped him on the shoulder.

"If you're looking for Mr. Emral, he's in Ward 5," she told him then walked off.

The old man was propped up against his pillows, his eyes closed. Mehmet sat beside him, attempting to spoon-feed yoghurt into his toothless mouth. The younger man's face was drawn, his shoulders hunched inside his padded jacket. He looked up. His right eye twitched.

"Have you news?"

Os attempted to read his face. Usually the brother gave little of his emotions away but this evening he appeared worried. "About what?" Os asked.

"Natalia! Have you found her?"

Os shook his head.

"Shouldn't you be out there looking for her? It's been several days now. Something must have happened."

Os frowned. "You now think that she was your brother's girlfriend?"

Mehmet jerked his head. "I didn't say that. I've no idea, but you should be doing something. Have you asked about her at work?"

"Several times. No one seems to have any idea where she is."

Mehmet put down his father's bowl and stood up. "What about her friends? Have you talked to them?"

"You mean the people who work in the Casino?"

Mehmet nodded.

"Yes. No one admits to knowing where she might have gone."

"Someone must know something. She must have a special friend - women always do."

"I don't understand why you're so worried about her."

Mehmet turned to look out of the window. "It's just strange, that's all. First Jamil is killed and then my father's attacked." He chewed on his lip. "And then a woman, who my brother was friendly with, disappears. I would have thought that it's obvious that her life could be in danger."

"We've put out a search and I'm talking to her boss tomorrow morning. He might be able to help."

Mehmet spun around. "You mean Mr. Kucuk? You're talking to him?"

"You know him?" Os asked.

Mehmet suddenly looked uninterested. "I've seen him in the Casino. He's the main manager."

"How's your father?"

Mehmet's eyes suddenly watered, before he pulled the covers up over his father's shoulders. "Not good. The doctor's think that if he does recover, there'll be permanent brain damage." His voice shuddered. "It means he'll have to go into a home."

"I'm very sorry to hear that, Your brother seems to have been involved in something big. Are you sure you had no idea what?"

Mehmet blinked several times. "Do you think I would keep something like that to myself?"

"You'd be very foolish not to tell me what you do know. Your father was the first casualty; let us hope that this Natalia isn't the second."

The temperature in the ward was not particularly high, but Mehmet was sweating. Os glanced at his watch. It was seven o'clock. "I'll leave you, but think about what I said. I don't want anyone else to get hurt."

Mehmet's tone was a mixture of pain and anger. "Why do you think that I know anything?"

Os walked to the door, calling over his shoulder,"You're his twin brother."

Chapter Nineteen

The cold engulfed him as he opened his front door. For a brief moment he considered turning round and going out again, perhaps having a solitary meal in one of the numerous restaurants within walking distance. But it was too early and he had done too much of that over the last six months. He had to get used to living on his own, and once spring arrived, the apartment would be more inviting.

He lit the gas fire and then turned on the TV; the room filled with the latest news. He fetched a beer, then stretched out on the sofa. There were at least five hours to kill before he could reasonably expect to go to bed. He picked up his mobile and considered whom he could ring. He had already seen Aka in the last few days, so in fairness he couldn't ring him; he did not want Cassie to become irritated by how much he took up of her husband's time. There were other friends of course, but most of them lived in Nicosia. Despite the prospect of a lonely night ahead, he had no inclination to drive over the mountains in the cold and dark just so that he could sit in a bar with a friend.

His mind flipped over to what he had been trying to block out all evening, his meeting with Rose. This was the first time that he had seen her in six months, which was strange since her closest friend lived in the flat below him. Why had she suggested that he should call round to see her when they really had nothing to say to each other anymore. Once, they would have spent night after night, talking into the early hours, but that was before she found out that she was pregnant, and within days her attitude to him changed.

He still felt the pain. If anything, she had looked more beautiful than he remembered, her translucent skin flushed from her walk and her blue eyes sparkling. Could she be seeing someone else? Maybe it was not the walk, but the excitement of a new man. His gut twisted.

He crossed over to the French window and went out on to the balcony. Lights glowed in the harbour below. With tourists in mind, some restauranteurs had lit braziers of logs. Few Turkish Cypriots would have any inclination to sit outside, however many fires were lit around them. Several of the large yachts had lights running up the masts left over from the New Year celebrations. The aroma of cooking food drifted up from the open barbecues below. He went back in, pulling the thick curtains closed.

He wondered what he was going to eat. He'd had a pizza at lunch-time so his usual take-away was out of the question. He went into the kitchen and rooted inside the freezer. His spirits lifted as he pulled out the last of the cooked meals his mother had made for him. He slid the plastic box into the microwave and flicked on the defrosting button. She had suggested rice to go with what he knew to be a spicy stew, but instead, he sliced two thick pieces of bread from the loaf he had brought yesterday. While he waited, he changed into jeans and his thickest jumper and then took his tray of food to sit in front of the TV.

At eight the next morning, working through a pile of paperwork, he felt surprisingly upbeat. An early night and one beer obviously suited him. There was no reason why he could not live a healthy life, now that he was a single man again; he had done it before. But then he had lived in Nicosia where his mother had cleaned his flat once a week and kept his freezer full of home cooking. He grinned to himself; he was not quite the modern man that he made himself out to be. He reached out to answer his land-line.

"There's a man to see you, Sir," the desk sergeant said, "a Mr. Kucuk."

Os glanced at his watch; if this was Kucuk, he was an hour early. Was this a good or bad sign? "Which interview rooms are free?"

"I'll send someone down to number two, to make sure that it's clean for you. Sir. Do you want Mr. Kucuk to be taken straight there?"

"No, I'm coming now, Sergeant. Tell him, I'll be a couple of minutes." Os stood up and checked himself in the wall mirror. His brown eyes were clear and his curly, dark brown hair springy from its morning shampoo. His white shirt was freshly starched from the launderette, and his black suit and colourful silk tie were to his satisfaction. He had made time to dress carefully this morning, his focus on the impression he would give the mainland Turk who wielded so much power in his domain.

Os had the advantage of examining Kucuk before he was noticed himself. The tall, broad-shouldered Casino manager stood in the middle of the corridor, talking on his mobile. He was dark, both in hair and skin tone and wore designer jeans, along with a thin denim shirt, topped with a long, tan-coloured greatcoat. Os sniffed the strong scents of a citrus aftershave. Kucuk turned round, a clean-shaven man in his early forties, with a face, that might be considered good-looking by some, despite the bags under his blue eyes. Did this man have regular facials to achieve his smooth skin? Certainly, the hand holding the mobile had been manicured.

"Mr. Kucuk?" Os asked.

Kucuk said something, in what Os guessed was Russian, then snapped his phone closed.

"I'm Chief Inspector Zahir. If you would like to come this way, we can talk somewhere more privately."

Os led the way down stone steps to the row of interview rooms, then opened the first door. He waited for a few seconds as the porter finished wiping the table and emptying the ashtray into a plastic bag.

"Thank you," Os said. "We'll take the room now."

The porter pushed his cleaning trolley into the corridor and Os's nose turned up at the mix of disinfectant and nicotine. He pulled out a chair for Kucuk and then sat down opposite him.

"Thank you for coming in, Mr. Kucuk. How was your trip?"

"Successful. But, I'm obviously concerned to hear that Natalia has disappeared. You haven't heard anything more since we spoke on the phone?

I've just talked to both my managers and neither of them has heard anything. Her passport is with the Casino, so she can't have gone far. But she hasn't slept in her bed for three nights and she's obviously not turned up for work."

"Tell me about Natalia, I need to get a better feel for her. Did you personally employ her?"

Kucuk pulled out a cigarette packet and took some seconds to light up. " I use an agency that's based in Odessa. Most of our staff are from Russia or in that area. They're good workers; they've not had a soft life so they know how to work." His eyes met those of Os. "The women are often beautiful, which is important in the gambling world, it attracts the punters."

"Natalia is beautiful then?"

"Oh yes."

Os thought he heard pride in the manager's voice. Did he see her as his property?

"The agency send me photos and their CVs and I choose who I want. Natalia and her friend, Alexandra applied together, which was fine by me; they tend to stay longer if they come with a friend."

"So how long was it before she became your mistress?"

Kucuk raised an eyebrow. "Is this relevant, Chief Inspector?"

Os spread his hands. "I'm sorry, but in a murder inquiry all niceties are put aside. I've got a dead man, an old man who will never walk again and a missing woman. I don't want any more fatalities."

Kucuk blinked. "Do you think she's dead?"

Os sighed. "At the moment she's disappeared and has a tenuous link to a murdered man. That's all. You weren't tempted to take her to Istanbul with you? I would have thought it would have been an ideal opportunity to have some time together?"

Now Kucuk sighed. "I have done in the past, but to be honest with you, Chief Inspector, I was thinking of calling it a day."

"Really? Why? You say she's a beautiful woman."

The man adopted a bored tone. "There are many beautiful women in my business and she was no longer fun. She wanted me to divorce my wife and marry her." He spread wide his large soft hands as if to suggest how impossible such a thing could be. "I have two children. I'm very fond of Natalia, but no more than that."

"I'm sure your wife will be pleased."

Kucuk face blanked. He took one last drag at his cigarette then ground it into the ashtray. "Is there anything else, Chief Inspector?"

"What about Alexandra? Are you surprised she says that she doesn't know anything about her friend's disappearance? Are they not close?" Kucuk creased his brow. Os noticed that some parts of his face remained smooth. Was this man using Botox to keep himself young?

"I am surprised, yes. They're very close. Though, Natalia told me that they have had some big arguments. Alexandra wanted to go home, but Natalia wanted to stay. Because of me." Kucuk flicked ash into the tray. "But, as soon as I get back to the Casino, I promise I'll talk to her."

"If Alexandra tells you anything, obviously you'll pass that information to me. We'll keep in touch."

Perhaps reading that as a dismissal, Kucuk leapt to his feet. "If that's all, Chief Inspector, I'd like to see my children and wife before I go into work."

"Of course, I'll see you out."

As they retraced their steps, Os asked, "Where are you from, Mr. Kucuk?"

"Izmir. I came over here with my family, a couple of years ago, to set up the Casino. You?"

"Nicosia."

Os watched through the glass door as Kucuk hurried

to his Mercedes. Was the man just an excellent liar? Was he really tired of Natalia? Somehow Os did not think so. He would wait until Kucuk had spoken to Alexandra, and then, if he did not come up with anything, Os would bring her into the station for questioning. But now he could no longer put off the unpleasant task ahead.

Chapter Twenty

Assistant Superintendent Ismail answered on the first knock; stomach clenched, Os walked in. Ismail's thin eyebrows rose as he looked up from the papers on his desk.

"Chief Inspector?"

"Just a few moments of your time, if that's alright with you, Sir?"

Ismail placed his pen on the desk in a manner which suggested that he found the interruption tiresome. "Yes?"

There was no suggestion that Os should sit, a position which suited him anyway; he wanted to be out of the room as quickly as possible. "I'd like permission to put out a search for Natalia Sakalova - the Russian croupier who has gone missing. I've just talked to the manager she's had a year-long affair with, and he claims that he has no idea where she is. My sergeant has been to the Casino to collect her passport, so she's definitely not left the country legally."

Ismail pursed his lips as if he had just eaten a lemon. "And you still think that she's linked to the dead man? These searches are costly, you know."

Os took in the well-cut suit and white crisp shirt of his superior, his dark hair slicked back with oil. He looked as if he had just come back from the barber, having had a haircut and shave with hot towels. Perhaps he had. What a contrast from Superintendent Atak, who preferred to spend his working day in one of his baggy suits. How he missed him as his line manager.

"There's a lot of conflicting facts in this case, Sir. But it's essential that we discover whether she really was a friend of Jamil's. We can't just dismiss the coincidence that she's disappeared."

Ismail sighed. "Very well. I'll inform Head Office in Nicosia." He flicked his hand as if to suggest that he had more important things to talk about. "Now, I did need to speak to you."

Os tried to smile, but could not quite get his muscles to obey. Ismail waved his arm expansively. "Please, take a seat." He waited, then said, "Have you ever thought of a change in career, Osman?"

With a face as blank as he was able, Os answered, "I'm quite happy in the job I'm doing, thank you. Why?"

This time, Ismail's sigh was more elaborate. Well, as you know, I've been brought over here to look at ways of cutting back on the force. If I can be of any assistance in helping officers find a new profession, then it would make things easier. You, I see," Ismail tapped the folder on the table in front of him, "You have an excellent law degree. You could earn far more as a lawyer, perhaps set up your own law firm?" Ismail smiled and Os found himself comparing the smooth face and black eyes to that of a crocodile.

"I am well aware of that, Sir. However, I'm in the police force and I'm happy here."

Ismail nodded. "Of course, many factors will go into my recommendations. We mustn't forget that you are the only single inspector in the station."

Os stared back at the assistant superintendent.

Ismail shrugged his narrow shoulders. "It must seem unfair to you, but it's something I obviously have to consider."

Neither man said anymore, then eventually Ismail stood up. "Well, that's all for now. I'll let you get on." In an unnaturally bright voice, he added, "I'll ring Head Office now about the woman, Sakalova. Every station in Northern Cyprus will be informed in the next few hours. I'll also let the desk sergeant know. Have we a photo?"

Os slid one of the photographs he had removed from

Natalia's room. Ismail picked it up.

"A beautiful woman." He raised a long thin finger. "One more thing, Osman."

Os cringed at the way his name was pronounced. "Yes, Sir?"

"Sergeant Rafiker will be working for me for the moment. You have your other sergeant. And of course you can commandeer a constable where necessary."

Os would have liked to ask what Sener would be doing, but the atmosphere in the room was suffocating; he needed to get out of there as quickly as possible. He nodded and the assistant superintendent let him go.

Sener was already in the café, a cup of coffee in front of him. Os threaded his way between the metal tables and chairs, apologizing to a few elderly men that he disturbed. He grinned at Sener, realizing that he was inordinately pleased to see him.

Os took a few moments to take in the familiar surroundings - the peeling plaster of the whitewashed walls, the traditional, large-framed photo of the founder of Northern Cyprus, President Denktas. They were the youngest customers by at least two decades. And, instead of the hustle of the station cafeteria, here was all calm. There was little chance of anyone listening in to their conversation; the men were far more interested in their games of backgammon. And there was absolutely no chance of some police officer tapping them on the back and asking their opinion on the redundancies that were promised.

Sener broke the silence. "So how's it going?"

The wooden chair creaked as Os pushed back against the wall. "I've just interviewed Kucuk. She didn't go to Istanbul with him, that's pretty definite. But I'm not sure whether the rest of what he had to say was the truth."

Sener lifted his coffee cup to his lips, but said nothing. Both men knew each other's ways.

"He says that he was losing interest in her because she wanted to marry him." Os stared across at the shop on the other side of the road. Bales of cloth were stacked in the window alongside a dressmaker's dummy. An elderly woman, in a shapeless black dress and headscarf, was sitting by the door, crocheting.

"But you don't believe him."Sener answered.

Os shrugged. "Your new boss is putting out a national alert for her now. He wasn't too keen at first - he seemed more bothered about the expense. How's it going with him, by the way?"

Sener blew out a lungful of smoke. "I feel as if I'm being set up to be the station snoop. Assistant Superintendent Ismail has told me that I am to report to him, no one else. I'm supposed to look into the backgrounds of everyone in the station - see if there are any black marks against them. He thinks that I'm going to report conversations I've overheard. Well he can go and swing. I can't wait to get back to the training centre at Yenicekoy."

Their eyes met; Os recognised deep misery in those of his friend. "I just wish that there was something I could do."

"He doesn't like you, you know, Sir." Sener's voice was flat. "I don't know why. I think he'll try and get rid of you."

Os's stomach contracted. But this was not news to him. "I'll just have to get on and solve this case and hope that Atak stands up for me."

"Superintendent Atak wouldn't allow you to go, would he, Sir? Why not speak to him, try and warn him somehow?"

Os shook his head. "Let's forget about it. I'm not going to be like all those in the canteen, spending their time worrying about whether it's going to be their name that comes out of the hat."

To suggest that the subject was over, Os held up his hand to re-order more coffee. "So, any insights for me?"

Sener pulled cigarettes out of his pocket and lit up. "You always told me to look at motive, Sir. What's behind this, greed, sex, money? Jamil obviously wasn't killed by mistake. Finding that money in his garden proved that, wouldn't you say? Why was there no photo of Natalia in his wallet? A girl as beautiful as that - you'd want to show her off, wouldn't you?" Sener flicked ash into the metal dish. "I just don't get the connection between him and Natalia; it doesn't make sense to me. Maybe we're getting sidelined by her, maybe she's not who we should be looking at."

Os stared at the burning cigarette and realised that, at last, the urge to smoke was weakening. "Perhaps. But nothing stuck out when we interviewed the people he worked for; most of them said the same thing, that he wanted to set up his own business or get married, though to whom we don't know."

"He didn't treat his boss very well, did he, Sir." Sener's eyes narrowed. The man must be gutted. He takes Jamil on because he is a friend of the father, bends over backwards for him, and then the bastard double-crosses him."

Os grinned. "Don't tell me that human nature still surprises you, Sener. Not after you've been in the job as long as you have."

Sener shrugged. "I just don't like to see people being abused, that's all."

"He wanted Jamil as his son-in-law and Jamil could have done a lot worse. Love wouldn't necessarily have to come into it."

Sener's eyes widened.

Os laughed. "I'm not talking from my point of view."

"There must have been some reason for him to be working so hard. To amass the kind of money he did, we're talking serious hours."

"Yes, and a big chunk of it was not accounted for."

Sener pursed his lips. "What do you mean?"

"Just that. Although he kept very accurate records from all the jobs he did, there was ten thousand lira more bundled up in that oven."

"Why do you make of that, Sir?"

"I don't know. Possibly, there's another book of accounts somewhere. Maybe whoever broke into the father's house, took it. Maybe Jamil just didn't write it down. It's strange though, wouldn't you say, when he was so particular?" Os drained his coffee. "A pity you didn't come up with anything on that Englishman, Joe Hains. He's a dodgy character, however charming he tried to make himself."

"Do you want me to look up anyone else? I can easily do

it in between what I've got to do for the assistant super."

"Be careful, Sener - make sure you keep a low profile around that man." Os plucked some notes from his wallet and slid them under his cup. "Come on. We'd better get back. I don't want him hauling me into his office, accusing me of stealing you away. He couldn't have said more clearly that you were working for him not me."

Os slid into the leather driving seat. As he moved off, the throaty voice of Leonard Cohen filled the car. Should he bring in Natalia's friend, Alexandra? Away from the prying eyes of Kucuk, she might be persuaded to talk. If not, he would have to threaten her with something; deportation wouldn't work. Northern Cyprus's charms seemed to have run rather thin with her.

Cohen started on the first lines of *'Hey, that's no way to say good-bye.'* Instantly, Os thought of Rose and her invitation to call round? Did she just want his company, or was she missing him as a lover? He even missed the dog. Os shook his head, as if to dispel such a ridiculous thought. He was Cypriot, for God's sake. Dogs were for guarding, not pets. Nevertheless, the memory of the lopsided grin of Tramps, made his chest tighten. But he would not be visiting. No way could he be friends with her now that their relationship was over; there was too much emotion between them. And they would just revisit the same old arguments again and again.

The roundabout with the fountain in the centre loomed up ahead of him. As usual he was irritated by the idea of using water as a decoration when the country regularly introduced water bans. He took the first exit on to the road leading to the station and was just about to turn into the car park when his phone rang.

"Chief Inspector Zahir?"

Os recognised the voice of the duty officer. "Yes, Sergeant Peksolu?"

"A body of a woman has been found - up at the top of Lapta, in a gully. Two foreigners were walking their dog. I don't know any more than that, Sir. But, it could be the woman you're looking for."

Os dragged the wheel into a U-turn."Give me the instructions, will you."

"The local police are there now. The Lapta constable said that someone would wait for you at their station. It would be easier than you trying to find the site and the local sergeant is already at the scene."

"Get hold of Fikri, will you. If he's not in the sergeants' room, he'll be in the canteen." For a brief moment he considered ringing Sener, then dismissed the idea. Instead, he turned off the music; somehow Cohen's lamentations no longer seemed appropriate.

Fifteen minutes later, the Mercedes was swinging up the hill to Lapta. Os turned left into the main street, barely noticing the row of shops selling anything from metal pans to clothes. Despite the cold, several men, thick coats buttoned up to their necks, sat outside cafés, talking or just sipping their coffees and contemplating life. He turned into a small square, passed the house that he had visited only yesterday, and pulled up outside the police station.

The Lapta station was a fraction of the size of Kyrenia, but then it was only there to service the population of a very large village. A uniformed policeman came out, locked the station office door, then ran down the steps to Os's vehicle.

Os pushed open the passenger door. "I'm Chief Inspector Zahir. Are you waiting for me?"

"Yes, Sir! Shall I come with you?"

'Why not.'

The constable, his young face alight with enthusiasm, climbed in. "If you turn left at the top, Sir and then right, I'll show you where to stop."

"Who's up there with the body, Constable?"

"Sergeant Alican, and the couple who found it?" He corrected himself. "Actually, it was the dog who found the body. Its owner rang us on his mobile."

Os pulled over as a car came down the narrow lane; it slipped past, the two cars' side-mirrors narrowly missing each other. Os drove on.

"Have you seen the body?" Os asked.

"No, Sir. Sergeant Alican reported it to Kyrenia and then told me to wait here for whoever they sent."He hesitated, then added, "I've never seen a dead body before."

Os glanced across at him. "I'm not sure that it gets any easier after the first time. And maybe it shouldn't. Manage it the best way you can. Don't think that you're feeling any different than anyone else."

The tension in the young constable's face eased and he smiled. In silence, they passed a couple of houses at the edge of the village and then turned on to the mountain road towards Baspinar.

"It's there, Sir, on the left."

A police car was parked on the grass kerb. Os pulled in behind. He turned off the engine, then buttoned up his leather coat, sensing the nervousness of the man next to him. "We'd better go and look for them."

It was significantly colder and damper up here in the shadow of the mountainside. A kestrel hovered high above and then dived into a cluster of pine trees clinging to the rock. A tortured screech ripped through the air .

They both moved to the edge of a gully, then stared down at three people and a dog looking up at them. Aware that he was wearing one of his more expensive pairs of shoes, Os shuffled down sideways, grabbing at the thicker branches of bushes as he went. The constable followed behind.

As Os neared the bottom, he saw her. Her waist and legs hidden under a bush. He recognised the face, but still he took out the photo from his wallet to double check. It was definitely her. Natalia Sakalova was lying dead at the bottom of the gully wearing an expensive-looking fur jacket over an emerald-green, mohair jumper. Soft leather brown boots had been pulled over tight designer jeans. Her blue eyes stared unseeing at the sky.

Os was aware that everyone was waiting for him to say something. But instead, he crouched down and closed her lids. The sergeant crouched beside him.

He lowered his voice so that only Os could hear. "I'm afraid they disturbed the body – pulling her out to see if she was still alive. It couldn't have been easy for them so I haven't said anything They're German. They don't speak any Turkish, but their English is okay."

Os wondered how fluent the sergeant's own English was. Both men stood up and Os held out his hand."Chief Inspector Zahir. You're Sergeant Alican? Thanks for handling this. Did the couple tell you anything else?"

The sergeant shook his head. They're both very shocked. I'm wanting to let them go home, Sir, if it's alright with you? I'm sure they haven't got anything to do with this."

"That's fine by me. I'll just have a quick word and then perhaps your constable can take them home. We'll know where they live then, for the future."

Os glanced across at the couple. Both of them had the appearance of people in their seventies, though they looked fit for their age. The woman was small, with blonde, cropped hair feathered around an elfin-shaped face. She chewed on her lips and once or twice wiped her eyes with the back of her hand. The man stood with his arm protectively around her shoulders.

"I believe your English is very good." Os gave a smile of apology, "I'm afraid I don't speak German. Thank you for reporting this. I'm sorry, but I'm going to have to ask you to repeat what you must have already said to the police here. Afterwards, I'll get the constable to run you home."

The woman gave a sob. Her husband pulled her closer and answered. "It was Heini who found the body. He kept barking, so in the end I came down here to see what was happening. Margot came down after me."

It was a steep climb down. Had the wife made the effort to support her husband, or had it been ghoulish curiosity?

"We've never seen this woman before," the man lamented.

"Do you walk along here every day with your dog?" Os asked.

The German shook his head. "We haven't been on this path for a week. We live in Lapta. We have many walks that we go on."

"And you're sure that you have never seen this woman before. She used to run along the roads around here most weeks, I believe."

The German's eyes narrowed. "No. Never. Why do you think that?"

Os smiled, attempting to defuse the sharpness in the man's voice. "No reason. Please don't concern yourself." Os waved his arm towards the gully slope they would have to climb back up. "That's all I need to know. The constable here will take your names and address in case we need to talk to you in the future. But, thank you again for ringing us so promptly.

The German appeared surprised that he was getting off so lightly. And then, as if he expected the policeman to change his mind, he spoke rapidly to his wife in German. Os instructed the constable to drive the couple and their dog home, and to take their address and mobile phone number.

As the three of them scrambled up the slope, the dog racing in front, Os turned back to the sergeant. "This is the woman I'm looking for. Have you already contacted emergency services?"

Sergeant Alican nodded. "A doctor and an ambulance are on their way."

Os turned back to study the body. Even in death it was obvious that she had been beautiful. "She'll have to go to Nicosia. I want a post-mortem done on her as soon as possible."

"You think she's been murdered then, Sir? I haven't examined her closely; I didn't want to disturb her any more than she had been. But I couldn't see any blood."

Os looked at the blonde hair now tangled with twigs and grass. Her skin was waxen-yellow and there was a smell of rotting flesh. "Oh, she would have been murdered, all right. This won't be an accident or a suicide."

"Do you think she was killed down here or thrown from the top?" Sergeant Alican chucked his chin towards the top of the ravine where the Germans and constable were now climbing into the police car.

"I'd have thought that she would have been killed elsewhere and then dumped here. But I need you and your men to search both areas - see what you can come up with."

Os snapped on a pair of rubber gloves, then rolled Natalia on to her side He found what he was looking for immediately. "You're looking for a gun, or at least you might find the shells. I think it's the same one that was used to shoot Jamil Emral. My guess is that the murderer might be holding on to it in case he needs it again."

"I heard about the Emral case, Sir. One of my mates was part of the group that searched the old man's house. He told me about finding the money in the outside oven. Amazing, storing all that cash in the garden."

The screech of an ambulance siren made both men look up. A police car, followed by an ambulance and an old Fiat were coming towards them. Os recognised the elderly doctor hunched over the wheel. Several men climbed out of the various vehicles and made their way to the edge of the ravine. The doctor handed his bag to the policeman and then, using both hands to grasp passing shrubbery, he edged his way down the bank.

Os went across to meet him. "She's been shot in the head. I've no idea how long she's been here though."

The doctor was breathing heavily. "So it's murder again. I suppose this body is linked to the man I looked at on Sunday morning?"

"We've been searching for her since Sunday morning. I'll need you to confirm her time of death," Os grimaced. "I suppose we're lucky that it's not summertime. God knows what state the body would have been in then."

Os stood back while the doctor did his examination. High above them a kestrel screamed. At least it was not a vulture, Os thought, but he shivered nevertheless. He resisted the temptation to cadge a cigarette from the ambulance men. Finally the doctor clambered to his feet.

" I'd say she's been dead approximately forty-eight hours. We're lucky that a wild animal didn't start on her. Amazing really."

Os grimaced at the thought.

The doctor jerked his head towards the ambulance men. "They can take her to Nicosia now. I'll send my report over to you by the end of the day, though it'll be for the pathologist to remove the bullet. There are some cigarette burns on her arms as well - I think she was tortured before they shot her." He blinked rapidly then snapped off his rubber gloves and pushed them into his pocket. "Are you near to solving this? We don't want any more like her."

Os cleared his throat. "Not really. But her death is going to frighten a few people. Maybe someone will talk." Os shook the doctor's hand. "I'll look forward to receiving your report."

Os held a farewell hand up to the others, then started slowly back up the side of the ravine .

He caught his breath at the top looking back down at the crime scene. The body of Natalia Sakalova was being lifted on to the stretcher, and then belts were used to secure her. It was not going to be easy to get the body back up. But now he had to go to the Casino and see what effect the news of Natalia's death had on people there.

It was late afternoon when Os drew into the Casino car park. The sun had set over the mountain range, and though it was still light on the coast road, Os buttoned up his jacket against the damp. He had thought about ringing ahead, to make sure that Kucuk was available, and then decided against it. The element of surprise would be more informative, and if Kucuk was not on duty, then he would have to go to his house.

The woman behind the front desk was different to the one that had been there on previous visits. He was greeted with a big smile until he flashed his badge.

"Mr. Kucuk, please," Os said.

She picked up the phone and spoke in Russian. Os waited. Sometimes he felt that he was not even in his own country. She replaced the receiver and then told him in stilted Turkish, that he was to go up to his office.

As the lift doors opened, Os came face to face with Salinsky. The Russian muttered a greeting, and then stepped into the space that Os had just vacated. Kucuk stood waiting by his desk.

"What can I do for you, Chief Inspector? Have you found

Natalia?"

"We found her body a short time ago."

Kucuk fumbled behind him for his chair and slumped down. "Tell me."

Was he acting or was the news really a surprise? Os studied the widened eyes and paled complexion. "It seems that she was shot and then thrown into a gully."

Kucuk thrust his head into his hands. Os waited for a few moments before he continued.

"This is now obviously a murder inquiry as far as she is concerned. And I know that you will want to help in any way you can." Os did not wait for an answer. "Do you have any idea at all who could have done this to her? What would be the motive? You said that you were about to end your affair with her."

Kucuk's voice rose several decibels. "You think that I did this to her? You're mad, I loved her."

Unsurprised by the outburst, Os pressed further. "I thought that you'd had enough of her?"

Kucuk turned weary eyes on Os. "It's what we say when we know that we are losing someone, isn't it. She did her best to hide it, but I knew that she was acting. In the end I had to find out if there was another man."

Os's eyes narrowed. "And was there?"

"I don't know. I had her watched while I was away in Istanbul. I thought that if she was going to be indiscreet, it would be then. But she disappeared, didn't she."

His landline rang. Kucuk picked up the receiver then looked across at Os. "Your Sergeant's downstairs waiting for you, Chief Inspector."

Kucuk's habitual arrogance was temporarily absent.

"Tell him to wait there. I'll be down in a few minutes."

Kucuk replaced the receiver. "What now?"

"My men will be doing a search here. We will want to see any documentation relating to Natalia and, of course, we will want to speak again to everyone who works here."

Kucuk opened his mouth and then shut it. "Of course."

"Another possibility we have to consider is that she could have been killed to get at you. Have you offended anyone recently? The local mafia?

"You're a very hard man, Chief Inspector."

Os found himself grinning. "Coming from you, Mr. Kucuk, that's a compliment. How many people knew of your relationship?"

He shook his head. " I didn't discuss her with anyone, but people talk and we used her room. The Casino is a small community. We forbid any friendships with the punters, so naturally, as their time off is limited, this is their entire world. Gossip here is a way of life. If I'm honest, probably most people knew."

"And outside the Casino?"

Kucuk hissed out a mouthful of air. "You know what we're like with a beautiful woman, Chief Inspector. Sometimes I would take her to a restaurant on her day off. We went shopping occasionally. I didn't want her to think it was just sex with me."

"So anyone and everyone knew." Os did not add Kucuk's wife. Was she used to her husband infidelities? Perhaps she was also frightened of him.

Os made an effort to keep his voice bland. "I want you to think hard. Let me know immediately if you come up with a name. Now, I'd like to talk to Alexandra."

Kucuk opened his mouth, as if to object, and then closed it again. Instead he picked up a piece of paper and scanned the list of names. "She's downstairs. Where do you want to talk to her?"

Os followed the grey-suited manager into the gaming room. Again, he had the sensation that, even though the croupiers' eyes were down, they were aware that their boss had arrived with the policeman, the one investigating Natalia. Kucuk scanned the room and then frowned; Alexandra was nowhere to be seen. He crossed over to a woman sitting on a high stool, her eyes fixed on the players at the tables below. After a brief conversation, she took out her mobile. Minutes later, Alexandra appeared in a doorway. Os could see the strain in her face and, when her eyes fastened on him, he saw that she had been told.

She crossed over to him. "You want to talk to me."

Her voice trembled, so he softened his tone. "Can we go somewhere private please?"

Like Kucuk before her, she hesitated, and then perhaps realised the futility of refusing.

He followed her swinging gait to the room that she had just come out of. The staffroom was better than he imagined, with two sofas and a couple of armchairs. Old magazines and three full ashtrays cluttered a low table. A kettle, with mugs and jars of instant coffee, were stacked on a counter. Stale cigarette smoke, mixed with cheap perfume and aftershave, made Os cross over to the window and wrench it open.

Alexandra slumped into an armchair. She was dressed for work, black cocktail dress low at the front, with the skirt ending just above her knees. Her makeup was thickly applied as before. She already had a lit cigarette in her hand. Os waited while she took a couple of deep drags.

"You've been told about Natalia?"

Tears streaked her face. "Vera said on phone just now." She blinked several times, but she could not stop crying. She then pressed her hand to her mouth while sobs racked through her body. Os sat down and waited.

After a few minutes she blew her nose. "Vera said that she been murdered, shot in the head?"

"I'm sorry. You realise that I have to ask you some questions."

She nodded and he thought that perhaps she would now tell the truth.

"Do you have some idea of what might have happened? You two were best friends; she must have talked to you."

Alexandra shook her head.

"Are you frightened of someone? Mr. Kucuk perhaps, or someone else? We can put you into a safe house if you want. You don't have to stay here."

She considered his question for a few moments. "I did know about Jamil. Natalia told me and I'd seen him in Casino. He always sat on Natalia's table." She shrugged. "It happens sometimes. A man comes in. He ask us out and we say no because we lose our job. Some of the casinos not as strict as here. But with him, how do you say, love at first sight. She broke the rule and saw him outside. He was a handsome man, but I told her that she was mad. She was having sex with Kucuk. He would be very angry, so she took up running. An excuse to meet Jamil." She paused. "I should have made her go back home with me. Now she'll never see her family again."

Os passed her his clean handkerchief.

She smiled weakly and took it.

"They presumably met somewhere besides here at the Casino. She couldn't have taken him back to her room, the caretaker would presumably have reported her."

She chewed her lip. " Jamil had a friend who was manager of hotel – just a few rooms." She stared wide-eyed at him. "I thought that was where she was, I should have told you."

"You're right: you should have told me. You're sure you don't know where this hotel is now?"

She shook her head. "Somewhere on the bottom road near the sea. She go out running and Jamil would be waiting on his motorbike. There was old house up in the hills. I never went there," she added hurriedly as if she expected that he would demand to see it.

More tears plopped on to her cheeks.

"Do you think Kucuk could have killed her?" Os asked.

Her voice became a deep guttural whisper. "I don't know. Please, I must go back to work. I'll be in trouble."

"You're sure you don't want to go back to your room? I could drop you there?"

She shook her head. "I don't think about Natalia at the moment."

"Will you stay or go back to Russia?" Os was interested.

"I go home. I stayed here for Natalia." Her voice jerked as she said her friend's name.

"Have you still got my card with my telephone number?"

She nodded.

"Ring me if you need my help."

She nodded again. He stood up and for a few moments he looked down at her. What had initially seemed like an adventure for the two girls could not have ended more cruelly. Instead of them both returning home with a large sum of money, it would be left to Alexandra to explain to Natalia's family that she was buried in Northern Cyprus.

Kucuk was waiting for him. Os decided to smooth the way for her. "Now that her friend is dead, Alexandra will want to go home. You haven't a problem with that have you?"

Kucuk's eyes widened. "She hasn't said anything to me, but she has fulfilled her contract. There will be no problem."

"I'm pleased that you're being so reasonable. No doubt we'll be speaking again."

Os shook the manager's hand and then walked out to the car park. For a few moments he stood by his car, breathing in the night air. He felt dirty and wanted to go home for a shower.

Instead he drove the thirty minutes to the village of Ozonkoy. It was rush-hour in Kyrenia and he found himself stuck in two separate tail-backs. He slipped in a Leonard Cohen CD and attempted to relax.

As soon as the opening notes of 'Suzanne' filled the car, his mind slipped back again to Rose. Maybe he should stop playing Cohen; the two were so closely entwined. Memories of them sitting outside by the pool, Cohen playing in the background made his body tense. Why was she still able to touch him? She had looked so fresh and beautiful when he had seen her yesterday in the pub. Even the sight of Tramps had given him pleasure. The dog had treated him like a long-lost best friend.

His headlights lit up the road sign for Ozonkoy. Os slowed down to negotiate the narrow lanes and a short time later he pulled up outside the Half Moon restaurant. The curtains were closed, but the lights were on. Os climbed out and walked to the front door.

He took in the interior at a glance. A fire burned in the large grate and a couple of mobile gas heaters gave extra warmth to the two occupied tables. Molly was standing behind the large charcoal grill turning kebabs. She looked flustered, wore no makeup and her hair was lank.

171

She looked up expectantly as the door opened, then her welcoming smile vanished when she saw who it was.

He crossed the dining room to join her, detecting the usual smell of damp mixed with that of meat cooking.

"He's with his father, Chief Inspector," she said."If you come back in a couple of hours, he will definitely be here. Or go to the hospital and talk to him there."

Os studied her face. "I called by to tell you both some bad news and to keep you up to date. Natalia Sakalova, the Russian croupier you mentioned, was found dead today. Murdered."

Molly yelped as her hand brushed a hot skewer. She then hurried to the sink and ran water over her burn. Her voice shook as she asked. "Where was she found?"

"In a gully - at the top end of Lapta. She'd been shot and then thrown into the undergrowth. Two murders and your father-in-law seriously attacked. Someone means business, Molly."

One of the customers called for more drinks.

Harassed, she said, "I've got to work. Please, come back when my husband is here. We can't afford to lose this custom."

She looked near to tears, so he nodded and left her.

An old Fiat pulled in to the spare parking space next to his own Mercedes and Mehmet climbed out, his skin was grey and his shoulders hunched.

"How's your father?" Os asked.

Mehmet's tone was terse. "He might not last the night."

"I'm sorry to hear it," Os's tone softened. "Will you go back to the hospital tonight?"

"If Molly can manage without me." He chucked his head in the direction of the restaurant. "Are there any customers?"

"Two tables."

As Mehmet moved to the front door, Os held up his hand. "I stopped by to tell you the latest news."

Mehmet's jaw tightened.

"Molly seems to have been right about a connection between your brother and the Russian croupier, Natalia."

Colour flushed to Mehmet's cheeks.

"I'm afraid she was found dead today. She was murdered, shot like your brother."

Mehmet span around and howled, the sound stopping as abruptly as it started. He then dragged cigarettes from his jacket pocket and lit one, keeping his heaving back to Os. Finally he turned round.

"Who found her?"

Os felt a surge of irritation. "Two people dead, and your father in the state he's in. What are you keeping back from me, Mehmet? Either one of you could be next."

"How many times have I got to tell you?" Mehmet hissed. "We know nothing about what's gone on. Why can't you leave us alone?"

Os shrugged, suddenly tired. "Have it your own way, Mehmet. You know where I am if you change your mind."

Os opened his car door.

Mehmet called after him. "Have you looked at the people he worked for?"

Os turned around. "The computer shop?"

Mehmet opened his mouth, closed it, then answered, "Or the people he did jobs for on the side. It might be one of them behind this. Why don't you look there instead of always hounding me? You must have some idea who's doing this."

"We're following several lines of enquiry. That's all I can tell you, that is until you start being straight with me, Mehmet."

Os tempered his irritation. Was the man a fool that he did not realise the dangers, or did he really not know anything? His mobile rang as he clicked in his seat belt.

"Yes, Ali. What have you got for me?"

His friend from Customs spoke quietly as if fearful of being overheard. "I've done that research. Hains has crossed over into the South - probably about once a month over the last five years. Whether he's flying out to the UK, or wherever, from Larnaca or Paphos, I wouldn't know. And I've got no way of finding out. The Greeks would never give me that kind of information."

Os could hear phones ringing and voices in the

background.

"I found it interesting though, that in the five years that he's lived here, he's never used Ercan airport to fly to England. He's booked himself into the Istanbul flight every couple of months but there's no record of whether he just stays there or flies on to any other country. Has he run away from something in the UK and so can't go back there?"

"He was up in court - accused of supplying drugs in Birmingham, but the case was dismissed. He sold his business soon after that and came out here." Os spoke cynically. "You can make what you like of that. Since there's no extradition here with the UK, he knows he's safe."

Os grimaced to himself. Since the UK had always sat on the wall over Northern Cyprus becoming part of the EU, he certainly did not think that they should have the right to extradite whoever they wished. However, the ruling meant that criminals were attracted to what they saw as a safe haven. "When was the last time he flew to Istanbul?"

"Several weeks ago, late November. He was gone five days."

"Thanks Ali. Anything I can do for you, let me know."

Os backed the car in to the road, then headed back the way he had come. It seemed a long time since he had had a couple of coffees with Sener that morning. But food would have to wait. Speaking to Hains came first. The man niggled at him and yet there was nothing concrete. Hains had used Jamil to sort out the electrics in his apartments on numerous occasions but that was hardly a crime. Jamil had paid no tax on the extra work he had done and, equally, that was nothing to do with Hains. Nevertheless Os travelled in the opposite direction to the station, no doubt, he thought, on a fool's errand.

The idea of listening to music did not interest him; instead he ran the case over in his mind. Two murders and one serious assault that would probably end in death, and now a dead-end as far as Ali's investigations were concerned. How much easier it all would be if he could negotiate with the Southern Cypriot police. But it seemed now, more than ever before, that there would never be peace between the two countries.

As he waited at the lights, Os glanced down at the paper that he had not yet had time to read. The headlines were similar to what they had been for the past week. *'Peace talks break down. Southern Cyprus shortly to take over the Presidency of the European Union. Turkey refuses to negotiate.'*

If those foolish EU politicians had not agreed to let only a part of the island in to the European Union, there might have been a chance of unification. But why would the Greeks Cypriots now put themselves out at the negotiating table? They already had the grants and the power. If the Turkish Cypriots would not bend to their wishes, then it was no loss to them. The old fury rose inside him as he churned over the injustices shown towards his country. He had voted for the Annan Plan in 2004, but would he do the same again? Northern Cyprus becoming a permanent part of mainland Turkey was looking increasingly attractive to him and his friends.

His mobile brought his attention back to the present. When he recognised Sener's number, he pulled into the side of the road.

"I've got something for you, Sir."

Os's adrenalin raced to the excitement in the sergeant's voice.

"Go on."

"I've dug up some interesting information about your man Hains. I don't suppose you knew that he's part-owner of a brothel out here."

Os stared up at the mountain range to his left, noticing that the low winter sun sent shadows across the craggy grey rock. His stomach contracted. "Where is it?"

"This side of Nicosia. Not far from the roundabout - you know, the first one you come to," Sener answered. "The other name on the form is Damdelen, a Turkish Cypriot." A pause. "Are you there, Sir?"

"I know the place. I've been there with Inspector Ure. It's taking time to sink in, that's all. How long has he been in partnership?"

"Three years. From the documentation I've got here, it looks as if Hains put up most of the money."

"That doesn't surprise me," Os answered. " ...Damdelen will just be the front man. Hains would have to have a Turkish Cypriot partner to get permission to operate."A thought occurred to him. "What are you doing at the moment?"

"Completing this dossier on the station for the assistant superintendent." Sener's voice quickened. "Do you want me to do something for you, Sir?"

Os knew it would probably get him in trouble with Ismail, but he said it anyway. "Any chance of you coming with me to Hains's villa now? Maybe I'm just reading him wrong, but I'd like your opinion on him."

Chapter Twenty-one

Os stood by the side of his car eating a doner kebab, leaning forward so that the juices did not splash on his suit. Perhaps he should have given the raw onions a miss, but it was too late now. Wiping his hands on the paper serviettes he had been given by the stall holder, he walked up the road to stuff the kebab wrappings into a bin. Lights had come on in the hill-villages. His eyes slipped over to the west, to where instinctively he knew was Rose's house, and then away again. He turned back as Sener's car pulled in behind his, and the sergeant climbed out. Despite feeling a rush of affection towards his friend, he gave a curt nod. Both men knew each other's ways.

"Leave your car there and I'll drop you back later."

"Okay, Sir. I'm going home afterwards, anyway - the assistant super doesn't keep long hours. He left half an hour ago and said he wouldn't be back."

"Where's he staying?"

"A small hotel just outside Kyrenia. He told me that he preferred that to an apartment, having everything done for him." Sener paused. "Do you think he's married?"

Os pulled out to overtake an open truck piled high with furniture tied on with rope. "Why do you ask?"

"He asks a lot of questions about Inspector Ure. It doesn't sound like a professional interest to me."

Os heard the distaste in the sergeant's tone and was surprised by his own flash of jealousy. Then Hains's villa

177

came into view and he swung the car across the road so that the bonnet was edged up against the steel barrier. A camera pointed straight down on them. Both men climbed out of the car.

"A lot of security, "Sener remarked.

Os pressed the button in the security pad, but instead of their identity being asked for, the side-gate swung open. Sener glanced across at Os, his eyebrows raised.

The same man who had met Os the day before, walked down the drive towards them. "Mr. Hains has asked me to take you into the house. He's on his yacht at the moment, going through some papers, but he'll be across in a few minutes. I'm to offer you a drink if you'd like one."

Both men declined. They followed him into the house to the same large living area that Os had been in the day before. The curtains were open and the flood-lights on, lighting up the launch moored up against the private jetty. Os walked up to the French windows and looked out.

"That's quite a boat. I take it Mr. Hains is a keen seaman."

The minder remained by the door, his arms crossed. "I believe it was why he bought this house, Sir, it having a jetty. He didn't want to risk any damage to the boat down at the harbour."

Suddenly, Hains appeared on the deck of the boat, jumping down on to the jetty. The paid-help unlocked the French windows. Gusts of cold air followed Hains into the room. Pulling the glass door closed behind him, his eyes slid first to Sener, then to Os. "Chief Inspector, what can I do for you now?"

Os introduced Sener. "This is Sergeant Rafiker. We're letting you know that there's been another murder. She was a Russian croupier at the Ruby Royal Casino - possibly the girlfriend of Jamil Emral."

Hains looked concerned. "How dreadful. He did tell me that he was hoping to marry." When neither officer answered, he added, "I'm surprised you felt it necessary to call in and tell me specifically though. I liked the man, but he was only someone who did occasional work for me." He sounded puzzled. "I'd have thought that you would have better things to do with your time."

"How long have you owned the brothel in Nicosia, Mr. Hains?" Os said.

The skin around the eyes of the Englishman tightened. He sat down in one of the armchairs and crossed his jean-covered legs. When he spoke, the forced warmth of a few seconds ago had gone.

"What's your interest in my business, Chief Inspector? I'm registered with the government here. I pay my taxes - there's never any trouble with the girls." He leaned over to a small table and took a cigarette from a silver box.

Os sat down opposite Hains. "Did Jamil ever do any work for you there?"

Hains pursed his thin lips. "I'm not sure. Let me think. He might have. Not recently - I'd remember. But I've known him for a couple of years now, so it's possible. But I've certainly never met the Russian girl you've just mentioned."

"The thing with my work, Mr. Hains is that everything is relevant until it's proved not to be. Believe me, I'm not accusing you of anything. I am merely trying to gain an understanding of Jamil's life. It was far more complicated than I first thought."

Hains uncrossed his legs then re-crossed them. His tone became less confrontational. "Well, as I've told you before, anything I can do to help. I'm as puzzled as you that a simple man like Jamil could be murdered. Why would anyone want to do such a thing? Now, I don't mean to rush you, Chief Inspector, but I've got an appointment in Nicosia in an hour. I need to shower and change before I go."

Os's mouth slid into a smile. "Of course, Mr Hains. Don't let us make you late. We'll get out of your way."

Os glanced across at Sener whose eyes flicked back. "Sergeant?"

Hain's man led the way back out through the house and to their car.

Rain hammered against the windscreen. Os was parked up behind Sener's car but now the two of them remained in their seats, staring ahead at the rivulets of water coursing down the glass.

"What do you think then, Sir?"

Os grinned across at the sergeant. "You think I'm barking up the wrong tree, don't you."

Sener grinned back. "Hains looked uncomfortable, but that's not so surprising. Having a stake in a brothel is not something you would necessarily want to make public. And he's been quite open about the fact that Jamil did quite a bit of work for him. And what does that prove anyway. Jamil seems to have done work for half of the population of Kyrenia. No wonder he didn't have time to go to his day job."

Os grunted. "You're probably right. I don't like the man though."

Sener threw back his head and laughed. "I didn't take to him myself, but that doesn't make him a murderer. And what possible reason could he have for killing Jamil?"

Os shrugged suddenly, not wanting to discuss it further. "Anything new on redundancies?"

Sener's smile disappeared. "I've been trying to think what I could do if it was me that had to go. It's the only proper job that I've ever had. And because I left school at fifteen, I've not got qualifications like you, Sir. I'm not sure how we would survive."

Os stared at his sergeant. He had been too occupied with the case and also Ismail's unhealthy interest in himself, to think properly about what was happening to the station. If Os was made redundant, he'd be devastated, but he could retrain. He had savings, his apartment in Nicosia was rented out to another policeman, and he still had his bedroom in his parents' house that he could fall back on. It certainly would not be easy, but very manageable. But for Sener, and people like him, it would be disastrous. Sener was the only wage earner and he had five children. They rented their house and the bit of land on which Sener grew all their vegetables. There would be no savings. How could there be.

As if he could sense Os's sympathy, Sener sat up

straighter in his seat. He had unbuttoned his overcoat in the heated car and the worn collar of his jacket was visible. Fatma always made sure that her husband went to work with his clothes clean and pressed. But his wardrobe was limited and often his collars were frayed.

Os changed the subject. "So you're off home now?"

" I might as well ingratiate myself with Fatma for once. She's keen on the idea of extra money if I ever make inspector, but she doesn't like it when I'm away." Sener grinned. "I can't blame her, looking after our lot on your own is not easy. Come back and have a beer if you want, Sir. Fatma would be pleased to see you and the kids are always asking after you."

Os was stopped from answering by the ringing of his phone. "Yes, Zelfa." The line was muffled, but he was loath to open the car door to improve the connection. "Where are you?"

Despite the crackling, he heard the lift in her voice. "In a bar in Nicosia. I've just been talking to Viktoriya, the woman who found Katja."

Os felt his mood lift a little.

"She decided that she wanted to be more honest with me than she'd been last time. I'd left her my card and she rang me this afternoon. But I had to promise that I would get her passport back from the manager before she would talk. She's desperate to get out. She's got a man friend in the South she thinks will look after her, a Russian working down there. She thinks that she will be safe with him. She's been very scared since Katja committed suicide."

Os interrupted her. "She doesn't now think that Katja was murdered does she?"

"No. But I'm bringing her back to Kyrenia before she changes her mind. Will you meet me at the station there?"

Os glanced at his watch. "If you set off now, you should be here by 6.30. I'll get the duty sergeant to make sure there's an interview room ready. Take care."

Os turned in the driving seat to face Sener. "You heard most of that?"

Sener pulled a face. "This reminds me of the Karpas. I

hope that Inspector Ure will be alright."

Os's memory flashed back to the previous August. After all these months he still did not understand why she had driven the Syrian workman, on her own, all the way back to the Karpas from the Nicosia border-crossing. A policeman had been killed because of her actions, and she had been lucky to survive herself. It had nearly cost her job. The fact that she was seconded from Istanbul had probably been the reason why she had not been sacked. Turkey paid her wages, so she was treated very differently to everyone else in the station.

Os attempted to sound confident. "She'll be fine."

"I've never dealt with the brothels, how do they work?"

"My experience is that their treatment varies," Os answered. "But the girls' passports are always taken from them as soon as they land in Northern Cyprus. Their contracts are usually for a year to begin with, the reason given being that it's not otherwise financially worth it as the women's flights are paid for them." Os sighed wearily. "I've seen some of these contracts the girls sign so readily. Either they're desperate for work, or they don't read the small-print close enough. Probably both."

Sener's face showed his disgust. "What kind of a country are we turning into. I was never aware of any of this happening when I was a teenager."

"I tell you, it all changed when the Turkish government threw out the casino mafia because they couldn't control them. We invited them here hoping to make money out of them, and the brothels followed. Not very impressive is it!"

They both stared out of the car window in silence.

"So have you got anything on tonight, Sir?" Sener asked at last.

Os shook his head and grinned. "I'm becoming a sad individual. I'll have to do something about it."

Sener's eyes sparkled. "I don't know. Your life sounds very attractive to me. Nobody but yourself to look out for. Being able to go out whenever you want. Not worried whether you have enough left over at the end of the week to pay the bills. I wouldn't knock it I were you."

Os grinned. "Well go on. Get back to your ball and chain. You know you wouldn't be without them. And I've got work to do."

Sener flashed a smile then opened the door. "I'm off over the weekend so I'll see you Monday, Sir."

Os drove off, thinking about his sergeant. He and Sener were the same age, but their lifestyles were totally different. Sener had married Fatma as soon as he had returned from his military service; they had been at school together. Apart from arguments about the children, and the constant shortage of money, they seemed happy enough. They lived frugally, never eating out, keeping a few chickens, a couple of goats, and growing their own vegetables. They seemed happy enough, more than he was anyway.

Chapter Twenty-two

He shook his head in self-disgust as he swung into the police car park and into one of the many empty parking places. Friday evenings were not a time that many officers hung around. The weekend ahead would also be quiet, the station managing on a skeleton staff. If the North ever managed to become part of the European Union, work ethics would have to change.

Os pulled open the front door of the station to be faced with the superintendent striding down the corridor towards him. Os found himself pleased to see him.

Superintendent Atak faltered in his stride, then stopped. "I was on my way out, but I need to speak to you first."

The superintendent spun around neatly on his heel for such a big man, then led the way. A few minutes later, Os was sitting opposite the big desk, while his boss re-lit the mobile gas heater. He must have only turned it off a few minutes ago, but already the air in the room had cooled. The door to his secretary was closed, so presumably she had already gone home. The curtains had not been drawn and Os now stared out at the black outline of the mountain range.

Having lit the gas fire, Atak linked his hands over his large stomach. "Tell me how the case is going? Now that you answer to Assistant Superintendent Ismail, I'm out of touch."

Atak listened. Once he popped a boiled sweet into his

mouth, but otherwise he just stared at his chief inspector and made the occasional note.

"So, Inspector Ure is bringing in this …," the superintendent glanced at his notes, "Viktoriya. And you're sitting in on the interview? You think she's linked to your case? "

"She works in the same brothel that Hains has a major stake in."

Atak's eyes narrowed. "You're an excellent detective, Osman, but are you spending too much time on this Englishman? Both Jamil Emral and the Russian croupier were shot with a Russian gun. I assume you haven't found it yet?"

"Sergeant Alican of the Lapta station, has searched the area where they found the woman. Nothing." Os thought there was sadness in the man's face.

"I just hope you're not missing anything, Osman. I want you to solve this case and quickly. Assistant Superintendent Ismail is looking for names for his redundancy list."

Suddenly, Os realised that the sadness in his boss's face was to do with him, It seemed that redundancy was a real possibility. If Atak had been a smoker, he would have asked him for a cigarette.

Atak splayed out his hands. "I've got no say in all this -they're closing down one of the smaller stations in Nicosia, so a superintendent has to go." He shrugged. "I'm a few years off retirement. I'd be an obvious choice. But you have a career ahead of you in the force, or you should have." The folds in the superintendent's face deepened. "I would expect you to be sitting in my place, or up in Head Office one day. You can't give Ismail any excuse to get rid of you."

"Things are changing here,"Atak said. "Unions can bang on as loud as they like that the Turkish government have no right to change things. But that's naivety. They've been bankrolling our lifestyle for the last forty years, and to be honest I can't blame them for having had enough. People expect to have a government job that pays them fourteen months of salary a year. Did you read that article in the Haberdar last week?"

Os shook his head. It was not a paper that he had sympathy with.

"A young salesman for a small computer business, here in Kyrenia, asked his girlfriend's father for her hand in marriage. The father said that the only way that he would agree was if the lad took on a job for life with the government. In fact he got him a job working in the same department as himself. Because the lad had been such an excellent salesman, the business collapsed after he left and now the owner is scratching a living selling dog food." Atak's huge jowls settled into a scowl. "This is the people we've become. And Turkey has made up its mind. However much we march in the streets and yell, they're not going to alter their decision. The good times are over and perhaps we can only blame ourselves."

Os could not disagree that they had become a nation that had become used to subsidy and now thought that it was their right. He still felt the injustice of the situation though. "This is what happens when the rest of the world cuts a country off. When the Greek Cypriots scuppered the Annan Plan in 2004, free trade should have at least been granted to us. The fact that we're still not even allowed direct flights is beyond belief." His chest hardened. "It's not surprising that the people here now take what they can get. They've been let down so many times by world politicians it's affected their spirit."

Atak nodded. "We all know the reasons why we're where we are." His leathery face suddenly split into a wide grin. "But despite all the money the South had when they joined the European Union, from what I'm hearing they're as broke as us. It seems that they have not managed their expensive workforce any better than we have."

Os grinned back. It was true. The news had been full of it for weeks. The South was closely linked to the Greek economy and their politicians were no better than those in the North, inexperienced and corrupt. His mobile phone vibrated in his shirt pocket. Zelfa's number flashed up.

Her voice sounded tired. "I'm at the front desk now, signing for the interview room. It's number two. Will I see you there?"

"I'm coming down now."Os looked across at the superintendent. "Inspector Ure's arrived, Sir. Can I just check something out with you? This Russian woman wants us to get her passport back and then get her to the border to meet a boyfriend of hers who lives in Larnaca. Are we able to legally do that?"

Atak's pursed his lips. "We can get a court order if it's necessary. Her boss will probably just give her passport back for an easy life. None of these people want to get on the wrong side of the police. You'll have to drop her at the border and she can walk through. Take her to one of the busy crossings in Nicosia. She needs to carry just her bag as if she's going across for the day shopping." Atak's eyes suddenly narrowed. "Take notice of what I've told you, Osman."

Os pulled the door behind him then strode down the corridor his conversation with Atak still buzzing around his head. He passed no one as he descended the stone steps. As he pushed open the door of Interview Room Two he made a mental note to thank the desk sergeant. The gas heater had already been lit and the table cleaned. And amazingly, the only smell was that of a pine air-freshener.

He went to pull the gas heater nearer to the table when the door opened. A tall, slim, dark-haired woman, in her late thirties, stood in the doorway, but despite her makeup-enhanced, good looks, she was a woman who had seen too much of the bad side of life. Wearing a short skirt, long, high-heeled boots and a red leather, zipped-up bomber jacket, she walked into the room.

Immediately behind her was Zelfa. The tiredness he had heard in her voice was evident in her face and eyes. Her brown eyes widened and she gave a little smile when she saw him. She indicated to Viktoriya that she sit down and then she took the seat opposite her. She introduced Os.

"This is Chief Inspector Zahir who I told you about. Between us we'll be able to help you. I know that you've already talked to me about Katja but I'd appreciate it if you could go over it again."

For a moment, it seemed that Viktoriya was going to refuse. She stared down at her long painted nails and chewed on her lipstick. Os glanced at Zelfa. Wait, she mouthed.

Viktoriya swallowed and her eyes filled with tears. "I was too scared to say anything before. But things got worse there. They'll know I'm here, I can't go back." She looked from Zelfa to Os. "If I help, will you take me to the South? My friend, Alek, will look after me."

Zelfa placed her hand over Viktoriya's. "I've told you everything will be alright. We'll get your passport and you need never return there."

Os stared at the large photograph of the now-dead, President Denktas hanging on the opposite wall. According to Atak, Viktoriya would be able to walk through the crossing and not have to return to the brothel.

Viktoriya looked uncertain and then nodded. "I told you that Katja always needed more money. She was popular with customers and I know that they gave her presents, but she wanted the best for her children – so that they would not end up like her. She always carried a photo of her children with her. Mr. Celik, the manager, had a soft spot for her. He was always asking after them and when she told him that her son wanted his own violin, instead of having to go into school to practise, he paid for it. He told her that he'd wanted to learn the violin as a child so knew how much it meant. He organised the whole thing. The children live with their grandmother, so she gave him the address. "Why she did that I don't know" She pulled out a handkerchief and blew her nose.

"Would you like something to drink, Viktoriya? Some tea?"

She nodded. Os went into the corridor and talked to the policeman outside. He then took a seat by the wall. This was Zelfa's case and she had developed some kind of trust with the Russian.

"Can you go on, Viktoriya?" Zelfa asked.

"He offered her cleaning jobs to make more money. Then one day she came into my bedroom all smiles. Mr. Celik had offered her an extra job. She wouldn't have to do the cleaning any more, but she could spend several hours a week with some children. She didn't know the details then except that they spoke Russian. I think she thought that they were from Afghanistan." Viktoriya shrugged. "I never found out if that was true. Just after that, I was on a special assignment. A rich Turk from Ankara came over here for two weeks to gamble. He wanted a companion and Mr. Celik sent me. I stayed at the hotel with him." For the first time her tired face lit up with animation. "It was fantastic. It was called the Kaya Artemis Hotel out at Bafra. I've never seen anything like it. It's huge and done out like something from the Roman times. Our bedroom was enormous. Mr. Celik never normally sends me on one of these trips; he usually chooses one of the younger girls." When I got back he told me that he had good reports about me and, when another request came up, he would send me again. I tell you, I had the best time and I had loads of presents." She creased her nose. "It's much easier being with one man. And this one was easy to please." She lifted her head and stared at Zelfa. "Maybe I'm being neurotic, but now I wonder whether he chose me because he knew I was friendly with Katja."

A knock on the door made her twist round like a startled rabbit. But she relaxed when she saw it was a man carrying a metal tray with three tea glasses.

"So go on, Viktoriya. What happened when you got back?" Zelfa asked.

"Well, that was just it. I hadn't spoken to Katja for two whole weeks. Mr. Celik told me that I was not to contact anyone back here while I was away. I had to give my whole attention to my client." She gave another little shrug. "I didn't mind. Everything was so exciting there and he gave me money to gamble every day. But when I got back, I couldn't believe the difference in Katja. She looked older and her eyes - they would never look at yours. She said that she wasn't sleeping, that her children were missing her and she didn't know what to do about it. But actually she didn't really want to talk to me at all. I know she had seen the doctor and she asked me if I had some sleeping tablets I could lend her." Tears flooded her eyes. "Stupid, stupid! But then I had no idea that she would kill herself. Her children needed her too much." The tears slipped down her face plopping on to the formica table.

Her own handkerchief was like a rag, so Os crossed the room and placed his own clean, folded one in front of her. She looked up at him and gave a weak smile. He glanced at his watch. It was eight pm. Zelfa's face was white and pinched, but he could see that she was determined to finish the interview. Viktoriya would talk as long as they wanted her to, Os was sure. Now that she thought she was safe, they would probably have difficulty shutting her up.

"So did you believe her when Katja said she was worried about her children?"

Viktoriya narrowed her eyes.

"Viktoriya?" Zelfa nudged her.

"Yes, I did. But she wouldn't give me details. She was always worried about them. It's natural for a mother, especially when she's not living with them, but this was different. I can't tell you how."

Os pulled out the chair next to Zelfa. "So you arrived back in Nicosia just before she died?"

Viktoriya twisted a large silver ring round her thumb. "The same night. She wasn't working; she had told them she was ill. I'd gone into her room earlier to say I was back. She didn't seem up to hearing my news. I thought it was because she didn't feel well so I went off to have a bath and when I came back a few hours later . . . .," she paused and pushed her handkerchief up against her face.

Zelfa touched Viktoriya's hand. "Are you okay?"

Viktoriya nodded though the memory was etched on her face. "I found her dead."

Os glanced at Zelfa and then sat down at the table.

"It is really important that you answer this question truthfully," he said firmly. "Did you pick up anything in the room? Had she left a note or was there anything in her room that you took to remember her by. I would understand if you did. You had been good friends for a long time."

Viktoriya's right hand drifted down to the gold chain around her neck. Os examined her face. He wondered how much longer she had at the top end of prostitution. If she needed to, she could go on for years, but life would become much tougher for her. He had seen prostitutes still working in their fifties, but by then the light had gone out of their eyes and they only managed to continue with the help of drugs.

"I took this chain." She pulled it over her neck and handed it to Os. "Do you want it back? If I'd left it there, someone else would have taken it."

Disappointed, Os weighed the gold links in his palm. He had hoped for a note or that Katja might have told Viktoriya why she was so desperately unhappy. But they were not really any nearer to the truth. It seemed the superintendent and Sener were right. He was not going to find the answer to his case here. He handed the chain back to Viktoriya.

"I'm sure she would want you to have it."

A tear slid down her made-up face. "I posted her letter for her. At least her family would hear one last time from her."

She spoke so quietly that Os nearly missed it. His voice was so sharp that she backed into her chair. He repeated himself more gently. "What do you mean?"

She'd written to her family and left it on her dressing table. There was no stamp so I paid for it. It was the least I could do. Something like that would get lost once they cleared her room, and they did that today. Apparently a new girl is arriving." She gave a shrug though her sad eyes belied her casual tone. "In Russia we say the waters close over very quickly."

Os felt as if he had been given a present and then before he had opened it, it had been snatched away. "So you posted it and have no idea what was inside?"

She spoke indignantly. "I would never read her letters."

Os sighed. "You haven't told us a great deal, Viktoriya. Are you using this as an excuse to break your contract? Have you had enough of the work and now want to take up the offer of this boyfriend? Who is he anyway"

He face became sulky. "He's one of my clients. He comes over once or twice a week to see me. He's old, but he's rich and he loves me. He's wanted me to go and live with him for a while now."

"And why haven't you?" Os asked, already having guessed the answer.

She spat out the words. "Celik won't give me my passport. Bastards! I've done over a year." Her voice suddenly trembled. "But it's not just that. He's been funny with me ever since I told him that I posted that letter. He asked me the same as you, did I read it? I don't think he believed me." She creased her nose again. "A couple of the other girls asked me the same question." She widened her eyes and looked at Os in a manner he suspected she used on her clients. "I'm scared," she whispered.

Os turned to Zelfa and saw in her white face the same disappointment that he felt himself. He raised his eyebrows and she nodded.

"We'll leave it there for tonight, Viktoriya. I'm going to take you to a house where you will be safe. You'll be with women who have been beaten by their husbands. You can tell them whatever you want about why you're there. The alternative is a cell here of course. I'm not sure how clean it will be and you'll be the only woman, I think."

"I'll go to the house."

Zelfa pushed back her chair and rolled her shoulders. "Come on then, let's go. I'll talk to you again about this in the morning."

Os would have liked nothing better than to go home, have something to eat and stare at the TV, but the sight of a despondent Zelfa made him ask, "Do you want me to come with you?"

She nodded. "I don't know if you've been - it's in the Turkish quarter."

"We'll go in my car," he said. "I'll drop you off back here afterwards."

"Thank you," Zelfa muttered.

"I need to go to the loo," Viktoriya interrupted.

"I'll wait in the car for you both," Os said and walked out

of the room.

He turned on the car heating and kept his eyes the entrance of the police station. As the two women came down the steps from the front doors, Viktoriya folded her arms, perhaps to give her extra warmth against the driving rain and January cold. Zelfa was wearing a full-length woollen coat, the collar pulled up around her dark hair. He got out of the car and held the back door open for Viktoriya. Zelfa climbed in on the other side of her. Seconds later he was back behind the wheel and pulling out into the main road.

The drive along the bypass in the direction of the Turkish quarter was done in silence, apart from music from the radio.

"You'll have to direct me," he called to Zelfa.

"Turn left, before the garage."

A few seconds later, he swung down a narrow road. A small tavern, its door and shutters closed against the cold, was open for business. Nearby was a garage lit by a single wall lamp, the workers having gone home.

"Turn right at the end," Zelfa said.

They were now in the centre of the old town. On either side were stone houses. This area was where many of the Turkish population had lived before the Turkish intervention of 1974 but in recent years it had become fashionable and the houses renovated. The architecture had an Arab influence and it was an area that Os had always liked.

"Pull in where you can, now," Zelfa called.

There was a row of shops, a butcher, a baker and a barber. All were now closed so Os found a space outside.

"I'll wait here for you," he said.

Both women got out and, with Zelfa holding on to Viktoriya's arm, they crossed over to an unmarked door. Zelfa rang the doorbell. Immediately the door opened and the two women went inside. Os turned off the radio and slipped in his Leonard Cohen CD. As the strains of 'Bird on a Wire' filled the car, he leaned his head back and closed his eyes. It had been a roller coaster of a day.

The sound of the passenger door opening made him sit up.

"Well, she's settled I think. Thanks for bringing me, it made it easier. Do you want something to eat? I don't know about you but I'm starving."

"Where do you want to go?" "Why don't we leave the car here and walk back to that restaurant we just passed. I've eaten there before, it's good."

Os turned off the music and opened the car door. Rain bounced off the road splashing up against his trousers. He ran back to the boot and grabbed a large umbrella, pushing it up and holding it over Zelfa's head. She linked her arm in his.

The restaurant was half full. A large fire roared in the stone grate and the pungent smell of olive wood hung in the air. There was an empty table nearby and Zelfa sat down. Os scanned the room, relieved that there was no one he recognised. It would just take one officer to see the two of them having an evening meal together for the station to be rife with rumours.

He shrugged off his raincoat and hung it over the spare seat, she did the same. He then unbuttoned the jacket of his suit and pulled off his silk tie.

Zelfa took the chair nearest the fire. "I feel like getting drunk," she said, looking straight at Os.

Os turned to a hovering waiter and ordered a bottle of Yakut red. The heat of the room was already bringing a blush to her pale cheeks. As was his habit, he took his mobile phone out of his pocket and placed it on the table.

"How do you think that went?"

She pulled a face. "I was hoping that Viktoriya would tell us more. We'd already been sitting for two hours talking in the café before I rang you. But she gave the impression that she had more to tell. Maybe she's just playing me along so that she gets her passport back."

Os told her what the superintendent had said. The waiter poured some wine into her glass. She sipped, nodded and thanked him. After he had taken their order and left, she said, "Did he tell you that I'd asked for four weeks leave?"

Os shook his head.

"I've got to leave for Istanbul within a few days. I've talked on the phone to all the women who've applied to look after mother and narrowed it down to three. Now I need to meet them and decide on the best person. It'll all take at least a week, so I'll spend some time with my mother. It's been months since I saw her. I'm owed some leave, so that's not a problem." Zelfa broke off a piece of bread . "I just wanted to find out why Katja killed herself before I went. Will you help me?"

Os swirled his wine glass. "Atak's on my back over this case. If I don't find out who's behind these killings, there is going to be trouble with Ismail. You might be coming back to an office on your own or they could move someone else into my desk." Os smiled to show that he was only half-joking. "Inspector Salim has been looking for a new office ever since Ismail took his.

Zelfa's hand reached out and touched his arm. "I'm sorry. I'm being selfish. I just feel I should have done something when Katja asked for help. Of course, you're busy. It would be terrible if Ismail found an excuse to get rid of you. You're the best there."

She said it with such conviction that he had to smile. He looked at his phone then turned it off. For once in six days, he would relax and forget about Jamil, Natalia and all the others. He was sat opposite a beautiful woman and he was going to enjoy himself. As if she sensed his change in mood, she lifted up her glass and clinked his.

Her voice became husky. "Let's talk about something else."

"Have you bought your plane ticket?"

"No, I'll do it on Monday. I'm sure there'll be a seat on one of the flights on Wednesday or Thursday. There are six a day."

"Will you come back?" Os was not sure where the question or his hesitancy came from.

"Do you want me to?"

"Of course." He grinned. "I've got used to you."

"So you'd no longer prefer to share your room with a

burly male inspector?"

"I've never wanted to share my room with anyone. But somehow it's worked out with you." He grinned. "And of course there are added attractions."

Her nose furrowed slightly and then her eyes widened. "Oh, you mean the air-con and heater."

Os laughed. "It's changed my whole attitude about going into work." He was not going to tell her how he also looked forward to seeing her each day.

"Sir!"

Os leaned back so that the waiter could slide the plate of steak and chips in front of him. Seconds later, another waiter appeared with fish for Zelfa. Os shook salt on his chips then glanced around him. Although it was a wet January night outside, inside the restaurant was heat and noise. Turkish music emanated from speakers hanging from the whitewashed walls and the diners' voices were raised in order to be heard over it. It was a perfect place for discussing a case or any private business; they certainly would not be overheard.

A waiter placed another three large logs on the fire. The wood spat for a few seconds and then succumbed to the flames. Os's shoulders dipped and his stomach relaxed in anticipation.

Zelfa was watching him. "You okay?"

He grinned and then cut into his steak. "How's yours?"

"Good."

He could see that the lines had softened around her eyes and mouth. For once she was wearing no lipstick. He had a huge urge to lean across and kiss her, but instead he sat back in his chair, away from temptation. She caught his eye and smiled, a wide smile that showed her white even teeth. She knows, he thought; she knows that I want to take her to bed. And admitting it to himself, he realised the strength of the emotion. The very good reasons why it was not possible had formed a barrier between them but now, inexplicably, that barrier had fallen away. He had kept it firmly in place for months, perhaps since the first time he had seen her. But then there had been Rose and he would never have been unfaithful to her. Strangely, the thought of Rose did not affect him tonight, but nevertheless he pushed her image away.

He felt the need to ask. "Will you look up your old boyfriend when you get back home?"

Her eyes widened in surprise. "No. A friend emailed me a few weeks ago. He's engaged to someone else now. It seems that he needs to be engaged."

Her soft brown eyes locked on to his. He did not feel the need to turn away.

"Your steak is going cold." She purred.

He wondered whether she would ask about Rose, and he suddenly regretted his own question. But thankfully it seemed that she had no intention of going there. Instead, she topped up their glasses and then sipped hers.

"It will be good to go home for a while. Do some shopping, see some friends. Apart from you, there isn't anyone in Kyrenia I feel I can talk to. The women are quite cliquish here - I suppose I'm the outsider."

Os had heard the comments about her, or some of them at least - people were careful what they said in his earshot. She was different and people didn't like that; maybe it threatened them. She was young and beautiful and obviously possessed money beyond her salary. How else could she afford all the beautiful clothes that she wore to work? The long woollen coat with the real fur collar - that she had thrown carelessly over an empty chair - must have cost a month's salary.

She had done a full day's work and it was well into the evening but her dark- red, silk blouse looked as if she had just put it on. Had she really worn it like that all day, with the top four buttons undone to reveal the swell of her breasts?

"You're the only female inspector and the women are wary of you."

"And the men?" She shook her head in irritation.

He shrugged. "We're just a little country with a history that affects everything we do. I think we live in the past too much - it makes us resentful. But I'm sorry that it's been like that for you."

"Hey." Her voice lightened as if suddenly regretting that she had unwittingly changed the mood. "It's not your fault. This has nothing to do with how you've been. What's your steak like?"

He cut off a piece and held it out to her on his fork. He half expected her to refuse, or use her fingers, but she bent over and took it in her teeth. She kept eye contact as she chewed and suddenly he was aware of the sounds and business of the restaurant fading away and instantly they were just two people, cocooned in their own sexual energy. He finished his meal, no longer tasting it and then poured out the remaining wine .Again she touched his glass with her own and stared into his eyes as she sipped. "Do you want to come back to my place for coffee? I'm only a couple of minutes away in the car. I bought a good French brandy from the Istanbul Duty Free, months ago and I've not even opened it. Sad!"

She smiled as she said it, but her eyes gave her away. He turned to beckon the waiter for the bill.

She took out her purse. "Let me pay."

Os waved her offer aside with a shake of the head and a flick of his hand. He threw some notes on the table and stood up.

She drained her glass and then reached for her coat. He helped her into it, then put on his own leather coat and stepped back for her to walk to the door.

He was aware that heads had turned towards them. For an instant he thought that people recognised them as police officers, and then he realised that they were watching Zelfa. She walked ahead of him, her unbuttoned coat flowing behind her and her shiny, dark head of hair held high. She wore her usual high heels, this time a pair of patent black-leather court shoes. Despite their height, she moved with the same agility as if she was wearing trainers. He followed her out into the night.

The rain was not heavy, just a drizzle, but enough to put up the umbrella. She slid underneath and it seemed natural to slip his arm around her shoulders. She nestled comfortably into the crook of his arm. There was no one about. Despite it being the beginning of the weekend the weather was keeping people indoors. They walked along the narrow street in silence until they reached his car.

Chapter Twenty-three

She was right. It took less than five minutes to reach her apartment in a modern block overlooking the sea. As Os stepped on to the tarmac of the small car park, he heard, crashing against the rocks, the sound of waves reverberating through the damp air. This time she did not bother with the umbrella, but hurried ahead of him to the front entrance.

The door to the small lift opened and they both stepped into the mirrored interior. They stared at their reflections. She came up to his shoulder and even in her heels, she looked slight beside his chunkiness. The colour had returned to her high cheek bones and her brown eyes glittered. They were fixed on his, but she said nothing. And he recognised a look in his own eyes that had not been there for a long time. They both stepped out into a long, marble-floored corridor, with pictures of Northern Cyprus breaking up the expanse of the walls. She unlocked the last door on the left.

He'd had a pre-conceived image of the kind of place she would choose to live in and he had been right. The room he walked into was open-plan, like his own, but that was where the similarity ended. Now there was no doubt that she had a private income beside her police wage. The rental of this place would be twice as much as his own. The leather sofas, and smoked-glass dining table were quality. He walked across to the French windows and stepped on to the large balcony. The crashing of the waves was now ear-splittingly loud. Os looked down at the salty surf, as the rollers broke on the rocks below. It had stopped raining and the full moon had slipped out from behind a black cloud, sending a streak of gold across the water. He breathed in the fresh sea air and then turned to go back in.

She had flicked on some lamps and was now crouched down by the music centre; her coat was thrown over a dining chair. Her skirt had risen up her stocking-covered legs and the navy wool was stretched tight across her bottom. He stood by the window, watching her as the notes of a female singer filled the room.

"Brandy and a coffee?" she asked. When he nodded, she added, "Have a look around if you want."

Os opened a white door off the large living area and walked into her bedroom. Here the full-length curtains were pulled shut and a bedside light had been switched on. The bed was huge, with a satin covering, on top of which were large cushions. She was certainly tidy - all her clothes were elsewhere, but then he was not surprised. Having shared an office with her for so many months, he would have expected her living quarters to be the same as her work desk. A silver photo frame stood on the bedside table. Os picked it up. A middle-aged couple smiled out at him. The woman looked an older version of Zelfa, still shapely and beautiful, and the man, dark and handsome, looked down at her with love. Os put it back.

He hesitated then walked into the en-suite. White fittings, a large walk-in shower, toilet and washbasin. Bottles and tubes sat neatly on a couple of shelves. It was all, Christian Dior, Clarins and Lancome with a large bottle of perfume that he did not recognise. He suddenly wondered if someone had bought it for her and a flash of jealousy slashed through his stomach. He moved quickly to view a small second bedroom, a cloakroom and then returned to the living area.

Zelfa was curled up on one of the sofas, a brandy glass cupped in her hands. She had kicked off her shoes. On the low table in front of her was a tray with a coffee cup, a bottle of brandy and a glass. He poured himself a measure and then sat down at the other end of the sofa. She watched him with her soft dark eyes and he wondered how he had ever thought her intimidating. This woman, sitting within touching distance was totally feminine. All the doubts of the previous months had disappeared; he reached out for her and in an instant she was in his arms.

The sun, streaming through a gap in the curtains, woke him. He lay still for a couple of minutes, feeling the length of Zelfa against his back, skin against skin. Moving, as little as possible, he reached for his watch. Ten o'clock. He grimaced. He should have set his alarm, but that had been the last thing on his mind last night. And, of course, he had turned off his phone in the restaurant, so there had been no calls. He gently prised her arms from around his waist and slipped out of the bed. For an instant, he allowed himself a few seconds to look down on her sleeping form. Her hair was messed around her face and he realised that he was looking at her for the first time without make-up. She looked younger and vulnerable. And it occurred to him, as it had done once before, that she wore make-up for the same reasons that he wore his white shirts and expensive suits, as a kind of barrier between himself and the kind of work he did. He pulled himself away and went into the bathroom.

Her eyes were open when he came back, a towel tied around his waist. The sleep was still in her voice. "Where are you off to?"

"Nicosia. I'm going to be late, but I told Dr. Gok I'd come. She always starts early, so she'll have the results on Viktoriya by the time I get there."

"It's Saturday!" Zelfa pulled up the covers and snuggled further down into the bed.

Os shrugged. "This isn't Istanbul. They work on bodies as soon as they come in; they haven't got the storage to allow them to back up. And anyway, she's doing this as a favour."

Zelfa's eyes had closed again but now they snapped open. "She likes you, doesn't she."

It was a statement not a question. He shrugged again.

"She's good at what she does. I like working with her." He grinned. "Perhaps she thinks the same about me."

Amazingly, considering the speed that they had thrown off their clothes the night before, he had thought to sling his suit and shirt over a chair. If he was going to catch the American pathologist, he would not have the time to go home and change. Zelfa sat up and leant back against the bed board, the sheet tucked up under her arms.

"Are you still on for tonight?"

Os faced the mirror and knotted his tie. He scanned his shirt for stains, but again, it did not look exactly fresh. However, it would do "Of course. I'll come and pick you up about six. Just make sure that the manager is there. There's no point in hiking all the way out to Nicosia again if he's not going to be around."

"I'll treat you to dinner afterwards. I really appreciate this, Os."

He looked at her reflection in the mirror and grinned. The last thing he wanted to do was go all the way back to Nicosia again that evening, but, at this moment, there was not much he would not do for the beautiful woman watching him from her bed. In fact it took all his self-discipline not to throw off his clothes and climb back in with her.

Instead, he asked, "What are you going to do today?"

She grinned again. "Read the papers, relax. I'll have to collect my car from the station of course. And then, I'm booked in for a massage this afternoon. Before last night I needed something to make me relax."

The image of her lying naked on a massage table, with strange hands pummelling oil into her skin, decided him finally that he should go. He bent across the bed and kissed her lightly on the lips. "I'll see you at six then."

A few minutes later he was behind the wheel of his car. It was a lovely sunny, winter's day, the kind of day that made you feel good about being alive. Os wound down the window so that he could feel the fresh warmth.

The residents of the Turkish quarter were also responding to the halt in the rain. He took care to give the pedestrians a wide berth as he manoeuvred through the narrow, waterlogged streets. Middle-aged and elderly woman were returning from the Saturday market, their shopping bags over-flowing with fruit and vegetables. The metal seats and tables of pavement cafés had been wiped down to allow the coffee drinkers to enjoy the sun. Os pulled into a space by a row of shops, to allow a delivery lorry to pass. A butcher leant across his window display to unhook one of the hanging carcasses . He threw it on a wooden slab and then picked up his cleaver. The lorry passed and Os drove on.

Once he got on to the dual carriageway which led out of Kyrenia, he accelerated. The road rose steeply ahead of him, snaking through the Besparmak mountain range, dividing the Mamounia plain from the sea. The sun glinted off the familiar metal statue of a soldier, high up on the mountainside. With thousands of Turkish soldiers resident in camps on the island, it was impossible to forget the country's violent past. But on such a beautiful day, he could forget politics for a while. Soon he was descending towards the emerald-green plain below. There had been so much rain in the last couple of months that the damage of the summer drought was now repaired. From his high vantage point, Os could see a flock of sheep grazing on the new green shoots, the shepherd slouched on his donkey nearby. The sun seemed to shine even more brightly through the windscreen this side of the mountains.

Os pulled over and, with the engine still running, rooted through the car's glove compartment for his sunglasses. His mobile phone lay on the passenger seat. He turned it on and then, after waiting for a car to pass, he pulled back on to the road. Rolling his shoulders,he felt better than he had done for a long time. For a few moments, he allowed himself to luxuriate in the memories of the night before. Why had he waited so long? He must have been mad. And then his phone began to ring.

"Yes Fikri?"

"Sir! Where are you?"

"On my way to see Dr. Gok. She's doing the autopsy on Natalia this morning."

"Haven't you got my messages?"

The bubble of contentment started to leak. Os slowed down and again came to a stop by the side of the road. "No."

"The father died last night about nine o'clock. Apparently, Mehmet lost control of himself. He went beserk, screaming and throwing over one of the tables in the ward. He ran out before the nurses could get one of the security men. Then they reported it to us. The duty sergeant tried to get you on your phone, but it was turned off."

Os clenched his teeth.

"The sergeant rang me. I said we might as well leave it until the morning when I would go round and see how he was. You know, caution him, but under the circumstances, leave it just as a warning. He's under huge pressure and we don't want to muddy the waters."

Still Os waited. Instinct told him that there was more.

"I got to the house not long ago. Only the wife was there. She'd been crying, looked terrible actually, Sir. She made it obvious that she didn't want me around. Mehmet hadn't come home from the hospital, though the wife knew that her father-in-law was dead. She said that he had rung about midnight to tell her the news and that he had sounded drunk. She swore that she had no idea where he was."

"Do you think she was telling the truth?"

"I'm not sure, Sir. I think you should have a word with her."

Os stared out at a single olive tree. He finally asked, "Where exactly are you, now?"

"By my car, just down the road from their house."

"If you were to sit in the car, could you still see the front door?"

Os heard a car door open, then heavy breathing; he presumed it was Fikri, easing his bulk into the driving seat.

"Yes, Sir."

"Right. Stay there. I've got to make a phone call and then I'll join you."

"I'm not actually on duty, Sir, I'm on overtime. I thought

that I'd better let you know." Fikri's voice became animated. "But it's fine by me, waiting for you here. I was supposed to be taking my wife shopping in Nicosia this afternoon, but I'll tell her that I have to cancel. No problem."

"Just make sure that you aren't distracted, Sergeant. If Molly leaves the house, you need to follow her."

Having disconnected the line, Os scrolled down until he found the American pathologist's number. It took her a few seconds to answer.

Her tone was condemnatory. "I understood that you were coming over here, this morning, Chief Inspector."

"I'm sorry I didn't ring you before, there's a problem at this end. Is there any way we can do this on the phone? If not, I could come over later."

Her answer was as he expected.

"I'm leaving here in half an hour. I've just finished. So after I've scrubbed up I'm off for lunch with some friends. This is an extra for me; it's Saturday in case you've forgotten. I won't be back until Monday."

It was his fault that he was late so he could not blame her. "What are your findings, Doctor?"

"She's been dead for approximately forty-eight hours. Shot in the head, as no doubt you saw." The doctor's voice sharpened. "That's what killed her, but she suffered considerably before she died?"

"What do you mean?"

"Her breasts are covered in deep cigarette burns. Whether her murderer was a sadist or wanted information, is for you to find out. Poor woman! It would have been excruciatingly painful."

"Was there anything else? Was she sexually molested?"

"I was surprised about that. Whoever captured her was a brute. But no, there's no evidence of recent sex at all. A couple of bones broken in her legs, but that happened after she died. She was found at the bottom of a gully wasn't she, so that's not surprising." Dr. Gok paused and then asked, "Have you any idea what's going on here? I assume this woman is linked to the death of the man I examined on Monday."

"Yes, she is. And to answer your question, there's still a way to go with this inquiry. I'm hoping that there will be further developments this afternoon."

Her tone became warmer. "I'm sorry that you won't get over here this morning, but no matter. I'll write this up over the weekend and email it to you Monday morning. I now take it that you won't be having a weekend, Chief Inspector?"

Os sighed. "It's looking increasingly unlikely. I look forward to reading your report. You have a good lunch."

The mention of food made him realise that he had not had not eaten or drunk anything since the night before. Both would have to wait. He did a U-turn then tore back up the mountain he had just driven down.

Instinctively, he knew that things had moved on a notch, yet the image of the cigarette burns on Natalia's breast counteracted any pleasure that he might have felt over this new development. What had the killer been so desperate to find out? The whereabouts of the money? Was this whole thing about the money in the oven? Kucuk had an alibi of sorts for when Natalia was murdered: he was in Istanbul. But it was unlikely that he could have inflicted those wounds. He appeared to have genuine feelings for her. Of course, Natalia could have been stealing from the Casino and given it to Jamil to look after. However much he loved her, Kucuk certainly would not forgive that. The money was not a fortune to such a man as Kucuk, but his pride would insist that she would have to be made an example of, a deterrent to anyone else who had similar ideas. But even if she and Jamil had been lovers, and there was reasonable evidence to suggest they had been, it was a lot of money to trust someone with.

He had reached the top of the mountain and was now descending the other side. The coastline stretched out below him, the sea not its summer azure-blue, but still inviting in the winter sun. For a moment its beauty took over, before he turned back to Dr. Gok's description of the corpse.

If it had not been for the dog, Natalia's body would not

have been found. Whoever killed her would have assumed that throwing her down the gully would have been as good a hiding place as any. And then there was likelihood that the wildlife would remove the evidence.

He had now reached the roundabout and turned right towards Ozonkoy. Os keyed in a number on his mobile phone. Fikri picked up on the third ring.

"Anything to report?" Os asked.

"She walked up the road to the restaurant a few minutes ago, Sir. But there's still no sign of Mehmet."

" I'll be with you in a couple of minutes."

Os threw the phone back on the seat then turned left on to the narrow road that ran through the centre of Ozonkoy village. He pulled into a space next to Fikri's car. The sergeant was leaning against the boot, but came round and opened the passenger door. As they both stared towards the restaurant entrance, Os filled him in on what the pathologist had said.

"I'm glad I'm retiring soon, Sir. I don't like what's happening in this country. It reminds me of when I first joined up as a young constable in Famagusta in the late sixties. People did this kind to each other then, the Greeks to the Turks and, if I'm honest, the Turks to the Greeks." He fumbled in his coat pocket and pulled out a packet of cigarettes. He lit one, passed the packet to Os and, when he refused, stuffed it back in his pocket. "I once had to take photos of a bath filled with cut-off penises, did I ever tell you, Sir?" He carried on before Os could answer. "I was attached to the British military police for a while. They were found in a deserted house. We thought the atrocity must have been committed by the Greeks, but of course we had no proof. It could just easily have been us."

Although he was always interested to hear about 'The Troubles' from someone who had played an active part, they did not have the time. Instead he interrupted Fikri's memories. "I know, Sergeant. But we had better get in there and see what she'll tell us about her husband."

Molly was sitting at a table, a mug of coffee and a half-full ashtray in front of her. She looked up as the door opened, but her face remained blank. She picked up the handkerchief on the table and balled it in her fist.

"I've already told him that I've got nothing to say." She jutted her chin in the direction of Fikri. "Why don't you stop bothering me?"

"But I think you have, Molly." Os pulled out a chair and sat opposite her. "I've just come back from the hospital in Nicosia. Jamil's girlfriend did not die easily. You need to know about it."

Molly hissed, snakelike, as she pulled away. "I don't want to hear."

"I insist that you do. They didn't just kill and shoot her in the head, as I told Mehmet yesterday; they placed lit cigarettes on her breasts to get her to tell them what they wanted to know." Os paused, watching her reaction with narrowed eyes. "It must have been unbelievably painful. The thing is, I'm not telling you this for my pleasure - I'm trying to get it into your head that you could be next. In fact it is a strong likelihood. Who else is there?"

She shook her head and pressed her lips together in a thin line, as if to emphasise that she had nothing to tell him. But fear had jumped into her eyes.

Os softened his tone. "What are you so scared about, Molly? What could be more frightening than reaching the same end as Natalia, Jamil and your father-in-law? I can protect you, you know. Once I get to the bottom of all this, find out who has killed three people, you can get on with your life. But otherwise, you'll always be living in fear. Where is Mehmet by the way?"

Molly looked around her. She looked as if she had not slept all night. The skin on her face was drawn paper-thin across her bones, and the lines which he had noticed before, seemed even more entrenched. She had aged over the last week. He would now have put her in her fifties. She pulled at her handkerchief

"Where is Mehmet, Molly?" Os repeated.

She behaved as if she had not heard him.

Should he arrest her for withholding evidence? Would

that bring her to her senses? Then her shoulders slumped and her body shook. The sobs continued for several minutes. Then she talked.

"I don't know where he is. He went off last night. He didn't tell me where he was going. I've tried to ring him on his mobile, but it's turned off. I've left loads of messages, but he's not rung back." She threw back her head and wailed. "Maybe he's dead now."

There was no place for sentiment here. "It's certainly a possibility.""Mehmet's not really my husband."She wailed louder and more animal-like this time.

A bolt of understanding clicked into place. Os waited.

"Jamil was my husband, except it was Mehmet."

Os glanced up at Fikri who seemed bemused.

"So tell me what really happened last Sunday, Molly," Os said. Had it really only been six days ago?

Jamil was here as I said, helping us as he normally did. He was worried about something and was drinking more than he usually did. A lot more actually. Mehmet had already said to me that if Jamil carried on, we'd have to tell him to go to bed because it wouldn't look good in front of the customers."

Os knew what was coming next.

"Then a neighbour rang to say that Dad wasn't well and could Jamil go and look after him."

"Jamil knew this neighbour?"

She narrowed her eyes. "No, he didn't. How did you know that?"

Os shrugged. Fikri cleared his voice. Os held up his hand to silence him.

"Go on," he encouraged.

"Well, Jamil obviously couldn't go - he was too drunk so it had to be Mehmet. He liked riding Jamil's bike. I made him get rid of his own when I married him. They're far too dangerous and we needed a car."

"When did you and Jamil realise what had happened?"

Mehmet was just going to drive over there, see how bad his father was, then ring me. He never did. When I had cleared up here, I rang him myself, but he didn't answer. I just had this feeling that something was wrong. So at about four o'clock in the morning, I got in the car and took Jamil with me. I nearly ran over Mehmet's body." She pressed her handkerchief to her mouth. " He was dead. I wanted to ring you, the police, but Jamil wouldn't let me. He took my phone and made me sit in the car. I've never seen him like he was that night, but he's been like that ever since."

"Like what?" Os asked.

"Telling me what to do. I'm scared of him now. He's changed. Or maybe he was always like this, I just didn't know him properly before."

"You watched him through the car windscreen?"

"He told me to turn off the headlights; he didn't want anyone seeing us. But the moon was bright, so I saw enough."

"He changed the identification, made Mehmet into Jamil."

Molly nodded. "Then he drove me home and told me what I had to do."

"What did he threaten you with, Molly? It was a lot to expect you to be quiet about your husband being shot dead."

"He told me that whoever had killed Mehmet had meant to kill him. That he knew too much. He said that Mehmet was dead now and he was very sorry; he loved his brother, but if I didn't go along with him then they would definitely make sure they killed him the second time. He also said that he wouldn't tell these people anything so then they would go after me. But now it looks as if they've got Jamil this time and I'll be next."

"What are you both hiding? What do these people want?"

"I don't know," she wailed. "He wouldn't tell me. He's not told me anything because he said it would put me in danger. But I'm in danger anyway, aren't I?"

There was no point lying to her. "So you don't think it was the money they were after? Did he ever admit where it came from?"

"I think some of it was from the Casino. Some of it anyway. He and that girl must have been in it together, stealing it. Why else would she be killed? But I was telling you the truth before; he's never brought her here, I never met her." Her eyes narrowed."Stupid man. He should have known they would come after him. He had money from his extra jobs, how much did he need for God's sake. Maybe she made him do it?"

"Who?" Os asked.

"That Russian woman, Natalia. She was probably using him. He's admitted that he loved her. And after you left yesterday, he went berserk, throwing things around in here. I was terrified. Then he cried and told me all about her. They had been intending to go to Turkey to get away from the manager in the Casino; she'd been sleeping with him before she met Jamil. Stupid man was playing with fire and now he's destroyed everything. Everything!"

"Did he tell you who he thinks is doing this?"

She shook her head. "No. He didn't tell me anything. He said it was for my own safety. That's not going to help me though is it - if they do to me what they did to that Natalia."

"Have you got any friends that live outside Kyrenia?" Os asked.

She wiped her nose across the back of her hand. "In Esentepe. Why?"

"I want you out of here in the next hour. My sergeant can drive you. He'll go across to your house with you and let you pack a bag."

"But what about my business?"

"What's more important, your life or here?" Os glanced around his surroundings. In the daylight the place was depressing. "You should have told us all this before."

"What will happen to me?" she asked.

"I don't know. You'll be charged, but it depends on your lawyer. He might be able to argue that you were bullied into changing the evidence. I'll need your passport by the way."

"Why?"

"To keep you in the country of course. I don't want you disappearing back to Newcastle just yet. When you lock up here, Sergeant Fikri will take the keys. You won't be opening up again for the foreseeable future. If there is anything you need from here you had better get it now."

She scurried into the small kitchen. Os turned to Fikri. "Can you manage this?"

Fikri nodded. "What do you think, Sir?"

Os shook his head. 'Well it's a criminal issue with him now, isn't it. We can officially put out a search."

"If he's still alive, that is, Sir."

"Yes, Fikri. If he's still alive."

"I'll get down to the station. When you're driving over to Esenteppe, make sure that you stress the need to be careful. She should never go out on her own."

"Would it be better to lock her up here, Sir?"

"She's had a hard time. I know she's caused us a lot of problems but I feel very sorry for her. Just make sure you get her passport when you go over to the house. I'll leave you to it then."

Os climbed into his car and sat there for a few minutes. He then took out his phone and keyed in a number. He stared out at the front of the Half Moon restaurant listening to the dialling tone. Then there was a click and the automated voice of Assistant Superintendent Ismail's voice telling him to leave a message. Os felt a surge of relief before he connected to another number. This time it was answered immediately.

"Superintendent Atak. It's Chief Inspector Zahir. I need permission to send out a nationwide search for Jamil Emral."

It took a few minutes for him to explain as he watched Molly and Fikri come out of the restaurant. Fikri took the key from her and locked the large wooden door. Then the two of them walked down the street to her house. Fikri looked across at him and nodded, but Molly was crying again, her handkerchief pressed to her mouth. The phone call over, he still did not turn on the engine. Should he contact Zelfa or Sener? They were the two people he always used to bounce off ideas. Both were as good as each other but he made his decision. Sener picked up immediately.

"What are you doing?" Os asked.

"Child-minding. Fatma has gone to visit her mother."

Disappointment coursed through him.

"Why, Sir."

Os explained what Molly had just told him.

Sener's tone lightened. "You could come around here, Sir. As long as I'm in the house, they tend to look after each other. Fatma's taken the two youngest with her."

"I'll be there in fifteen minutes." As Os started the engine, he picked up the strobe and slapped it on the roof.

As predicted, it took him fifteen minutes to get to Alsancak. Sener lived down by the sea, in a house inherited from Fatma's grandfather. The long path was flanked on either side by rows of winter vegetables. The usual collection of rusting car parts, that was often to be found outside Cypriot houses, was absent here, replaced by containers of flowering plants. The front door opened and Sener stood waiting, a four- year-old child peering around his legs.

Os chastised himself for not bringing something for the children. Instead he ruffled the child's hair and followed Sener into the house. Despite the size of her family, Fatma kept everywhere clean and tidy.

"We'll sit outside if that's alright with you. Fatma has developed a thing about me smoking in the house."

Os grinned. Fatma came up to Sener's shoulder, but she ruled in the home. They passed by the sitting room and Os spied two boys watching a film. They smiled shyly at him. Os visited rarely, but Sener's family was always friendly. Sener paused in the kitchen.

"Can I get you anything?"

Os shook his head. He wanted to talk this through and Turkish coffee took too long to make. As if sensing his boss's urgency, Sener moved out into the garden to sit at a hardwood table, under a large olive tree.

Chapter Twenty-four

"I don't know what to say, Sir," Sener said, after Os had finished. "Of course it explains a lot: the woman, Molly and her relationship with the man we thought was her husband. She was scared of him, but not as we thought. It was her husband's brother who she was frightened of. The reason she was crying all the time was because she had lost her husband, not her brother-in-law. Will she get a jail sentence, do you think?"

Os sighed. "I don't know. If we'd known all this from the start, we would probably have solved the case by now. But at least, when we find Jamil, we'll know it all. He knows who the murderer is, there's no doubt about that."

Sener took out a pack of cigarettes. "Do you want to go through it again, Sir? Now we have this information, somethings might seem more obvious." He glanced at his watch. "I'm going on duty in two hours' time, but I've got nothing on before then - besides keeping an eye on the kids that is." He grinned. "I've offered myself for overtime. We're having a bit of trouble managing with the new one."

How Sener and Fatma provided for themselves and five children on a sergeant's wage was beyond Os. And now that there were to be all these cutbacks, it could be a long time before Sener made inspector.

"That would be very helpful," Os said. "I don't suppose, Tahir has still got that blackboard?"

Sener grinned and went back into the house. Os leaned

back in his chair and looked around him. Despite all his other commitments, Sener had cultivated the land at the back. He had left a section for the children to play in, but the rest had been dug over and planted with vegetables, the same as the front. A couple of goats, their collars attached to long ropes, cropped the grass nearby, and Sener had constructed a large hen house by the dividing fence. The family only ate meat once a week, most of the family meals consisting of beans and vegetables. But he very rarely had a day off for illness, so the diet was obviously doing him good. How different was this from his own present lifestyle. Os subconsciously patted his small stomach; he might have more money, but his diet, heavy on the pizza and beer, supplemented by meals in the freezer that his mother had prepared for him, was not so healthy. He watched the goats pulling up the grass both chewing methodically.

Sener set his son's blackboard on top of the table. He then went back into the house, returning with a tray holding two beers, a piece of chalk and a cleaning cloth.

"Tahir says, hi!" Sener said, as he snapped the top off the beer bottle and handed it across to Os.

Os grinned as he pictured the four-year-old watching the TV. He must remember to give them all some money for sweets when he left.

"Right, how do you want to do this?" Sener asked, as he rubbed off the children's drawings.

Os took a swig of cold beer. "Put Jamil in the middle and then we'll surround him with the people he has dealings with to see if anything comes up and hits us in the face."

Sener printed Jamil's name in yellow chalk. "What do we know about the man?"

Os answered. "He's twenty-eight, hopefully not dead. Had a twin brother, Mehmet and worked in a shop installing computers and servers."

"Could the shop owner be the killer?" Sener asked.

Os's eyes narrowed. "Jamil certainly double-crossed him. He spent a lot of time and some money, training Jamil because, one, he had designs on him as a son-in- law, and two, he was doing a favour for Jamil's father, an old friend of his."

"So it was a double betrayal. He might easily have realised before what Jamil was up to. He must have wondered why so many of his clients were no longer coming back - business must have fallen substantially. Someone might have seen Jamil and Natalia together and told him. We don't know for certain that there was a romantic relationship there, but the assumption would be made." Sener put two small ticks by the name. "In a way, he could have seen Jamil's savings as his by rights. After all, they were his customers and Jamil had been taking time off, presumably with sick pay, when he should have been working."

Os pictured the shop owner. Could he really have committed these murders out of revenge? The man had been pleasant enough, but from experience he knew that people were capable of anything.

"Put Kucuk down." Os drank more beer as Sener printed the name. "Kucuk was in love with Natalia and probably guessed that she was losing interest. He says that he didn't know about Jamil, but for all we know, he could have had Natalia followed. A man like Kucuk has to keep up appearances. Also, there was a possibility that Natalia and Jamil were stealing from the Casino. Kucuk could never forgive that. He would have to make an example of them."

Again, Sener put two ticks by the Casino manager's name. "Who else could have wanted him dead?"

They looked at each other. Sener chewed the inside of his lip. "What's the motive here? Money, jealousy, love? Revenge?"

Os suddenly grinned. "All of them I suppose. And we've never accounted for all the money we found, have we?"

"You mean the likelihood of him being up to something else besides doing IT jobs on the side?" Sener rolled his head on to his left shoulder and then slowly around the back to his right. He repeated the action.

Os knew this helped Sener to think. "Is there any significance in the fact that the gun was Russian? I would have thought that Kucuk could have been able to acquire such a gun."

"How easy is it to get a Russian gun, especially the standard one used by the army?" Sener asked. "A few years ago, I would have said impossible, but things have changed so much here now. And who else might have had access to it?"

Os pursed his lips. "There's Jamil's family, but as two of them are dead, it crosses them off the list of suspects, wouldn't you say. I can't see Molly behind all this." Os was diverted by a goat attempting to chew through its tethering rope. He pointed this out to Sener who dismissed it with a wave of his hand. "She's always doing that. I have to replace it about once a month."

Os dragged his eyes away from the domestic scene. "The only others that we've looked at are the people that Jamil did work for. Fikri and a couple of constables interviewed most of them and came up with nothing suspicious. And you know what I think about Hains."

Sener added the Englishman's name to the chalked list. "What's Hains's motive then?"

Os shrugged and gave a wry grin. "That's just it. I can't think of one. I've just got a bad feeling about him."

Sener picked up his beer. "My money's on Kucuk."

Os thought back to the urbane businessman he had interviewed only yesterday. "Yes, I think that might be a reasonable bet."

"Are you going to arrest him, Sir?"

"Not yet. I'm hoping that the nationwide search will bring in Jamil. The superintendent's going on the TV and radio today and there will be pictures in the newspapers. Even if this doesn't make Jamil give himself up, then someone will probably ring in with his whereabouts. They always do." Os grimaced. "That's if he's not dead."

"Hello, Os." Fatma, dressed in jeans and jumper, cut across the grass towards them.

Os stood up, giving her the traditional kiss on both cheeks. "I'm borrowing your husband's brains as usual. But we've finished now, I'll leave you both to it. I believe he's back at work shortly."

She looked affectionately at her husband. "The sooner

he's promoted the better."

Remembering his promise, Os called into the sitting room and placed two notes in the oldest child's hand." That's for sweets for you all." He grinned. "Split them equally between you." As he walked to the front door, choruses of 'thank you' followed him.

Sener accompanied him out to the car.

"Thanks for your help."

"What will you do now, Sir?"

"I'm not sure. Probably go for a walk and think." He decided not to mention that he was driving across to Nicosia later with Zelfa, to interview the manager of a brothel. The sergeant would want to know why Os was involving himself in a case that was not his own. He could hardly tell him it had been a promise made last night in bed. He climbed into his car and started the engine.

Sener thumped the roof. "See you next week, Sir."

Os drove back up the unmade road until he reached the highway. With no car behind, he dawdled at the crossing. Finally, he made a decision. He turned left and headed back to Kyrenia. He would go home, change out of his suit and do some chores. It was a waiting game now.

Chapter Twenty-five

Fikri rang as he was pulling into his apartment's parking spot.

"I've just left her with her friend, Sir - in a house on the hill to Esentepe. Very nice."

"You've got Molly's passport and the address?" Before the sergeant could answer, Os added, "On your way back, just call into the Esentepe station. Have a word with the sergeant in charge. I shouldn't think they've got a huge workload out there; it would help if they could pass by where Molly's living and make sure all is okay. It won't do any harm to know that we're keeping an eye on her." When Fikri agreed, Os added, "And then you had better clock off. I don't want the assistant superintendent on my back for a huge bill in overtime. Enjoy the rest of the weekend."

Os locked the car door behind him and then walked the short distance to his front door. He entered the flat, slumped down on the settee and picked up the newspaper but within five minutes his eyes had closed.

The ringtone of his mobile phone woke him. He pushed the open newspaper on to the floor and sat up.

"Yes, Sener."

The sergeant's voice sounded brisk. Os shook his head to clear the muzzy feeling.

"I thought that you would be interested, Sir. Two things. Superintendent Atak will be on the news in a few minutes time and I've just been logging all of yesterday's reports from the small stations as they've come in. Last night there was a phone call to the Lapta station from a neighbour of that man you're interested in, Hains. Someone torched his boat. The station sent a couple of men down, but by the time they got there, the fire had been extinguished. The constables insisted that they had a look, but the report says that they felt that it was all under control. Hains denied that it had been arson and said that the fault was his. He apologised and said he didn't want anything doing about it. What do you think, Sir?"

Os clicked the TV remote button until he found the programme he wanted. "I think that I'll call and see Mr. Hains again this afternoon."The time of five o'clock flashed up in the corner of the screen; he had been asleep for three hours. "I'll get round there myself and let you know if anything comes of it," he said hurriedly."But thanks for letting me know."

Superintendent Atak's portly frame came into the camera's view. Os turned up the sound. Atak spoke confidently into the microphone, explaining that the Kyrenia police needed to speak to Jamil Emral and that he should report to any police station as soon as possible. A photo of Jamil filled the screen as Atak added that if anyone knew of his whereabouts, they should also let the police know. The camera then moved onto other news items.

Os scrolled down his phone memory until he found Zelfa's number. She answered on the first ring. She had just arrived home, but agreed to come with him to Hains's house before going off to Nicosia. She even offered to drive. Os went to get changed.

Twenty minutes later she arrived and they set off. Os briefed her about his conversation with Sener and if she was put out by his decision to have the discussion with his sergeant rather than her then she hid her displeasure well.

Arriving at the house, they both stared through the windscreen. Lights had already been turned on in the house against the descending twilight. "Ready?" he said to Zelfa.

Os rang the intercom bell. A man's voice rattled through the speaker. Os held his badge up to the camera and the gate swung open. He and Zelfa strode up the path, Zelfa's heels grinding into the gravel. She wore her full-length coat, buttoned up to protect her from the cold, now that the winter sun had gone down. One of Hains's minders was waiting for them at the open door, his wide fleshy face devoid of any expression. From the pathway there was no view of the jetty, they would have to wait until they went into the sitting room.

He stood aside so they could enter. "Mr. Hains says that he is going out shortly, but he can give you fifteen minutes." After closing the front door behind them, he knocked, then opened one of two doors off the hallway.

The large room had been prepared for the evening, the long curtains drawn and the fire lit. Hains sat in an armchair, a newspaper folded on the arm and a glass on the table beside him. He stood up, but did not move across to shake hands. In the two previous occasions, Os had met Hains, he had made an attempt at joviality, but this evening his face was verging on the hostile. His eyes flitted to Zelfa but she seemed to hold little interest for him.

"Good evening, Chief Inspector. I have to say, I'm beginning to feel harassed. I've only a short time to give you, so shall we dispense with the niceties. Could you tell me what you want this time?"

Os glanced towards the drawn curtains. "I heard about the incident with your boat. I've called in to see how we can help you?"

Hains sneered slightly. "Help me?"

Os kept his tone light. "I assume you'll be wanting to make an insurance claim. You'll need a police report and I'm quite happy to sort that out for you - a thank-you for the help you've given me with Jamil Emral. I'll need to check the boat over of course but otherwise I can't see any problems."

When Hains remained silent, Os said, "It is insured I take it?"

Hains gave a little shake of his head and then forced a

smile. "Okay. If you want to have a look at it now, I'll just have to be a little late for my meeting."

He walked over to the French window and flicked two switches. The curtains slid back automatically and a security light, on the patio outside, clicked on. The boat that Os had seen before was now lit up, but the shiny-white fibreglass was blackened, presumably by smoke. Hains pulled open the glass door and led the way across to the jetty.

"What happened exactly?" Zelfa asked.

"Some stupid vandalism," Hains snapped. "I'm lucky that the whole boat didn't go up. I don't know how the person got in and how they got away so fast afterwards. Jack," he jerked his close-cropped head back in the direction of the house. "...was quick off the mark. There's a couple of powerful fire extinguishers in the house. He alerted Ben, the other man I keep here, and they managed to put the fire out."

"No sign of whoever did it?" Os asked.

"They had the choice to either look for him or put the fire out. Luckily for me they chose the right option."

They were now on the timber jetty. Hains led the way along a short gangway and leapt on to the boat. Although it had happened the night before, a whiff of fuel still hung in the air.

"Someone threw a bottle of burning petrol on to the deck. Maybe it was the way it landed, who knows. But it set fire to a pile of rope instead of blowing the boat up. I assume that's what the intention was anyway."

Although the boat had lamps, Os took a torch from his pocket. It was obvious that there had been an attempt to clean up the mess. But gauging from the still- evident, black smears it would need at least another couple of goes.

Os turned back to Hains. "Can I have a look inside?"

"Downstairs seems to have escaped, thank God."

"Nevertheless, I'd like a look. I've not been on a boat like this before."

Irritation flashed across his face, then Hains unhooked a key from the back of the cabin door. "A couple of minutes then. I can't spare you any more time."

Hains stepped inside first, and a second later a light was switched on. Os following closely behind, found himself in a large cabin. There was a living area, cooker, sink and a small bathroom. This led into an area comfortable enough for four people to sleep in. Although the interior was in need of a good tidy and clean, the boat was obviously worth a great deal. If the arsonist had been successful, millions of lira would have gone up in smoke.

"Who hates you so much?" Os asked, following Hains back on to the deck.

"I'm sure I've got my fair share of enemies. I've done well for myself - I'm sure I've offended a few people on the way. I couldn't give you specifics though."

"You told the constable yesterday that you didn't want anything doing about it. Why's that?" Os asked.

Hains made a clucking noise at the back of his throat. "I wouldn't have bothered the police at all if my neighbours had not interfered. They saw the flames from their side of the fence and made the phone call. Next minute, a fire engine and a police car are tooting at the gate." He made eye contact with Os. "No offence, Chief Inspector but I've never been a man to ask the police to help me out with life's little problems. But as you say, I might as well save myself a few bob and claim on the insurance. After all, I've paid for it. Now if you don't mind, I've got to go."

Os took one last look round the boat and then followed Zelfa down the gangway. "You can see yourself off the premises can you?" Hains said. "And I'd appreciate the police crime number as soon as possible. I'm surprised that you're spending your time following this through, Chief Inspector. I'd have thought that you would have had better things to do with your time."

Os smiled, then said goodnight. He followed Zelfa back to her car.

She had reversed on to the main road and was heading in the direction of the bypass, her headlights sweeping the road ahead of them, before she said, "Well, what did you think?"

"Do you think he knew who had done it?"

"He certainly didn't want us poking our noses in, did he?" she answered.

"If it was Jamil, then what's his gripe with Hains? Wouldn't he be grateful for all the work he's been given. I'm sure Hains has enemies, but why Jamil?"

"He certainly didn't want us there, did he," Zelfa said. "And if you hadn't gone on about the insurance, he would have thrown us out. Is he always like that?"

Os grinned. "Quite a change in behaviour, I'd say. This boat thing has rattled him."

The interior of the car had now warmed up and Zelfa's perfume encompassed them. She looked across at Os several times as she spoke and once she touched his arm. They were now near the turning for the Nicosia road. The moon was rising and newly turned on house lights were illuminating, both the mountainside, and the lower road and coastline. Rain splattered their windscreen.

"You obviously decided not to mention that we were going across to his establishment in Nicosia?"

Os shook his head. "We don't want him warning the manager that we're on our way. How do you want to handle it?"

"Get in to the building, retrieve Viktoriya's passport and tell the manager that she won't be coming back. I also want to ask him about the extra work Katja was doing for him. Maybe her death was suicide, but I might feel better if I found out exactly why she took her own life, especially as she has two children back in Russia that are dependent on her." She lowered the gears as the car took on the extra incline. "And then, if you are up to it, I'll cook you a meal back at my place. I bought a couple of beautiful steaks today after I called in to see how Viktoriya was."

"Sounds good. How was she?"

"Calmer. Obsessed with getting her passport so she can join her friend in the South." Zelfa sighed. "I hope she's not going to be disappointed; she thinks he's got money, but being a paid lover for a few hours every week is very different to living with him permanently. I told her, that, once she gets her passport, she needs to hold on to it, in case she decides to go home."

"So she would prefer to stay in a country she's never been to before, with a man she barely knows, rather than go home?" Os asked.

Zelfa mouth twisted. "I don't think she has much to go home to. Her parents are dead and there's no money."

Os's phone rang. "Yes, Sener?" Os glanced at his watch. It was seven o'clock. The sergeant still had several hours of his overtime to complete.

"We're in luck, Sir. Jamil Emral has turned himself in."

Os stared out at the black mountains that rose up from the side of the road. "Where, Kyrenia?"

"No, Sir, Karsiyaka. The constable there has just rung."

Os blew out a lungful of air. "My God! Is he alright?"

"As far as I know. I haven't heard anything different."

"Bring him across to Kyrenia, Sener. Get one of their officers to drive him. Or you send someone from Kyrenia station. I was on my way to Nicosia but I'll come back now. Put him in a cell on his own and book an interview room."

Os turned to Zelfa. "Did you hear that?"

She had pulled into the side of the road, waiting for a car to pass, before doing a U-turn. "I'll take you back."

"I'm sorry, this will take some time. I intend to get the whole story out of him tonight. But I don't want you going over there on your own. Take a constable with you. Or, I could probably manage to come with you tomorrow. If that's not too late?"

"I'd prefer to go with you, if you think you can make it then?"

He remembered his promise to eat Sunday lunch with his parents. Zelfa could come with him and then they could go on to the nightclub afterwards. His mother would probably read far more into the visit, but he would just have to ride that. Things had changed between him and Zelfa. However, he was certainly a long way from taking her home as his girlfriend.

Zelfa accelerated, and seconds later they were heading back down the mountain the way they had come. "I can feel your excitement," she observed.

He keyed in another number knowing that he would probably be in trouble later for ignoring the line of command. Os heard the TV in the background.

"Have you been told, Sir? Jamil Emral has given himself up. He must have seen your appeal this afternoon."

The superintendent's usual heavy breathing rattled down the line. "No. Have you spoken to Ismail yet?"

"I tried to but he didn't answer," Os lied.

Atak sounded immediately more cheerful. "I'm coming down myself. I want to see this. Are you at the station now?"

Os explained his whereabouts and then rang off. He looked across at Zelfa. "I've not heard him so excited for a long time."

"I'll drop you off at the station and then go home. I'll wait for you there."

He realised how good that sounded. Why had he waited so long?

Zelfa smiled again and pulled into the police car park. Not caring that he might be seen, he leaned across, kissed her and climbed out into the wet night.

Despite it being a Saturday evening, Os could feel the buzz in the entrance hall. The duty sergeant called over from his desk.

"Emral has just come in, Sir. Sergeant Rafiker has taken him down to cell five until we are ready for him.

"Is Superintendent Atak here yet?" Os asked. Os felt the cold air on his neck and turned to see the imposing figure striding through the front doors.

"Chief Inspector, Sergeant?" There was a purpose in the big man's movements that made Os feel good. Whatever trouble he might get from Ismail later, it would be worth it.

"He's already downstairs, Sir," Os answered.

"Well lead the way. This should be an interesting evening."

He's enjoying himself, Os thought, as the two of them took the stairs down to the basement. The superintendent was dressed casually in thick trousers, a jumper and a jacket instead of his usual baggy suit. He appeared quite happy to have been dragged away from his night in front of the TV.

Sener came out of a room, followed by Jamil Emral. He had aged in the last twenty-four hours, paler with dark shadows under his eyes. His hair needed washing and there were stains on his clothes. Os opened the door to Interview Room One and led the way.

"Hello Jamil," he said to the man he had previously known as Mehmet . "I'm glad you decided to help us with our enquiries. We've all been worried about you."

"I've told Mr. Emral that Molly's safe, Sir," Sener interrupted.

Os kept his eyes on Jamil. "It's just a great pity that you've misled us about your identity. If you'd been upfront with us from the beginning, your girlfriend would probably still be alive. She was your girlfriend, wasn't she?"

A tear streaked Jamil's face, followed by another and another.

Os handed Jamil his handkerchief."You've lost your brother, your father and, you say, your girlfriend. Are you going to tell us what it's all about?"

Jamil stared at the wall ahead of him. Os had always found the man surly, but now his eyes showed no expression at all.

"Who killed them?" Os persisted. "Who tried to kill you?"

Still Jamil stared in front of him. The superintendent shuffled in his chair while Sener leant against the wall. Os could hear the superintendent's breathing.

"Come on, who are you afraid of Jamil? Kucuk from the Casino? Was it him who murdered all these people? Men like him don't take kindly to being double-crossed."

Jamil had developed a twitch in his left eye; every few seconds he put his hand to it as if to calm the nerve.

Jamil's voice became agitated. "What will happen to me if I tell you what I know? Will you protect me? And what if his lawyers get him off? What then?

Os glanced at Atak, who nodded.

"Okay Jamil," Os said. "If it's a deal you want, then,

depending on what you tell us will depend on what kind of protection we give you."

Jamil nodded miserably.

"Okay," Os continued. "You came in on your own accord -whatever you've done, that will count for something. If you make it worth our while, we'll authorise your protection. Now, what have you got for us? It's getting late and we're all tired."

"It's Hains."

Os thought that he had misheard; then he felt a surge of elation. His instinct had been correct. "Did he kill all three of them?"

Jamil nodded. "I don't know if he actually did it himself, and that's another reason I'm scared. His kind of man will pay people to do his dirty work. Those two gorillas who live in the house with him, they could have murdered them."

"Tell me how you got involved with him in the first place, Jamil. If what you're saying is true, you can leave that side to us."

Jamil shivered. " There's far more than you think. I liked him - that was until I found out about the children."

Os eyes narrowed. Was Jamil wasting their time? Taking them away on a tangent? Os decided to let him continue for a while.

Jamil's voice sounded full of shame. "But when that woman told me about what was going on - asked me to bring in the police - I said I could but I wouldn't."

Atak shifted again in his chair.

"What woman?" Os asked.

"She wouldn't tell me her name, she was too scared. But I know she was Russian, like Natalia."

Os wondered whether Jamil was deliberately being obtuse. "Where are we talking about now? Not in the Casino?"

Jamil shook his head impatiently. "No, near Nicosia. In a house in the countryside."

Os felt his earlier disappointment. "Not one of the nightclubs then?"

Jamil's own eyes narrowed seemingly confused by Os's

questioning. "It was just a house with children in; I think it was some kind of orphanage. I don't think any of them were Turkish."

Os clamped down on his irritation. "What nationality were they?"

Jamil shrugged . "I heard the woman talk to them sometimes and she was Russian."

"What were you doing there?"The deep voice of the superintendent cut across them both.

Jamil's eyes flitted across to the older man. "Working. Some of the building needed rewiring. It was in a terrible state."

"Take us back to what the woman said to you," Os said. "Why did she want you to bring in the police?"

Jamil fixed his eyes on the table as if trying to distance himself from what he was about to say. "She said that they were being abused, the children. By men."

Os felt the static in the room. For a few seconds, Atak's heavy breathing stopped. Sener sat up straight.

"Did she say anything else?"Os asked.

Again Jamil shook his head. "A man came into the room then and said that she shouldn't be there. That she should take the children into another room."

"So you only saw this woman the once?"

Jamil nodded. "I was there for a couple of weeks on and off, but I never saw them again. I never heard them playing, you know like you normally do when there's children together."

"But you didn't go to the police?"

"I was going to report it later, when I got to Turkey. I couldn't risk that not happening."

"You and Natalia?" Os guessed.

"I had to get her away from Kucuk. He would never have let her go. And she thought he was beginning to suspect us. We loved each other."

"But the Casino had her passport."

" Hains promised to take us in his boat. He was going to drop us on a beach near Mersin and then we could have gone anywhere. I'd been saving for a long time. We could

230

have set up our own business."

"So that money we found in your garden, was yours. You earned it?" Os asked.

"Most of it, yes. And Natalia and I had a little scam at the Casino. We only took small amounts each time, but it added to what I earned with my extra jobs."

"But you think that you were found out?"

"I don't know really who came to my house and attacked my father. Kucuk's men or Hains."

Os shook his head. "What a mess. Do you know why Natalia was tortured?"

Jamil blinked then pressed the handkerchief to his eyes. "I don't know. Maybe it was Kucuk wanting his money back."

"Or Hains? Did Natalia know about the children?"

"No." Jamil shook his head sharply as if to emphasise that he was telling the truth. "If I had told her, she would have made me go to the police and then we would never have got away. I told you: once I was in Turkey I would have reported it."

"But Hains might have thought she had known, wouldn't you say? Perhaps it was him who tried to make her talk?"

Jamil's mouth puckered and his eyes swam with tears."Maybe."

"So presumably that's why Hains sent you out to do that job for him. He knew that if you came across the children, you wouldn't say anything - you had too much to lose."

Jamil twisted the ring on his finger. Superintendent Atak turned to Os with hooded eyes. He held up a thick index finger, implying that Os should wait.

"He knew that I knew. We should have gone last Friday, but on the Thursday he rang me and said that the journey would have to be delayed. Natalia and I had got it all planned. We couldn't wait any longer. So I told him that if he didn't take us by Monday, I'd go to the police with what I knew. I'd been going to that place for a week, I knew exactly where it was ."

"What did he say?"

"He agreed. He told us both to meet him on Sunday

morning. There's a place above Lapta, an empty cottage where Natalia and I used to meet. I'd put a lock on the door and we'd cleaned it up. Put a mattress in there. Hains knew about it, I'd told him all about Natalia, how I wanted to marry her. He encouraged me to go for it. Anyway, he said he would bring the four-wheeled drive up there and collect us."

"So you think that Natalia kept to the agreement?"

"I don't know. I tried ringing her in the morning, but she didn't answer. I left message after message, but I had to say that I was Mehmet and that I had something to tell her. I couldn't take the risk of anyone finding out that I was still alive." His voice moved up an octave. "She'd never met my brother, but you would have thought that she would have recognised my voice."

"So, it was Hains who shot your brother, thinking it was you? To stop you going to the police?"

Jamil nodded. "I think so."

Os breathed out. "Why didn't you come straight to us then?"

Jamil hung his head.

The superintendent pushed back his chair. "You're sure you can find this place tonight?"

Jamil nodded.

"Then, I'll get things organised, Chief Inspector. Sergeant, wait here with this man."

"If it's alright with you, Sir," Os interrupted. "I need Sener and two other officers to come with me to Hains's house." Os thought of the two men that Hains always kept near him. "We'll need to be armed. If I could leave the other business in Nicosia, to you?"

The superintendent nodded.

Os turned to Sener. "Sort things out and then give me a call when you're ready. I'll finish up with Jamil here."

As soon as the door closed behind the superintendent, Os asked, "Tell me about the jobs you did for Hains, Jamil. How did you meet him in the first place?"

"I put in a satellite dish at his house when I was working in the shop. He was having some trouble with his electrical box while I was there, so I sorted that out too. He offered me a coffee and we got talking."

"What about?"

"What skills I had basically. He had several apartments in Kyrenia that he rented out. He needed someone he could trust if anything went wrong."

"By your records, he paid you regularly over the two years."

Jamil appeared genuinely surprised. "You found my book?"

"Of course," Os responded. "We talked to your boss and found your accounts book in your locker."

Jamil flushed. "I'm sorry about that. He was a good man, but he wanted me to marry his daughter." Jamil squeezed his lips together. "She's a nice woman, but not for me. Maybe I would have considered it if there hadn't been Natalia."

Os leaned back in his chair. "No guilt about what you did? Taking over his clients when you should have been working for him?"

Jamil blushed again. "What will happen to me? Will I go to jail?"

Os did not bother to soften his words. "I really don't know. It will depend on the judge. You came in voluntarily, and you're helping us with this house in Nicosia, so you might be shown a little leniency; you should have come to us immediately. The judge will probably say that your behaviour has led to the loss of three lives. Your attitude to your boss won't help either. You won't be able to bring him in to give you a character reference."

Jamil hung his head. "I know. It's been a madness. When I saw her for the first time, I knew that I would do anything to get her. She was the most beautiful woman I've ever seen."

Os could feel little sympathy for the man. He had gambled everything for love and it had ended in the death of his girlfriend, his father and his brother. Perhaps he would have alerted the police to the children once he was out of the country, but not even that was certain. And when he came out of prison, what would he return to? His father's house, if it was not a rented one? But he would have no job and no family. And the locals would blame him for the deaths of his father and brother. Now Molly was free from his threats, it was unlikely that she would welcome him back to the restaurant, that is if she did not decide to sell up and go back to England. Without her husband, the hard grind of running a restaurant might no longer appeal.

Jamil took a sip of water. Although his clothes looked creased and in need of a wash, he did not look like someone who had been sleeping rough.

Os was curious. "Where did you go after you left Hains's house?"

Jamil blinked. "I've done a lot of work on a foreigner's house in Karsiyaka. She's never here in the winter and she keeps a key hidden at the back." He shrugged. "I let myself in. There were tins and stuff in the kitchen, so I didn't starve. It was only when I saw my face on the TV that I decided to come in." His tone was defensive. "I had no choice really, did I?"

"Not really, no." Sener's number flashed up on Os' phone. "Are you sorted?", he asked his sergeant. "Ten minutes, okay. I'll meet you by the desk."

Os keyed in the number of the duty desk. "Chief Inspector Zahir here. I need to speak to the superintendent. Any idea where he is?"

"In his office Sir. Do you want me to contact him for you?"

"No. It's okay. I should be able to get him on the phone here. It's extension three, isn't it?"

It took several rings for the superintendent to answer. "Sorry Osman, I was on another line. I've been in touch with Nicosia and they're getting a team of men, some ambulances and a couple of social workers together. I'm meeting them in an hour."

"I'm ready to go in a few minutes, Sir. What shall I do with Mr. Emral? Do you want me to put him back in his cell until you're ready to go?"

"Good idea. Leave the keys with the desk and I'll send someone down to collect him. Take care now, Osman.

Don't be taking unnecessary risks. We don't want another incident."

To his horror the memory, of when he was stabbed less than a year ago attempting to arrest a murderer, flashed across Os's mind. He pushed it rapidly away."Good luck yourself, Sir."

Os turned back to Jamil. "I'm sure that you heard that. Come on, you can wait in a cell. "

Chapter Twenty-six

Sener and four constables were standing by the duty sergeant's desk. Sener held out a bullet-proof vest and a gun. "I've signed for them, Sir, and the van outside."

Os acknowledged the two constables, sensing their tension and excitement.

"Let's go."

"I'll drive if you want, Sir."

Os climbed into the passenger seat while the two constables took the back. Os was still fastening his seatbelt when Sener pulled out into the road. "No strobe," Os warned, when Sener reached under the seat. "I don't want them to know we're coming."

Sener took the road up to the bypass where he pressed his foot to the floor.

A few minutes later they re-joined the coastal road. No one spoke as they flashed by the lights of familiar restaurants. Then, Os saw the sign for Lapta.

"We're nearly there, slow down now. We don't want to miss the house," Os snapped. Sener lifted his foot off the accelerator and Os lessened his grip on the door handle. "It's just a few hundred yards on the right."

Ahead, a man came out of a small shop carrying two plastic bags. He waited by the side of the road as they passed by.

Sener peered into the driving mirror. "Wasn't that one of Hains's men?"

Os twisted in his seat. The man was now crossing the road, but he was too far away to see his face. Sener braked and swung the car on to the kerb.

Os walked to the gates and pressed the intercom. Nothing. He buzzed again, sensing that it was a pointless exercise. Sener joined him.

Os pulled out his mobile. It took several seconds before his friend answered. "It's Osman here. Make sure you don't look at them, but are Hains and his two men in your restaurant?"

There was a pause before Kemal answered and then his tone had a false jollity to it. "What's that? How are you, what have you been up to?"

"I'm sorry - this is urgent."

Kemal lowered his voice. "Well actually, yes. The three of them have been here for the best part of an hour. They're just finishing their pizzas now."

"Is there anyone else in there besides you?"

"It's Saturday night. Of course there are people here. It's pretty much full. Why?"

Os sensed that as soon as Kemal had asked the question, he guessed the answer. Os heard fear in his voice as his friend asked, "You're not thinking of causing problems in here are you, Osman. This is my only livelihood. I can't have you fucking it up."

Os grimaced. "How much longer do you think they'll be?" Another pause. This time Os strained to hear his friend's answer.

"They usually have a couple of coffees. I'd say another half hour."

"Okay. We'll wait outside for him." Os heard the exhalation of air.

"Thanks Osman, I owe you one."

Os disconnected the line and turned to Sener. "You heard that, I suppose?"

Sener nodded. "You didn't have any choice, Sir."

"We'd better get down there. It could be our luck that this one time, Hains decides that he doesn't want coffee after his meal."

As they drove back, Os told the two constables what was happening. "So we'll wait outside until they come out. I'll step in front of the door so they can't get back into the restaurant and we'll arrest them. Handcuffs on as soon as possible. The two heavies will definitely be armed and possibly Hains." Os twisted round in his seat and made eye contact with the two men. "I don't want any mistakes on our side."

Sener pulled off the road opposite the shop, which a few minutes before had been frequented by one of Hains's men. Presumably he had been buying cigarettes or some such thing and then returned to the restaurant.

"No talking now," Os ordered, as he led the way down the path to the circular wooden restaurant below. The interior was lit up by electric lights and table candles. Through the glass, Os could see that most tables were taken. He just hoped that it was not so easy for diners to see out.

As he came nearer, he saw them. Hains and his two henchmen were no longer eating, but a waitress was setting out a tray of coffee. Os stepped behind a wide tree trunk, and indicated, with a jab of his arm, that the other three also take cover. He still had a reasonable view of the diners, and no one's body language gave any sign that they had noticed anything untoward outside.

Os breathed deeply in and out, focusing his mind. There was an occasional rustle of undergrowth as one of the other men moved to get more comfortable. A wind was building off the sea, swaying the branches and rustling the leaves. Os folded his arms and waited.

A couple got to their feet and went to the bar to pay the bill. Os stepped farther back into the undergrowth. The man took out his wallet, placed some notes on the counter, and then, after a few words with Kemal, went to the door. Seconds later, the couple could almost have touched Os as they started up the path. But they were too engrossed in their own conversation, and seconds later Os heard the sounds of car doors opening and shutting and an engine starting.

Os looked back at the restaurant. Hains was holding up

his hand to indicate he wanted the bill. Kemal hurried over to the table. Despite his own inner tension, Os grinned to himself; Kemal would want them out as quickly as possible. He would have been on tenterhooks ever since Os's phone call. Hains stood up and tossed some notes on the table, then shook Kemal's hand. He then stood up and shrugged on a tan overcoat. The two other men did the same. Kemal stood back, allowing them to make their way across the floor to the glass door.

Os tensed. "Ready everyone?"

Three voices whispered back. Os touched the gun in his pocket. The restaurant door opened. One of the men stepped out, followed by Hains, with the last man right behind.

Os moved on to the path, his body blocking any retreat. "Mr. Hains! If we could have a word?"

The three men spun back towards the voice and Sener and the two uniformed men appeared out of the undergrowth.

Os stared into Hains's blue eyes. "Sorry to interrupt your evening but I need you to come down to the station." Os heard the distinctive snap of handcuffs as Sener linked himself to one of the minders.

"Are you willing to come with us?" Os asked.

The question hung in the air. Os's hand slid into his pocket. One of the policemen stepped forward with a pair of handcuffs. He reached out to grab Hains arm but the Englishman moved. His elbow shot up and jabbed the policeman on the chin. There was the sound of bone snapping and the jangle of metal on stone. The other minder lunged at Os. Instinctively, Os jabbed at the minder's eyes; he screamed and turned away. But Hains was already moving up the path, his coat flying out behind him.

"Cuff him," Os yelled, and then ran, his leather soles slipping on the wet stones, but he kept his balance.

The pounding of Hains's feet were above him, though the Englishman was hidden by the curve of the path. Os leapt up the last few steps to find a car parked by the side of the road. Hains had reached the driver's door. Suddenly Os remembered that Sener had the keys to their own car, and he was at the bottom of the steps, handcuffed to one of Hains's men. If Os did not reach Hains now, he would be gone, with little chance of them catching him. But Hains paused, then turned and ran down the road towards his house. So Hains also did not have the car key; it had not been him driving. Spurred on, Os ran after him. Minutes later the two of them were on the floor. Gravel bit into Os's skin and then he felt Hain's boot in his chest. Os gasped but held on. Hains flayed out, his fists hammering on Os's chest, on his face. Os thought of the gun in his pocket, but dismissed it. He needed this man alive. His fist hit Hain's chin, jerking his head back. His eyes glazed over. Seconds later the cuffs were on and the pressure in his chest eased.

"Are you alright, Sir?"

Os stared at the heavy shoes of a constable next to his head. If his body had not hurt him so much, he might have grinned.

He looked up at the young man standing anxiously over him. "You took your time, Constable. You can give me a hand now."

Between them they hauled Hains to his feet. Os transferred the cuff to the constable's wide wrist. "I'll let you have him. I've no desire to be near him at the moment."

Sener and the other constable were waiting with their two captives.

"You had better ring for assistance, Sergeant," Os called out.

"Already done so, Sir," Sener answered. "There's a couple of cars on the way."

As if to reinforce what he had just said, they heard sirens in the distance. And then, out of nowhere, came the guilty realization that he had not rung Zelfa.

Os sat in the front seat, with Hains and a constable in the back. Nobody spoke during the ten minute ride back to the station. It was a journey that should have taken twice the time, but Os indulged the driver. He was also glad of the silence as it allowed him time to calm himself. His trousers were ripped and stained with blood and there was blood on his shirt. He touched the sticky mass on his right cheekbone.

The constable pulled up outside the station. Several police officers were already waiting in the doorway. Os grinned. It would only have taken minutes for the news of the arrest to have spread.

"You need any help, Chief Inspector?" one of them called out.

"Yes, Sergeant. "Hains's men need to be held in separate cells, but Hains himself can go straight into an interview room. " Os paused as the other two police cars pulled in beside them. "Sergeant Rafiker, let someone else take over from you, then come with me." Os led the way up the steps. Seconds later Sener fell in alongside him, the other officers stepping aside to let them pass.

"I just need to clean up a bit and then we'll question Hains," Os said.

Sener grinned. "That might be a good idea, Sir. You're a bit of a mess."

Os raised an eyebrow. "Thank you. I couldn't help but notice that I was on my own out there. After I'd been beaten to a pulp, but still managed to get the cuffs on him, that constable asked me if there was anything he could do. I'm thinking of transferring him to the other end of the Karpas."

Sener laughed. "I suppose it means that you're fitter than you thought, Sir."

Os looked down at his ruined clothes. "This time I'm claiming for a replacement suit...and new shoes. This pair cost me a fortune."

Sener's grin widened. "That's the downside for being such a snappy dresser, Sir. I haven't got that problem."

Sener's shoes would have been cheap when he bought them and, since then, had seen lengthy service. His jacket, also well-worn, was devoid of any rip or blood stain. Os grunted but said nothing. Instead, he pushed open the door of the toilets and went inside. Sener followed.

His reflection stopped him in his tracks. Os's thick hair stood up in clumps. His left eye was blackening and the blood on his right cheek was beginning to crust. But at least he still had all his teeth. Os went over to the sink and patted water on his face and neck.

"Should you get that seen to, Sir?"

Os pulled out his handkerchief and dabbed at the broken skin around his eye. "Maybe later."There was nothing he could do about his appearance now. Adrenalin was pounding through his body.

"He's not going to talk to you without a solicitor, Sir,"Sener reminded him. "He's too experienced to make that mistake. Give me a minute while I check."

He took out his phone and went out into the corridor. Os forced himself to relax, knowing Sener was right. He was not thinking properly. Better to find out how Hains was going to operate before they went in all guns blazing. To have to withdraw, while they waited for a lawyer, would lose the impetus.

Sener came back to the toilets. "He's rung his solicitor. He'll be here within the hour. Go home, Sir. You'll feel better after a shower and change of clothes."

Tentacles of lethargy crept over Os. "What about you?"

Sener grinned. "I'll hang around here. Get a bite to eat. If I go home, Fatma will have me doing all sorts."

"Well see if you can find out what's happening in Nicosia." He took out his gun and handed it to Sener. "Can you book this back in while you're about it."

As Os passed the duty sergeant's desk, a constable called out, "We're all hoping that you'll nail the bastard, Sir."

Os accepted the support with a wave of the hand. Everyone seemed to know that Hains was linked to the raid that was about to take place in Nicosia. Sexual acts against children were one of the few crimes that both the force and the criminal world were united against.

Chapter Twenty-seven

Fifteen minutes later, Os was standing under a hot shower, the grazes on his legs and face stinging as the soapy water coursed over him. After draping a towel around his waist, he went back into the bedroom and picked up his phone. A call would take too long and she would ask too many questions, but she did deserve to know what was going on, and why he would not be seeing her tonight. He texted his explanation and then pulled on fresh clothes. At exactly nine-thirty, he walked back through the door of the station.

"The solicitor's here, Sir. He's with the prisoner now," the duty sergeant informed her.

"Sergeant Rafiker?" Os asked.

"He said to let him know as soon as you arrived. One minute, Sir."

Os stared back out through the glass doors. For a Saturday night, the police car park was unusually crowded. Tonight's events had caused quite a stir. He suddenly thought of the assistant superintendent. Had Superintendent Atak kept him up to date? Os had the opportunity to ring him now, but he knew that he would not take it. Better a reprimand on Monday rather than have him interfering. Sener strode down the corridor toward him, his face drawn.

"I've got the low-down on what's going on in Nicosia."

Os opened a door into an empty porters' office; the smell of stale cigarette smoke hit him as he walked in. Sener followed him.

"Tell me," Os said.

"I didn't speak to the superintendent himself but Aysol Ozturk went with him - you know, he's just been made up to sergeant. Anyway, they met with a team of police from Nicosia an hour ago." Sener's voice edged. "There were twenty-five children, ranging from twelve down to four years old. Four years old," he spat out. "What sick bastards!"

Os's stomach tightened. "What nationalities? Did he say?"

Sener hissed out a mouthful of air. "Some from Russia, Afghanistan, a couple from somewhere in the Far East. Indonesia I think. They're taking them to Nicosia hospital now to get them checked out."

"We've got him then haven't we? Come on! We'll get down there and start."

Much, much later, Os sipped his brandy and stared into the flames of the gas fire. Zelfa was curled up next to him in a white towelling robe. It was two a.m., and they had been talking for nearly an hour. Tiredness enveloped him but he had to get it all out - a kind of cleansing and then maybe he could sleep.

"So Katja killed herself because she saw it as the only way out."Zelfa's voice was barely audible. "The nightclub manager had the address of her parents and her children. She knew that she couldn't report the paedophile ring. Jamil had been her only hope. She told him what was going on, but he did nothing about it. I suppose she just couldn't live with herself."

"Jamil will certainly have time to reflect."

Zelfa's face showed his disgust. "He deserves it. If he hadn't been so obsessed about getting over to the mainland with Natalia, four people would still be alive. And those abused kids would have had a few days' less misery." She refilled his glass and then rubbed his back. Os closed his eyes for a few seconds as the soothing strokes did their work.

"What will happen to Hains now?", she asked.

"He'll be in isolation in Nicosia prison for a long time."

"How many years has this been going on for, do you think?" she asked.

Os twisted the stem of his wine glass. "He bought the brothel five years ago and put Celik in as the manager. On paper, Celik was Hains's business partner, but it was Hains who dealt with all the money. After that, it was easy to establish a sideline. That was where the serious money was made."

Zelfa shivered. "Those poor children."

Os sighed. "Most of them were taken from overcrowded orphanages in Romania. Whether the money was fed back into the orphanages, or ended up in private pockets, I doubt that we will ever find out." Os paused, then said it anyway. "Men would fly into Larnaca from the Middle East, then cross over the border to use the place. That's why it was where it was - out in the countryside, ten minutes' drive from a border crossing. Hains promoted the place discreetly on the internet and then, of course, by word of mouth."

"And he judged Jamil right, didn't he," Zelfa said. "He had too much to lose by going to the police. That was until Hains decided to change the date he had agreed to take them to Turkey in his boat. Hains decided to shoot him then to shut him up, though he got the wrong brother. Presumably it was Hains who broke into Jamil's house?"

"Probably his men. But he needed to make sure that there was not anything there that would incriminate him."

"What I don't understand is why Molly agreed to go along with it. I couldn't have "She looked meaningfully at Os. "If my husband had been shot, I would be screaming blue murder. I'd be helping the police to solve the case, not going along with my brother-in-law's farce. "

"He terrified her into agreeing to it. He made her believe that she could also be killed or at least lose the restaurant. We were wrong about their body language. It was not because husband and wife were not getting on."

"I suppose it didn't help being a foreigner here. But I still don't understand her. And after what happened, she's certainly going to regret what she did. Will she do time?"

"I don't know. It depends on the quality of her lawyer and the judge. To be fair to her, I think that Jamil kept most of this from her." Os closed his eyes.

Zelfa pulled him off the sofa and led him into the bedroom. Within minutes, he was asleep.

Chapter Twenty-eight

The January sun splashed warmth as Os walked jauntily up the steps into the station. Lunch with Zelfa and his parents had gone well yesterday, and amazingly his mother, although fussing throughout the meal, had not embarrassed him. He felt better than he had for months. Zelfa was going back to her mother's in Istanbul on Wednesday, but she would return within the month. Hains and his two henchmen were now ensconced in Nicosia prison, waiting for their court cases, and Os had nothing to do but tidy up a little paperwork. He might even treat himself to an afternoon off and go down to the hamman for a steam and massage, maybe even have a shave in town. He rolled his shoulders inside the soft material of one of his favourite suits, then pushed open the glass door and went inside.

"Assistant Superintendent Ismail wants you immediately in his office, Sir. He's been in since eight am."

Os attempted a smile, an action that would have been easy a few seconds ago. "I'll get down there now, Sergeant, thank you."

"Oh, and congratulations, Sir, on Saturday."

Assistant Superintendent Ismail's response was curt and loud to the knock. Os opened the door and walked in.

"Sit down, Chief Inspector." Ismail was behind his large desk, the surface covered in neat piles of paperwork. He twisted an expensive looking pen between his long tapering fingers. "I believe you arrested several men on Saturday night"

Os looked into eyes that reminded him of a dead fish. "Have you spoken to Superintendent Atak yet, Sir?"

"Of course. He had the good manners to update me on Sunday. As your line manager, I would have expected the same courtesy from you."

Os focused on the standard official picture of the late President Denktas on the back wall. Many people would not have called Denktas a physically attractive man, but the warmth and humanity in his face, contrasted sharply with that of the man opposite him. Ismail pulled a pad towards him and unscrewed his pen.

"I'd like you to tell me everything from start to finish."

As Os talked, the only other sound in the room was the scratch of pen nib on paper. Occasionally, Ismail barked a question, but otherwise he recorded everything in some kind of shorthand. When Os finished, Ismail continued to write for several more minutes, before closing his notepad and screwing the top back on his pen. He stared at Os for several seconds.

"I will be expecting your report on my desk by lunchtime, of course, unless that's a problem?"

Os shook his head. "Is there anything else, Sir?"

Ismail steepled his long fingers and sat back. "Well, since you're here, it seems appropriate to let you know that I have interviewed all the inspectors in this station. I've obviously had certain criteria to keep to, so unfortunately I've had to propose your name for redundancy."Ismail's face fell into a sneer. "You can of course take the decision to tribunal, but I think you'll find that they'll have no option but to back my recommendation - difficult as it may seem." The look on his face belied his next comment. "I'm very sorry."

Os's gaze returned to Denktas's photo as he stood up. "I'll get on with that report then."

He closed the door quietly behind him and then walked down to his own small office. Zelfa was already behind her desk. Her face clouded when she saw his expression. He would have preferred to have had a few minutes to himself, but he would have told her anyway.

"I'm being made redundant. Ismail's just told me," he said, as he sat down behind his desk.

"Just like that, when you've just solved this case?"

Her landline started to ring. She looked at it, her mouth tight with irritation. When the peal continued she grabbed the receiver. "Yes?" Her eyes flashed over to Os and her voice immediately softened. "Yes, Sir, he's here. I'll tell him now. Thank- you, Sir."

She put down the phone. "Atak wants to see you. He's not going to let you go, you'll see. He wants you in his office now."

Os stood up. Instinctively, he leaned across her desk and kissed her before he buttoned up his suit jacket, pushed back his shoulders and left to keep his appointment.